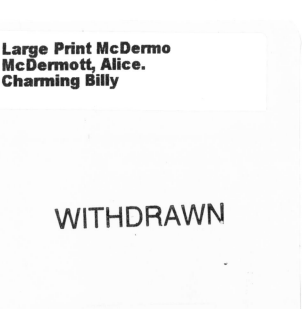

Charming Billy

Alice McDermott

Charming Billy

WHEELER
PUBLISHING, INC.
ROCKLAND, MA

★ AN AMERICAN COMPANY ★

Published in Large Print by arrangement with Farrar, Straus and Giroux in the United States and Canada.

Wheeler Large Print Book Series.

Set in 16 pt Plantin.

Library of Congress Cataloging-in-Publication Data

McDermott, Alice.
  Charming Billy / Alice McDermott.
    p. (large print) cm.(Wheeler large print book series)
  ISBN 1-56895-685-1 (hardcover)
  1. Iris Americans--New York (state)--New York—Fiction. 2. Alcoholics--New York (state)--New York—Fiction. 3. Family--New York (state)--New York--Fiction. 4. Bronx (New York, N.Y.)--Fiction. 5. Large type books. I. Title. II. Series
[PS3563.C355C48   1998b]
813'.54—dc21   98-44849
                                                                              CIP

Author's Acknowledgements

I am grateful to the Virginia Center for the Creative Arts for providing a quiet place; to Kevin E. McDermott for research assistance; and to Harriet Wasserman and Jonathan Galassi for friendship, wisdom, and infinite patience.

For Will, Eames, and Patrick

SOMEWHERE IN THE BRONX, only twenty minutes or so from the cemetery, Maeve found a small bar-and-grill in a wooded alcove set well off the street that was willing to serve the funeral party of forty-seven medium-rare roast beef and boiled potatoes and green beans amandine, with fruit salad to begin and vanilla ice cream to go with the coffee. Pitchers of beer and of iced tea would be placed along the table at intervals and the bar left open—it being a regular business day—for anyone who wanted a drink.

The place was at the end of a sloping driveway that started out as macadam but quickly diminished to dirt and gravel. There was an apron of dirt and gravel in front of the building, potholed, and on the day of the funeral filled with puddles, and the first ten cars parked here, including the black limousine Maeve had ridden in. The others parked up along the drive, first along one side, then the other, the members of the funeral party walking in their fourth procession of the day (the first had been out of the church, the second and third in and out of the graveyard), down the wet and rutted path to the little restaurant that, lacking only draught Guinness and a peat fire, might have been a pub in rural Ireland. Or, lacking dialogue by John Millington Synge, the set of a rural Irish play.

1

How in the world she ever found this place was a mystery, despite the question being asked again and again as Billy's friends and family filed in—the women, in high heels, walking on tiptoe down the sloping path, the men holding their wives' arms and umbrellas that had already been well soaked at the side of the grave. All of them, in their church clothes, giving a formal air to the gray day and the ragged border of city trees and wet weeds. All of them speculating: perhaps the undertaker had suggested the place, or someone from the cemetery. Perhaps a friend or relative on her side (few as they were) who knew something about the Bronx, or maybe Mickey Quinn, who had his territory up here. But Mickey Quinn denied it, shaking his head, if you can believe there's a bar in any of the five boroughs that he hasn't been to.

The place smelled slightly of mildew, understandable in this weather and with this thick (even in April) bower of trees, but the red-and-green tile floor was immaculate and the wooden bar gleamed under the fluorescent light. One long table draped with white tablecloths and set for forty-nine cut diagonally across the entire length of the room. One large window showed the parking lot full of cars, the other a wood that no doubt ended at a narrow side street or a row of dumpsters behind a row of stores, but seemed from in here to be dark and endlessly deep.

Maeve sat in front of this window, at the head of the table. She wore a navy-blue dress with long, slim sleeves and a round neckline, and anyone in the room who had not thought it earlier thought now—perhaps inspired by the perfect simplicity of what she wore—that there was a kind of beauty in her ordinary looks, in her plainness. Or, if they didn't think to call it beauty, they said courage—more appropriate to the occasion and the day—not meaning necessarily her new-widow's courage (with its attendant new-widow's clichés: bearing up, holding on, doing well), but the courage it took to look out onto life from a face as plain as butter: pale, downy skin and bland blue eyes, faded brown hair cut short as a nun's and dimmed with gray. Only a touch of powder and of lipstick, only a wedding band and a small pearl ring for adornment.

Of course, they'd thought her courageous all along (most of them, anyway, or—most likely—all but my father), living with Billy as she did; but now, seeing her at the head of the table, Billy gone (there would be time enough throughout the afternoon to say it's unbelievable still), her courage, or her beauty, however they chose to refer to it, became something new—which made something new, in turn, of what they might say about Billy's life. Because if she was beautiful, then the story of his life, or the story they would begin to recreate for him this afternoon, would have to take another turn.

My father sat to her right. Although Maeve had made all the arrangements herself—had found the place and chosen the menu and requested the fruit salad be served as soon as all the guests had arrived so there would be no long interval for speeches or toasts, only a quick blessing from one of the priests, he was the one the waitresses spoke to, and the owner of the place asked every now and then if anything was needed. He was the one who would settle the bill at the end of the afternoon and tip the waiters and the girl who took the coats and the umbrellas. He was the one who asked Maeve, after he'd already poured her a glass of iced tea, if she would like a drink, and then got up to fetch it for her, nodding to the undertaker and the driver, who were having their lunch at the bar.

She said, "Thank you, Dennis," when he placed the martini in front of her and then waited just a moment, her pale hand just touching the stem of the glass before she lifted it. "Good luck," he said, raising his own glass of beer. She nodded.

There's not much sense in pointing out the irony here—or even in trying to determine if everyone was either oblivious to it or so keenly aware that it no longer bore mentioning. Billy had died an alcoholic. Last night, in his casket, his face was bloated to twice its size and his skin was dark brown. (Dennis himself, my father, when he had identified the body two days ago at the VA, had said at first, momentarily relieved from the fact that Billy was dead, "But this is a colored man.")

Billy had drunk himself to death. He had, at some point, ripped apart, plowed through, as alcoholics tend to do, the great, deep, tightly woven fabric of affection that was some part of the emotional life, the life of love, of everyone in the room.

Everyone loved him. It was Mickey Quinn saying this, down at my end of the table. Mickey Quinn, who also worked for Con Ed, his territory being here in the Bronx, although he'd never heard of this place before. Mickey with a beer in his hand, and the irony either lost on him or too obvious even to bear mentioning. "If you knew Billy at all," he said, "then you loved him. He was just that type of guy."

And if you loved him, we all knew, you pleaded with him at some point. Or you drove him to AA, waited outside the church till the meeting was over, and drove him home again. Or you advanced him whatever you could afford so he could travel to Ireland to take the pledge. If you loved him, you took his car keys away, took his incoherent phone calls after midnight. You banished him from your house until he could show up sober. You saw the bloodied scraps of flesh he coughed up into his drinks. If you loved him, then you told him at some point that he was killing himself and felt the way his indifference ripped through your affection. You left work early to identify his body at the VA, and instead of being grateful that the ordeal was at long last over, you felt a momentary surge of joy as you turned away: This was not Billy, it was some colored man.

"He had the sweetest nature," another

5

cousin, yet another Rosemary, said at my end of the table. "He found a way to like everyone, he really did. He always found something good to say, or something funny. He could always get you laughing."

"He was funny, though." It was agreed. "God, wasn't he funny?"

"Everyone loved him."

Not missing the irony of the drinks in their hands and the drink that had killed him, but redeeming, perhaps, the pleasure of a drink or two, on a sad, wet afternoon, in the company of old friends, from the miserable thing that a drink had become in his life. Redeeming the affection they had felt for him, once torn apart by his willfulness, his indifference, making something worthwhile of it, something valuable that had been well spent, after all.

The fruit salad was canned but served with a little scoop of lime sherbet, which was refreshing, everyone agreed. It cleared the palate. The rolls were nice. There was some soda bread in one of the bread baskets, someone must have brought it. "Not as good as mine, but then I prefer it with caraway seeds, the way my mother used to make it..."

You could not redeem Billy's life, redeem your own relentless affection for him, without saying at some point, "There was that girl."

"The Irish girl."

"Eva." Of course, Kate, his sister, would remember her name.

"That was a sad thing, wasn't it? That was a blow to him."

"A girl he met right after the war. Right after he came home. Out on Long Island."

"An Irish girl," Kate said, "visiting her sister, who was a nursemaid for some wealthy family from Park Avenue. He wanted to marry her, even gave her a ring. She had to go back home first, her parents were elderly, I think. But they wrote to each other. Billy was a great letter writer, wasn't he? He was always scribbling notes and mailing them off."

"He'd write a note on anything, wouldn't he? A paper napkin, a train schedule, and mail it off to you."

"I have one," Bridie from the old neighborhood said. She dug into her patent-leather purse and found a greeting-card-sized envelope with two stamps that showed a harp and a fiddle. She looked at the postmark—June 1975—and then extracted a limp paper square of a cocktail napkin that contained Billy's looping hand. "He sent it from Ireland," she said. "From Shannon Airport." And there was the Aer Lingus logo in the corner. With a blue ballpoint Billy had written: "Bridie: Just saw your face pass by on a twelve-year-old girl in a navy-blue school uniform. Said her name was Fiona. She was meeting her father's plane from New York. Your smile, your eyes, your very face at that age—second edition. Love, Billy."

The napkin was circulated, held as delicately as a fledgling, some even reaching into a purse or a breast pocket for reading glasses so as not to miss a word. All the way up the table to Maeve, who read it with a smile and a nod, and all the way back down again. Bridie took it back and read it once more before placing it into its envelope and back into a side, zippered compartment of her Sunday pocketbook.

Other letters from Billy were being mentioned: a note scribbled on a *Playbill* page, on a business card. The long missives he'd sent home during the war, whole lines blacked out by the censors but the homesickness coming through. He was so homesick. The postcards from the Irish trip, the place mats and napkins from various Long Island restaurants and diners, that summer he and Dennis were out there, fixing up Mr. Holtzman's little house. You remember Mr. Holtzman. Dennis's mother's second husband. The shoe-store man.

Which was the same summer he met the Irish girl. Eva. The one he had hoped to marry.

"She went back to Ireland at the beginning of the fall." Kate would remember. "And not long after that, Billy took the job with Mr. Holtzman—Saturdays all day and maybe Thursday nights, I think it was. Dennis had arranged it for him. Billy was trying to put together enough money to send for his girl, to bring her back here, and Dennis set it up with Mr. Holtzman that Billy work at the shoe store when he wasn't at Con Ed."

"He was a great salesman," her younger sister, also Rosemary, said.

"Well," Kate explained, "Mr. Holtzman

8

had lost some business during the war—I don't know if it was rationing or his being of German extraction or what. Anyway, he was glad to get Billy, an ex-GI with that handsome face of his. Those blue eyes."

"He was a good-looking young guy," Bridie from the old neighborhood said. "Maybe a little shy."

"And that's where he met Maeve, wasn't it? In the shoe store?"

"Later on," Kate said. "She used to come to the store with her father, and I remember Billy telling me how patient she was with him because, you know, her father was a drinker, too."

"A redheaded W.C. Fields," sister Rosemary said. "I remember him at their wedding." Rolling her eyes.

"Poor Maeve has had her share of it."

A pause as a waiter reached between them to remove the fruit-salad bowls, every one of them whispering, Thank you, thank you, and then Thank you again as another waiter leaned in to put down the lunch.

"Doesn't this look good?"

"And the plates are nice and warm."

"They're doing a nice job, aren't they? I wonder how she found this place."

"The undertaker, I'm sure. He probably gets a commission."

"He sent her the money," Kate continued. "Eva, that is. The Irish girl. He sent her about five hundred dollars, I think."

"Which was a lot of money in those days." Someone was required to say it.

"It certainly was"—and to second.

"He sent her the money in the spring some-time, this would have been in '46. And she wrote back to say she was busy making plans, you know, arrangements for coming back over. Lord, he was like a man waiting for a bus in those days. The sun couldn't rise and set fast enough. He was hoping she would come over before the summer ended, so they could spend their honeymoon together, out on Long Island, in the little house, Holtzman's house, out where they'd first met. I don't know where he thought they were going to live after the hon-eymoon—remember what it was like, trying to find an apartment then?"

It was remembered. It was also noted that the roast beef was very tender, very moist. Better this splash of juice than a thick gravy.

"Rose and I were already living at home with our husbands and I had the baby, too," Kate said. "I don't know where Billy thought he was going to put her."

"I don't think," her sister Rosemary said, "he looked beyond her coming back to the U.S. and their getting married and going back out to Long Island."

"Maybe that was good," cousin Rosemary said.

Dan Lynch said, "Maybe it was just as well."

"Because he didn't hear another word from her all through the summer," Kate went on, "though I think he must have written to her two or three times a week, maybe more.

"In September, Dennis got a call from her sister, the one who was still minding the children on Park Avenue. He went into the city to see her and then came rapping at our door at about nine o'clock on a Sunday night. He asked Billy if he wanted to take a drive out to Long Island to check on the little house. I think he said there had been a storm out there. Anyway, Billy was always game. I remember he went out with his suit on a hanger because they were going to drive back first thing in the morning and go straight to Irving Place. I remember my mother ran after them with a sackful of rolls and butter and some sliced ham for their breakfast. All the way down the stairs.

"So it was dinnertime the next day before Billy got home, and that's when he told us that Eva had died—pneumonia. She was twenty-six years old. I'd like some tea instead," and the waiter with the stainless-steel coffeepot leaned away. "With lemon, please."

"Tea for me as well, please," Bridie said. "I'd almost forgotten this."

Mickey Quinn said, "None for me, thank you, maybe later," and then added that he thought only Midwesterners drank their coffee *with* their meals. He said he remembered how it was in the service, the Midwesterners guzzling coffee with every meal, it was a wonder they could taste anything. He paused to see who would rise to the bait, pick up the conversational thread, turn the talk away from Billy's lost girl to the Second World War.

11

But Dan Lynch said again, "It was a blow."

"I honestly thought he'd never get over it."

"But he stayed on at Holtzman's store, didn't he?" Dan Lynch said. "I mean, afterwards. Even when he didn't need the extra cash anymore. He stayed on. That was Billy all over, wasn't it? Loyal like that."

"Well, see," Kate said, "the money he'd sent her wasn't all earned. Mr. Holtzman had advanced him a good deal of it, and when Billy wrote to the girl's parents, to extend his sympathy—can you imagine that letter?"—Bridie shivered audibly—"naturally he told them to keep the money to pay the funeral expenses and to keep a fresh wreath on her grave."

"Like Joe DiMaggio," Bridie whispered.

Kate's eyebrows disapproved of the parallel. "For a while," she went on, "he talked about going over himself, but we discouraged it. Even Dennis said it would be awkward, maudlin. I was afraid it would just break his heart. Thank you. But working at the store was good for him, in the long run. It filled up one or two nights a week. And Saturdays. And, like I said, Holtzman was glad to have him."

"Billy told great stories about that place," Mickey Quinn said. "You know, the kids screaming and the women squeezing their toes into size fours or leaning down into his face when he was trying to fit them, nearly smothering him with their furs and their perfumes. I remember him telling me about one,

12

some big-footed woman who said to him when he measured her, 'Young man, I've always been told I'm a five and a half,' and he says, smooth as silk, 'That's five if it's halved, madam.'"

"A woman bit him on the ear once," Dan Lynch said. The information might have been on the tip of his tongue for twenty years.

"No."

"You're joking."

"Good Lord."

"It's the truth!" Delighted to finally get it out. "Billy must have blushed every color of the rainbow when he was telling me, down at Quinlan's. It seemed he was leaning over to pick up some of the shoes this woman had been trying on when she reached down, too, as if she was going to help him, and took a nip out of his ear. Can you imagine it?"

"He was good with the children," Bridie from the neighborhood said quickly, steering our thoughts down a more wholesome route. "He fitted all of mine, from infant shoes on. He had a way with children."

"And he met Maeve there," cousin Rosemary said.

Sister Rosemary confirmed it. "He met Maeve there. She always came in with her father. Getting him shoed, Billy said, was like fitting a mule, and no sooner would she be in to buy him a pair than they'd be back because he'd lost one of them. It didn't take Billy long to realize he'd lost one under a barstool somewhere."

13

"But Billy managed to ask her out," Bridie said.

"To the movies. You could have knocked me over with a feather when he told me he was taking her out to the movies. It had been what, Kate? Four or five years since the Irish girl?"

"Five years. It was 1950 and they were married three years later, in 1953."

"Thirty years, then," Mickey Quinn said.

Kate nodded. "It would have been thirty years in September."

"That's a good long run," said Mickey Quinn.

And all eyes went to Maeve, who, it seemed, had not touched her food but with her hands in her lap was leaning to listen to Ted, another of Billy's cousins, as he crouched beside her chair, speaking earnestly.

"She never had an easy time of it," sister Rosemary said, "especially recently. You know, toward the end."

"Toward the end it was a foregone conclusion," Kate said. "I think it was worse for her at the beginning, when she had her father *and* her husband to keep track of."

"She's doing beautifully today."

"Oh, she's strong."

"You have to hand it to her. She's got a lot of courage."

And a certain beauty, perhaps, looking up now to say something to my father, and to Father Ryan beside him, her pale hand in a fist on the white tablecloth. And if courage also meant beauty, then her presence in the shoe store was Billy's salvation, or at least his second chance that through willfulness and indifference he had let slip. But if she was as plain as they'd always said her to be during all the years Billy was alive, a plain girl approaching thirty with an alcoholic old father to take care of and no prospects—if Eva had been the beauty—then Maeve was only a faint consolation, a futile attempt to mend an irreparably broken heart. A moment's grace, a flash of optimism, not enough for a lifetime.

"I didn't know," cousin Rosemary whispered. "Was Billy having trouble even in the beginning? Even when they were first married?"

We all turned to Kate, whose memory had already proven keen. She was the older sister, the only one of them gathered here who had attained real wealth (although it had already been well noted that her husband wasn't here today, hadn't come last night), and so she could speak with some authority, while the rest might only venture a guess.

"Well, he always drank," Kate said. "But for a very long time it seemed he drank harmlessly. I remember him feeling no pain when he was on leave, before he went overseas, but that was understandable. I remember the night he came home and told us that Eva had passed away. He went straight to bed afterwards and I called Dennis to see if I could learn anything more and Dennis said they'd both had quite a lot to drink the night before, which was understandable, too. It was probably as hard for Dennis to tell him as it was for Billy to hear the news."

His sister Rosemary said, "I remember he had one too many at Jill's christening. I was worried about him riding the subway home."

"But for years he never missed a day of work," Kate told us. "And he was there to open the shoe store every Saturday morning from the time he started into the early sixties, when Mr. Holtzman finally sold the place to Baker's. I don't think Mr. Holtzman ever knew he drank. Certainly no one at Edison knew until near the end."

But Mickey Quinn held up his hand. "They knew," he said wisely.

"But not until fairly recently," Kate said. "Maybe when he went into the hospital in '73, the same year my Kevin graduated from Regis."

But Mickey Quinn frowned and shook his head slightly, apologetically, as if over something that was only slightly askew. "They knew," he said again. "We all knew. I left Irving Place in '68 and the fellows in the office knew Billy was a drinker even then. They covered for him, mostly in the afternoon. He'd go out on a call after lunch and not come back to the office and they'd cover for him. Everyone liked him. They were glad to do it."

"I think Smitty might have covered for him, too," his sister Rosemary said. "In the shoe store. Do you remember Smitty? Mr. Holtzman's assistant—the little bald man?"

He was remembered. "I went in there one Saturday, we were looking for Betty's First Communion shoes, and Billy was just coming in from lunch. I had the feeling he'd had a few. I mean, he was fine, and the kids were always happy to see him, but I noticed Smitty did all the measuring and got out all the shoes. Billy mostly sat. Which wasn't like him. He was sucking a peppermint."

"When was this?" Kate asked as her wealthy husband, trained at Fordham Law, might do.

Rosemary paused to calculate. "Betty was in second grade. 1962." Almost in apology: "He was drinking in '62."

Dan Lynch raised his hands. "Well, what does it mean? He was drinking before that, too. Down at Quinlan's. Saturdays after work. Sunday evenings. Hell, I was always there, too, and my liver's fine."

"So when did it become a problem?" cousin Rosemary asked.

"He started AA in the late sixties," Kate told her. "And then again around '71 or '2."

"He took the pledge on that Ireland trip. That was '75."

"What good did it do?"

"I thought it would stick. Maeve did, too."

Dan Lynch was chuckling, his hand around his small glass. "I remember Billy saying that AA was a Protestant thing, when you came right down to it. Started by a bunch of Protestants. He said he didn't like the chummy way some of them were always calling Our Lord by his first name. I drove him to the first

17

meeting and waited to take him home, 'cause Maeve didn't want him driving, and when he came out he said you could tell who the Catholics were because they'd all been bowing their heads every ten seconds while the Protestants bantered on about Jesus, Jesus, Jesus."

(And sure enough, up and down our stretch of table, heads bobbed at the name.)

Sister Rosemary said, "He didn't like them calling God a Higher Power, either—which I guess was the official AA term. Nondenominational, you know. He said it only proved that none of them had a sense of humor. He said you'd have to be God Himself to get higher than most of these guys had been."

There was a bit of low laughter. "Billy had an irreverent streak," Mickey Quinn said. "I liked that about him."

"The way Father Joyce explained it to me," Dan Lynch went on, "the pledge was the Catholic take on AA. He said it was like Holy Orders itself—you signed on and there was no going back. An unbreakable oath never to take another drink. Billy thought it was the real thing."

"But he broke it."

"There's plenty of priests that break their Holy Orders, too," Dan Lynch told them.

"Well, it got him over to Ireland, anyway," cousin Rosemary said. "I tried to talk him and Maeve into going over any number of times, but I never could do it."

"Maeve isn't one to travel," sister Rosemary said. "She's a homebody. Always has been."

Kate leaned toward us all, folding her hands on the table: a tasteful ring of diamonds, a gold bracelet, a professional manicure. "I often wondered," she said slowly. "I never had the heart to ask him, but I wondered if Billy went to visit the town Eva came from. While he was there."

Her sister shook her head. "Billy would have said so if he had. He wasn't one to keep things to himself."

Kate paused only a moment to consider this. "But he might not have wanted it to get back to Maeve, you know," she said. "He might have thought she wouldn't want to hear about a pilgrimage like that."

"Who would?"

"She knew about Eva?" Bridie said, whispering too, adding, "Thank you," as the waiter took her empty plate.

"I'm sure," Kate said. "Thank you." And then: "Actually, I don't know. I'd imagine she knew something about her."

"He must have told her something."

"Dennis would know," Mickey Quinn said. "They were always real close."

But Dan Lynch objected. "I was the best man at Billy's wedding," he said. "We were pretty close, too."

"Well, did he tell Maeve about the Irish girl?"

Dan waved his hand impatiently. "I'm sure he told her something. You know, it's not the sort of thing men talk about. And I'll say this for Billy, you never heard him mention that girl again, once he married Maeve."

19

"Ask Dennis," cousin Rosemary whispered.

The selected dessert was brought in: two scoops of vanilla ice cream in cold stainless-steel bowls. Hands in laps to make the poor man's job easier as he reached between their shoulders. Thank you.

"I remember watching Maeve come down the aisle," Dan Lynch said, lifting his spoon, holding it like a scepter. "She was on her old man's arm, but it was clear as you watched her that she was shoring him up, you know, keeping him straight. She was smiling as sweetly as any bride, but there was a determination in the way she walked, you know, the way she held her shoulder up against his, like it was a wall about to topple. She took hold of his arm when they got to the first pew, I mean a good grip, right here." He demonstrated, taking hold of his own forearm, spoon and all. "The old man banged his foot against the kneeling bench—you could hear it all over the church—and for a minute it looked like he'd go down headfirst. But she got him in there and got him seated. She maneuvered him. By sheer force of will, I'd say. And then she gave a little nod, as if to say, Well, that's done, and came up the steps to marry Billy." He sipped his beer. "Ready to take him on, is what I remember thinking. She was a plain girl, but determined."

"Very quiet," Mickey Quinn said. "Go over there for dinner and Billy would do most of the talking."

"He was lucky to find her," sister Rosemary said. "My mother always said there's nothing more pathetic than an old bachelor who's not a priest. That's what she thought Billy would be, after the Irish girl. An old bachelor. No offense, Danny."

And Dan Lynch laughed, blushed a little across his bald dome. Sipped his beer and shrugged. None taken—the story here being that Danny Lynch was such a connoisseur of beauty and behavior that no flawed wife could have pleased him and no flawless one could have been found.

"Did you ever meet her?" Bridie from the old neighborhood whispered. "The Irish girl?"

The two sisters exchanged a look across the table—the kind of look they might have exchanged had they been eyeing the last bite of a shared piece of cake. "She came to the apartment," Kate said, scooping it up. "It was just before she went back home. Billy borrowed Mr. Holtzman's car to go into the city to get her."

"She was very pretty," Rosemary added, taking a crumb. "Like Susan Hayward."

"Oh, I didn't think so," Kate said. "But she had nice hair, dark auburn. And big brown eyes. She wasn't very tall, even a little chubby. Billy brought her for Sunday dinner and then couldn't eat a bite himself. He was so—I don't know what—so delicate with her. The way he spoke to her, and watched her and listened to her. She did have a nice voice, you know, the poor girl" (a reminder to us all that she had died young), "with her brogue and

21

all. My mother's brogue got thicker just listening to her. They were good-looking together, Eva and Billy. A handsome pair. Better looking together than singly, somehow. He was lovestruck, that's for sure. We kidded him when he got home, after he'd taken her back to the city. We put his plate out on the dining-room table when we heard him coming up. We'd saved it. He'd hardly eaten a bite. We said, 'What was wrong with your dinner, Billy?'" She began to laugh. "We said, 'How are you going to marry this poor girl if her mere presence takes your appetite away? Billy,' we said, 'she'll be at your dinner table every day, breakfast too, when are you going to eat? You'll starve. You'll waste away to nothing. You'll have to sneak over here just to calm down enough to have your dinner.' We gave him such a hard time."

"And do you remember what Momma said?" sister Rosemary asked. Kate swallowed her smile, looked blank. Professional makeup, too. "No."

Well pleased, Rosemary said to my end of the table, "You know my mother thought herself a kind of psychic." She was getting her share of the story, after all. "She read cards and had dreams. And she said after Billy left that when she touched the girl's hand she felt four quick pulses in her own stomach, like baby kicks, which meant they'd have four children."

"Or that your mother had indigestion," Mickey Quinn said.

"More likely," Kate said. "You know how my mother cooked."

"She wasn't a much better prophet."

But Bridie shook her head. "I don't know," she said. "It might have been true. I mean, you could say if the girl had lived, that's how many children they might have had."

Dan Lynch said solemnly, "Which would have made this a different day."

"It would have been a different life," Bridie said.

Mickey Quinn shook his head and leaned back in his chair, as if to avoid all such speculation. "I'll have that cup of coffee now, please, when you get the chance," he said to the waiter's back.

"A different life," Dan Lynch repeated, and raised his beer.

The light through the window behind Maeve had begun to change now. A trace of shadow coming between the dark trunks of the trees, the clouds breaking up, perhaps.

"I don't agree with that," sister Rosemary said softly. "I've done a lot of reading in this regard, with Billy the way he was. Alcoholism isn't a decision, it's a disease, and Billy would have had the disease whether he married the Irish girl or Maeve, whether he'd had kids or not. It wouldn't have been such a different life, believe me. Every alcoholic's life is pretty much the same."

"Now I don't agree," Dan Lynch said under his breath, and Kate added, "It's not always fatal."

"I say it's a matter of will," Dan Lynch said, speaking up, keeping Kate from running away with the talk once again. "I drank side by side with Billy Lynch for nearly forty years. My liver's fine. Billy never had the will to stop."

Sister Rosemary frowned, shaking her head. "That's not fair. When he went to Ireland, when he took the pledge, he was truly determined. He told me so. You know what faith Billy had. And you know how seriously he took that trip. He was truly determined that time. But the disease had him in its grip." She raised a fist, showing them.

Dan Lynch poured himself and Mickey Quinn another beer. "Well, let me tell you what he told me," he said. "Down at Quinlan's, maybe a year or two after the Irish girl died. He told me," he said, lifting his glass, pointing around it, "that every year was a weight on his shoulders. Every hour was, he said." He pointed to Kate. "Remember when you said he was like a man waiting for a bus, when he was waiting to get her back here? Well, when you said that I thought: It never changed. He was still waiting, years after she'd died. But he was waiting to go to her now. Ever since the night Dennis told him the news, he was waiting to die. I'm sure of it."

"But there was Maeve," Bridie from the neighborhood cried.

"That's not fair to Maeve," sister Rosemary said.

Dan Lynch shook his head. "I'm not saying

24

a word against Maeve. She had a lot to handle, that's for sure. But if you ask me, Billy had a foot in the hereafter even before he met Maeve." He glanced up the table and then leaned forward, lowering his voice because the guests were beginning to thin out, Billy's friends and relatives getting up to have a few more words with Maeve, to go to the bathroom, or to get another drink before departing.

"We went to Mass together once. Feast of the Assumption. August 15. We'd both stopped into Quinlan's after work, a blazing hot day if there ever was one, hot as Hades, and both of us realized at the same time what the date was. We hightailed it over to 6:30 Mass at St. Sebastian's and, I don't know, I glanced at Billy, just after Communion. It struck me that it wasn't any thought of Our Lord or the Blessed Mother that put that look on his face. It was the girl. The Irish girl. When he turned his eyes to heaven, that's who he saw."

"Oh, nonsense," sister Rosemary whispered.

Mickey Quinn studied the ceiling. Down the table, a few heads turned, perhaps sensing a fight.

Dan Lynch took a sip of his beer, pursed his lips around the taste. "What's nonsense is all this disease business," he said. "Maybe for some people it's a disease. But maybe for some there are things that happen in their lives that they just can't live with. Things that take the sweetness out of everything. Maybe for some it's a sadness they can't get rid of or

25

a disappointment that won't go away. And you know what I say to those people? I say good luck to those people." He raised his glass, raised his chin. "I say maybe they're not as smart and sensible and accepting as every one of us," indicating every one of us with a sweep of his beer, "but they're loyal. They're loyal to their own feelings. They're loyal to the first plans they made—just like Billy was loyal to Holtzman and the job he gave him. And like he would have been loyal to her if she had lived and come back here and they'd gotten married. Just like he was loyal to Maeve: Billy never breathed another word about that girl after he married Maeve. But the girl was first, and for Billy she would always be first. That's the kind of guy he was. Maeve couldn't change him."

"I think he went to her grave when he was in Ireland," Kate said suddenly. "I just have the feeling that sometime while he was over there he went to the town she was from and visited her grave. I think it was the whole reason he made the trip."

Rosemary shook her head, appealed to Mickey Quinn, who was intent on dissolving the sugar in his coffee. "He went with Father Ryan to take the pledge," she said patiently. "To make the retreat. To quit drinking."

But Kate said, "Oh, Rose, think about it. Ireland's not the only place that has retreats for alcoholics. He could have made one over here. Maybe he thought if he went to her grave he could put something to rest, finally.

Put his feelings for her to rest so then he could quit drinking."

"But he couldn't," Dan Lynch said sadly, and poured another little beer.

"He couldn't," Kate agreed. "Which is why it didn't stick, as determined as he was."

But Rosemary's mouth was set. "No," she said firmly. "Look, there are faster and more pleasant ways of killing yourself. I tell you, I've read everything there is about this. Alcoholism is a disease, it's genetic. Our own father ruined his liver as well and probably would have died the same way if he hadn't gotten cancer. And Uncle John in Philadelphia was an alcoholic. And two of his sons—Chuck and Peter—go to AA. And Ted. And Mary Casey and Helen Lynch. And Dennis's father was no teetotaler either."

"Uncle Daniel died of cancer," Dan Lynch said indignantly. "He was no drunk." He turned to Bridie and Mickey Quinn. "He brought his six brothers and a sister over here and God knows how many other friends and relations. All on a motorman's salary."

"He was a saint," Bridie from the neighborhood said, nodding. "My mother always said so."

"Okay," Rosemary said. "God bless Uncle Daniel, but my point is that our family has what they call a genetic predisposition to both cancer and alcoholism. Billy had it in his genes."

"When he came back from Ireland," Kate

said softly, stroking the stem of her glass. "June of '75—I remember because my Daniel had just graduated from Fordham—he went straight out to Long Island. Out to the little house. Dennis was there, it wasn't long after he'd lost Claire. Remember how he used to rent the place back from his mother's tenant so he could spend his vacation? Well, Billy wasn't home for more than a day when he took the train out—and he hadn't been there in years."

"Meaning?" Rosemary asked coolly.

"Meaning he went back to the place he first met her. Eva. He was trying to work something out."

"Oh, honestly," Rosemary said. "It had been nearly thirty years. What was there to work out? It was a shame that she died, but Billy had had thirty years of living since then. I mean, come on, name me anything that's going to stay with you that strongly for thirty years."

Which seemed to silence our end of the table for a moment, as if the thing we would mention had only momentarily slipped our minds.

Cousin Rosemary poked her swizzle stick into the remaining ice in her glass. "It's all water under the bridge," she said, as if water from under the bridge was the very thing the tall glass contained. "What's the point of even discussing all this now? Billy was here and now he's gone, and I for one just can't believe it. Despite his troubles." Tears now. "I'll miss him. I'll miss his voice over the phone. I'll miss his smiling face."

"Hear, hear," Mickey Quinn said.

But Dan Lynch raised his beer again. He was whispering, his voice fierce. "I just don't think it credits a man's life to say he was in the clutches of a disease and that's what ruined him. Say he was too loyal. Say he was disappointed. Say he made way too much of the Irish girl and afterwards couldn't look life square in the face. But give him some credit for feeling, for having a hand in his own fate. Don't say it was a disease that blindsided him and wiped out everything he was." He bit off a drink, his face flushed. "Do the man that favor, please."

The clouds were indeed breaking up and a feeble bit of sunshine was striking Maeve's hair—you couldn't say lighting it up, but striking it and revealing it for what it was: a dull brown getting coarser with gray, and yet showing what it was so clearly that you could see a kind of appeal in it. Maybe it was just the honesty of it. A kind of beauty that was not a transformation of her simple features but an assertion of them, an insistence that they were no more than what they appeared.

My father stood beside her, his napkin in one hand, reaching behind her to say goodbye to another cousin, Ted from Flushing, who went to AA in order to die of cancer, not cirrhosis. Ted's little wife was right behind him, one hand on his back.

In the next half hour, my father would pay the bill and distribute the tips and take Maeve's arm when she walked out to the limousine that

29

would carry her home to Bayside. He would promise to stop in to see her later in the evening, just to make sure she was all right. He would shake hands with everyone, thanking them for coming, agreeing it was unbelievable, unbelievable still. In our car, crossing the bridge, he would listen with a slight smile when I told him about the debate that had gone on at our end of the table.

"Well, here's the saddest part," he would say, finally, wearily, as if he were speaking of an old annoyance that time had nearly trivialized, but not quite: "Here's the most pathetic part of all. Eva never died. It was a lie. Just between the two of us, Eva lived."

Telling the story, my father easily slipped from past to present: Billy was, Billy is, Billy drank, Billy drinks. Billy sets his heart on something.

In the front seat of Mr. Holtzman's car, on Seventieth Street, just off Park Avenue, my father watched Mary, Eva's sister, worry a small handkerchief, Irish linen (naturally), embroidered in one corner with three small shamrocks. Emblematic, sure, now, looking back, but in truth the children, her charges, had sewn it for her. She had shown them how to make the stitches. They had made one for their mother and their aunt. And one for her.

Her fingernails were round and white and always made him think that she had just come from giving all seven of them their baths, as she probably had. It was late September, late afternoon. The light the same that hung over the city now as we crossed the bridge into Queens.

"They're shamrocks," she said, showing him because he had asked her. She spread out the damp fabric. Her skirt was good wool, her sweater cashmere, hand-me-downs from her employer. "The children made it for me. I showed them the stitch. They made one for their mother and one for her sister up in Riverdale. And then they made one for me. Shamrocks."

"I know what they are," he said. And then added, "God, you're a silly woman."

The look on her face told him she was anything but. "Don't kill the messenger," she whispered.

It was Mr. Holtzman's car, an old humpbacked Ford: the wide cloth front seat, the old rationing sticker in the corner of the windshield that asked, Is this trip necessary? Something of the smell of the man's hair pomade on the back of the seat and the fabric around the window.

She said, "What will you tell him?" and if you're looking to blame someone for the lie, then you could as well blame her for putting it just that way: What will you tell him? As if there were options to choose from.

"I'd like to tell him she's dead," he said.

"She's dead to me."

This was Irish hyperbole, of course. This was the Irish penchant for pursuing any mention of death, any metaphor, any threat, the way a seal goes after a tossed mackerel. Because he'd had no real intention then. No plan. This was just talk.

"I knew about Tom," she said, the hometown boy Eva had married. "But I knew she liked Billy, too. She always said how sweet he was. She always talked about his great letters. I never would have believed she'd steal his money." To make a down payment, she had said, on a gas station on the convent road outside Clonmel.

He leaned across her lap, across the good

32

wool skirt, the soft cashmere, the still-lovely dregs of her employer's bottle of Chanel—and pulled at the bone-white handle of the car door. The handkerchief was in her hand, balled in her fist again. The tears starting again.

"I wish she had died," Mary said. "It would have been better." It was the Irish penchant for the word, sure, but also the fact that she was young enough to think that such talk proved her feelings were profound. "She's as good as dead to me now."

Leaning, he pushed the car door open with his fingertips. He still had one hand on the steering wheel. She put her hand on his arm, the linen handkerchief between them. "Will you call me?" she said.

He said he would. He kissed her. And then leaned to push the door open again, all the way now, so that it swung out over the sidewalk. So that there was nothing else for her to do but to get out, unassisted, and to walk with her head bent and her handkerchief to her eye, unescorted, back to the building's service door, where she'd been waiting for him just half an hour before.

Such rudeness meant something in those days. It's all ignorance now, but then it was intentional and it meant something to both of them. It meant the end of the thing.

EVEN CLIMBING THE STAIRS to Billy's apartment that evening, he had no real plan. He only knew he didn't want to deliver the blow with Billy's two sisters and their husbands and Aunt

Ellen, his mother, around. Imagine the night: your life's plans blasted, the baby crying in the next room, your sister and her young husband stirring in their bed, your widowed mother tapping at your bedroom door hour after hour saying, "Are you all right? Would you like a cup of tea?" Saying from behind the closed door, "Billy, there'll be plenty of other girls, believe me."

When Dennis had left Mary in the city that evening, he first went home to Jamaica, where earlier in the day Holtzman had wondered out loud if the little Long Island house had done all right in last night's storm. He'd grabbed his Dopp kit and a suit, a pressed shirt and a tie, and then told Holtzman he would drive out there tonight, just to see how the little house had fared.

Surprised, Holtzman licked his lips and ran a hand down his belly. He was a jowly German with slick hair and earlobes that could have held an entire thumbprint. *My mother's husband.*

"That's awfully kind of you, Dennis," Holtzman said slowly, full of hesitation. Wondering, no doubt, if there was a girl involved here, perhaps the very same girl who had called the house that afternoon. Wondering, no doubt, about the miles driven and the wear and tear on the machine and how many more years of accommodating her grown son would have to go into this marriage.

Dennis's mother was on the other side of the living room, going through the Sunday papers, smoking. She paused to watch the two of them.

"I'll take Billy along," Dennis said—no doubt killing the light in the projector that showed Holtzman some pretty young blonde stark naked against the brown upholstery of his car. There would be no such nonsense if Billy went along.

"Billy always loves a ride out there."

And Billy, opening the apartment door, grinned to see Dennis. There was a fountain pen in his hand, he was just getting off a note. He wore the trousers and the white shirt he had worn to Mass that morning. A drive sounded great, come in, come in. His sister Kate on the living-room couch with the baby, whispering that her husband had the bedroom, he was studying. Rosie and Mac, her husband, out to the movies because Kate's husband (shhh) was studying. Billy's mother coming from the kitchen with a book in her hands, whispering hello, reminding them to keep it low because poor Peter was in there studying.

The lie—still the only lie he'd intended to tell that evening—forming itself nicely around its little grain of truth: the storm last night. Mr. Holtzman, he said, had asked if the two of them would take the time to drive out there tonight to check on the place. They could spend the night and drive back in the morning, go straight to the office.

At the curb, they turned to see Billy's mother running down the stairs and into the vestibule with a brown paper sack full of rolls and butter and slices of the overcooked Sunday ham. What will you eat in the morning, way out there?

Dennis put the bag on the floor of the back seat, next to the bottle of vermouth and the bottle of rye he'd borrowed from Holtzman's cabinet. They both got in, the green light of the dashboard catching Billy's glasses.

His mother's vision of eastern Long Island, Billy said, was of wild black ducks and desolate potato fields and a mad, foaming sea. She'd never understand what he saw in it.

"Maybe she has a point," Dennis said.

He set landmarks for himself, places at which he would begin: once they reached the Jericho Turnpike, the Sunrise Highway, once they crossed into Suffolk. "I saw Mary today," he would say. "She had a letter from Eva. She got married, Bill, last month. To a boy she'd known since she was a child. She's spent your money. Put it into a gas station, if you can imagine. Probably hocked the shoes you sent her. Probably hocked your ring. It's a damnable thing, Billy, a damnable thing."

But his courage failed him. His thoughts, to be frank, going more and more to the other people he would have to tell once he'd given Billy the news. His mother first and foremost, who would say, What a shame, with that light in her eyes that would say, as well, I knew it all along. Who would then ask about Holtzman's money.

There was Holtzman. The man had already

composed a long list of things that he believed
Dennis and Billy and most of their generation
were incapable of doing: running a business,
making a fortune, shaking free of the lesson
they'd learned in the service that having
someone take care of you was equal to taking
care of yourself. Creating a future.

Writing the check he had given to Dennis
to give to Billy to send to Eva so she could come
back before the summer was over, Holtzman
had said, "You boys will never have any
money if you spend everything before it's
earned."

"This is an advance, sir," Dennis had told
him. "Billy will earn it back in no time at the
store."

Holtzman had looked wise, a maddening look
in a man so dull. "But first he'll spend it," he
had said.

Holtzman would have to be told.

And the fellows in the office. All of them knew
about Eva, Billy hardly able to go twenty
minutes without working around to saying her
name. The girls in the office, too, many of whom
(your mother included) had once had an eye
for him. Many of whom, no doubt, would
find the story of Eva's betrayal slowly changing
the way they saw him: if she preferred Tom,
might not I?

(His mother telling him through his closed
bedroom door, "Billy, there will be plenty
of other girls.")

The rest of the family would have to hear
about it, and Billy would have to endure for

37

some months, maybe years, both their sympathy and their studied silence whenever the subject of love and marriage arose. The neighborhood would have to know, too. Including Bridie, whom Billy was talking about now as they passed through Speonk—another point at which he had promised himself he would begin.

Bridie, it seemed, was engaged at last, to be married to a fellow named Jim Fox, from Staten Island, around Christmas. Which would make...Billy counted out loud, naming each couple off...the seventeenth wedding he'd been to this year.

"Everyone always thought she was holding out for you," Dennis said.

But Billy shook his head. Kate said Bridie would have married Tim Schmidt if he'd lived. They'd had an understanding, Kate said. Kate herself had sat up all night with Bridie the day the news came that he'd been killed. In Italy, in the winter of '43. Kate's own husband in the same division and unheard from for six weeks or more. Wasn't it easy to forget sometimes what the war had been like for the people at home? You know, Mike Breen was in the Battle of the Bulge as well. Saw him at Quinlan's. He had a hell of a war...

The night grew deeper and the headlights showed just the one dark stretch of road that carried them toward that mad sea. Better she had drowned in it, Dennis thought. Better the women gather around Billy in real mourning, sit up with him all night if they liked, moaning about fate and loss and the inevitability of death, than have them turn their gummy sympathy, their studied silence on him every time there's a mention of love and marriage. A gas station on the convent road. Better he be brokenhearted than trailed all the rest of his life by a sense of his own foolishness.

He told him the lie in the rutted, rain-filled driveway of the little Long Island house. The headlights showed only a single branch, its leaves already touched with color, that had fallen across the side yard. (He was surprised to see it, as if he had made up the fact of last night's storm as well as Holtzman's request that they come out here to check its effect, as if, were he to touch it, he would discover it was made of paper and paste.) Everything else around them was in utter darkness. Billy had just gotten the flashlight from the glove compartment. It was the roof he was most concerned about, he said. Considering all the ceiling plaster he'd slapped around last summer, the last thing he wanted to see was that it had all ended up on the floor.

"I saw Mary today," Dennis began. "She had a letter from home. About Eva." The details came easily enough, without much planning. Pneumonia, he said, the country being as damp as the relatives always said it was. She'd been sick for weeks, he added, which would explain why she hadn't written him for so long.

Billy sat for a moment, stunned, and then pulled his glasses off from around his ears and touched thumb and forefinger to the bridge of his nose. And then he blessed himself and cursed and said quietly that it was a damnable place, a piss-poor primitive country. He asked if they had at least gotten her to a hospital.

"I don't know," Dennis said, meaning, of course, that he hadn't thought the story through that far. He was stunned himself, at the audacity of what he had done, was doing. The breadth and depth of the lie he was telling, the world he was creating that even now he saw he would not be able to sustain. There would be a tremendous number of details, a tremendous number of opportunities for mistakes, misjudgment, for a sense of falsehood, inaccuracy, to creep in and bring the whole thing down. Billy would get a letter from her (let's hope with a check inside), or he'd run into Mary on the street, or Mary's employer, or he'd rush over to Ireland to throw himself on her grave, or she'd come back here with her husband and feel compelled to give him a call, to apologize. It was an audacious, outlandish thing he was doing, and he knew the workaday world, the world without illusion (except Church-sanctioned) or nonsense (except alcohol-bred) that was the world of Irish Catholic Queens New York, didn't much abide audacious and outlandish. Not for long, anyway.

He took the flashlight, told Billy he'd give him a few minutes alone. He reached into the back for the food and the drinks and made his way across the muddy path to the little house.

All was intact, no water stains that he could

see, no inordinate dampness. No mildew yet, which might or might not be because of the lumps of charcoal his mother had scattered along the baseboards when they'd closed the place up after Labor Day. Just three weeks ago now. When they were still saying Billy and Eva would be back before winter for their honeymoon.

He mixed a pitcher of drinks, made some sandwiches with the stringy slices of ham. At one point he heard the car door slam, but it was some minutes before he heard Billy's footsteps on the path. He didn't come in. He sat on the front steps as they had done nearly every night when they were first back from the war. The light from the living room shone through the screen and onto Billy's white shirt.

Dennis carried the drinks outside then, the plate of sandwiches balanced on top of one of them. He pushed the screen door open with his foot and Billy moved a little to make room for him. Billy took the drink. Dennis put the plate of sandwiches on the steps between them.

He asked Dennis to repeat the details, the letter, the pneumonia, the length of her illness—which Billy himself said would explain why he hadn't had a letter from her all summer.

"Her parents would have written to you themselves," Dennis added, looking into the darkness of the yard and the road, covering his tracks, "but they thought it would be better if they told Mary first and Mary thought it best that I tell you. She'll be going back over herself now, I suppose."

"You'll miss her," Billy whispered, and Dennis shook his head. Nothing he could say in that regard struck him as authentic.

He put his hand to the back of Billy's neck at one point. Refilled both their glasses more than once. Later, he led him into the house and put him to bed.

It was the next morning, on their way back to the city, when Billy said he couldn't understand how Dennis had managed to keep from telling him the news the whole time he was at their apartment the night before, the whole way out to Long Island. How he'd managed to drive and chat, to keep from telling him until they had reached the place. He didn't say he admired or even appreciated Dennis's restraint. He simply said he couldn't understand how he'd managed.

We were in our own driveway by now, and again my father was smiling, shaking his head at that old annoyance. He said it was a very long time ago. They'd been younger than he was now capable of remembering them.

"Did he ever find out?" I asked him. "That you lied about it?"

He nodded. "In 1975," he said. "When he was over there. He met her again. Had a cup of tea with her in the little shop she'd added to the gas station. I guess it had turned into quite a successful operation. She had four kids, too. All grown by then. He said she was still good-looking."

42

"Did she pay him back?"

"I guess she offered to. More out of embarrassment than anything else. Of course, he wouldn't take it."

"Was he mad, when he found out?"

"At her? Never."

"At you."

He considered this. "On the one hand," he said, "she was back from the dead. There was that. On the other, he'd lived thirty years with a mistaken belief. With that grief. But no, he wasn't angry. He ended up kidding me about it almost. We realized that it had all happened a long time ago."

He pulled open the door.

"Do you wish you'd told him the truth?" I asked.

"Yes," he said, without hesitation. "I suppose." He smiled again. "It's a bad business. A lie like that." And then he was climbing out of the car, the thin gray cloth of his suit jacket buckling between his shoulders. We went in the side door, into the kitchen. Our coffee cups and juice glasses were still in the sink. He'd left the radio on; it had become a habit, I think. I followed him through the kitchen into the dining room, where he stood before the mirror over the sideboard, pulling off his tie, raising his chin to unbutton his collar.

"Did you ever tell Mom?" I asked.

"I never told anyone," he said. "And Billy never told anyone, either, as far as I know. That was his choice, I thought. When I went down to the VA Tuesday morning, though, I was glad it had come out, back in '75. I was glad he didn't go through his whole life deceived about it. Didn't die thinking about some lovely reunion in the sweet hereafter."

"You think he would have? That's what Dan Lynch was saying, that he was waiting all his life to meet her in heaven."

Working with two hands, my father pulled off his tie, unknotted it, folded it in thirds, and placed it on the lace doily that covered the sideboard. "That's Danny Lynch for you" was all he said. He turned, leaned his two palms behind him, on the edge of the server. He spoke as if providing an antidote to Dan Lynch's utter nonsense. "I shouldn't have done it, I suppose. I should have told him the truth. He would have gotten over it and met Maeve anyway. He would have found something else to moon about when he drank. Rosie was right, an alcoholic can always find a reason but never needs one. I thought I was preserving his innocence, I guess. But I should have remembered that when Billy sets his heart on something there's no changing him. He's loyal. He's got this faith— which is probably why he drinks. The problem is, it's hard to be a liar and a believer yourself, at the same time. I didn't see it until your mother died, and it gave me some trouble then. I don't know if you remember."

I lowered my head. I remembered. And my father pushed himself away from the server, where he'd been leaning. Too much said. He headed upstairs to change. I went to the kitchen to stand there for a minute looking for

44

something to do. I put the kettle on—a genetic trait. When I called up to him, he said he'd just have a piece of toast or something before he went over to Maeve's.

THE LONG ISLAND HOUSE was my father's inheritance from a mother who, in a recapitulation that must have left even the heavenly host momentarily voiceless, decided during the closing days of her life to make an end run at heaven. It was not that she had been a bad woman until then. She had simply been indifferent, to her two husbands and her son, to her grandchildren, to most of the simple and complex joys of the life she had been given.

The house became hers during her second marriage, and according to my father, the only pleasure she ever got from it was her ability to withhold invitations to visit. The house itself was a modest affair, updated by my father and Billy right after the war, and except for an occasional dusting, an occasional coat of paint, hardly touched again until the early eighties. It had a single room divided into a living room and kitchen, with three tiny bedrooms stuck like postage stamps along the side. The small plot of land it sat on was mostly scrub, but there was a bay beach within walking distance and, especially at night, the tang of sea salt in the air, and for my grandmother's friends and family from Brooklyn and Queens it was a toehold in a world of spacious lawns and famous artists and summer colonies where wealthy people had once called their mansions *cottages*—of days at the shore that did not involve changing trains for Seagirt or waiting in line for two hours at the Jones Beach tolls.

The man she had inherited it from, Holtzman, her second husband, had bought it during the Depression from another city dweller down on his luck and then with money problems of his own had all but abandoned it for nearly a decade. Toward the end of that decade, a petite redhead somewhere in her late forties began to visit his store on Jamaica Avenue, looking for size fours. With her tiny heel resting in the palm of his hand, he learned she was a widow with a son overseas. He took her phone number in order to call her when something new in her size came in. He took her to lunch, allowing her to leave her box of shoes behind the counter while his assistant ran the store. He gave her some stockings, and a handbag. He took her to dinner and, driving past the house in Jamaica that had been his childhood home, had said that he also owned another place, a little bungalow out on Long Island.

She mentioned the house in a letter that reached my father while he was overseas. A regular laundry list, he said, of reasons why she should remarry. The house on Long Island was right up there near the top.

He said there wasn't anything at all about love.

She was, according to my father, the most unsentimental woman he had ever known or even heard of. He blamed this mostly on her childhood. The only child of Scottish immi-

47

grants with delusions of grandeur, she had been raised in genteel poverty, given ballet and riding lessons, lessons in deportment and French and violin, until tuberculosis made her an orphan at twelve. She spent the next six years being passed from one already-overburdened relative to another and at eighteen had married a forty-four-year-old streetcar conductor so full of blarney (as my father told it) and wild verse, of Tennyson and the Bard and Gilbert and Sullivan, that he'd had to import every brother and sister, cousin uncle niece and nephew from the other side simply to have enough ears in which to deposit it all. Which made him Holy Father to a tenement's worth of Irish immigrants but kept his wife and son mostly impoverished and never—what with one wetback mick after another being reeled in from the other side and slapped down on their couch—alone in their own home.

My mother might have been different, my father was fond of saying, if her life had been different (I was a teenager before I began to point out that this was true of us all), and I think that throughout his own life my father harbored in his heart a vision of his mother as a happy and pampered child whose bright eyes saw only the purest intentions.

As it was, as he knew her and as I knew her, she was a Geiger counter for insincerity, phoniness, half-truths. She could dismantle a pose with a glance and deflate the most romantic notion with a single word. She had no patience for poetry, Broadway musicals, presidential politics, or the pomp of her religion—although my father, his father's son, loved these things in direct proportion to her disdain—and she sought truth so single-mindedly that under her steady gaze exaggeration, self-delusion, bravado simply dried up and blew away, as did hope, nonsense, and any ungrounded giddiness.

Her philosophy of life seemed to be to get to the bottom of things, the plain, unadorned, mostly concrete and colorless bottom of things, and from there to seek to swat away any passing fancy that might cloud the hard-won clarity of her vision. Because she was also intelligent and witty, and because all her cynicism was bolstered by a keen logic, she gained in her later years a reputation as a sage, but one whose advice friends and family would seek only at the tail end of some experience when they were ready to be either reconciled to their disappointment or disabused of any vestige of hope for some unexpected change.

When Holtzman died in 1964, she found a year-round tenant for the Long Island place, because it was at the time the economically sensible thing to do. (Swatting away any sweet recollection of summer weekends spent there with her husband and her young grandchildren since—swat—the one was dead and the others growing so quickly that such weekends wouldn't be continuing much longer anyway, and if they were to continue, at the expense of the steady income a year-round tenant could provide, they would really be more

49

of the same, wouldn't they?—days at the beach and cookouts on the back-yard grill, taking strolls through the village, marshmallows to the campfire, bread heels to the duck pond, and really, when you got to the bottom of it, how many memories of pleasant summer days on Long Island does one person need? Isn't enough as good as a feast?)

Eventually, all mention of the house seemed to disappear and my parents began to suspect that she had quietly sold the place to her year-round tenant and found some far more practical and profitable way to store the money that had been tied up in it for so long. We had begun to spend our vacations in the Adirondacks by then, had even stopped reassuring ourselves that the mountains were far preferable to the shore. Children of a certain age are pleased to encounter nostalgia, I think, and the summer days we had spent with my father's mother in the Long Island house moved easily into our family's short but expanding list of things we used to do but did no more.

And so it was with some amazement that I learned on the afternoon of her funeral in 1971 that she had left the Long Island house to my father. My mother told me the news as we left the restaurant where her funeral luncheon had been held. I remember the greedy triumph I'd felt: a house, a piece of land, all unexpected and unsought and, most satisfying of all, unearned—the greedy and self-satisfied triumph of a lazy heir.

But my mother's triumph was that the inheritance was part of a package of changes my grandmother had made to her estate in the weeks before she died, a part of her deathbed conversion. The Long Island house, it turned out, was the only thing my father was getting. The rest of my grandmother's money, which was really Holtzman's money, was to go to the Church she had had, until then, no use for, to a number of charities whose mailings and TV solicitations she had always held up as proof positive of their misappropriation of funds, and even to her mixed-race former neighbors in Jamaica who took in foster children—for profit, she had always claimed. My mother was Catholic enough to be grinning as she told me all this, as if the satisfaction she felt in learning that my grandmother did, indeed, fear God was well worth the substantial sum of money that she had just described away. Money that otherwise would have been our family's alone.

My brothers and I saw it differently, of course. We saw our college tuitions dispersed. We saw her surprising change of heart not so much as a deathbed conversion but as a final-hour placing of bets, a closing-time rush (as my oldest brother, the philosophy major, put it) to get a piece of the action in Pascal's wager. A woman as clear-sighted as my grandmother would not go to meet her maker empty-handed, sure. But, we were certain, a woman as clear-sighted as my grandmother would know, too, that what she was going to meet might just as well be the void of a spent body and a finished mind. She was merely covering her options.

My father claimed it was an indication of the soft, even romantic heart she had carried and hidden all along. In support of this, he described how in those last days, after she had made her sweet intentions known, she had also said one morning when the hospital chaplain left her room, "Don't they send them to hospitals because there's something queer in their pasts?" Still her ornery self. But she had added, too, when she told him he was to have the Long Island house, "Get Billy to visit you there. He's avoided the place for too long."

I knew that in life she had pretty much ignored Billy, although with no more passion or purposefulness than she had displayed in ignoring us all, and so, by way of explanation, my father told me, perhaps for the first time and in a much abbreviated form, the tale of Billy's brief romance, and engagement, to a girl he'd met out there, right after the war. A girl who died of pneumonia before they could marry.

Billy was for me then merely one of my father's legion of cousins, distinguished not so much by his alcoholism (it had seemed to me that there were more alcoholics among them than there were Republicans, or even redheads) as by his wife, Maeve, who without many relations of her own relied so heavily on my father whenever Billy was giving her trouble. I suppose I made some connection, or that as my father told the story there was some connection implied, between that ancient disappointment and Billy's current need to drink, but as I said, that side of his family was full enough of alcoholics who had as far as anyone could tell married the girls of their dreams to make such a connection compelling.

"You think he's been avoiding the place?" he'd said to his mother, more intrigued by the fact of this kind of conversation, at this late date, than by any observation she might make about Billy.

"I think you know he has," she said. "And I'm sure you know why."

"Revenge," my father told us now. "Stubbornness." So he could say, whenever he was asked out there or whenever someone else had come, "I won't go back myself," and wordlessly remind them all of what he had suffered, found and lost, all those years ago. He never had to say the girl's name. He merely had to hold up a hand when he was invited and whisper a gracious No, no, in order to remind them all.

"Get Billy to go out there again," my father's mother said. "Make him bring his wife."

"My mother understood," he said, proving further that she had not been all she had seemed, that her cool exterior had hidden all along a warm heart. "She had Billy on her mind. Billy and Maeve, and that summer he'd spent out at the Long Island house, all those years ago. My mother had thought about him without ever seeming to. She'd thought about any number of things we never knew."

Of course, what he did not say then was that she, too, had been deceived. That despite her lifelong disdain for delusion and romance and teary-eyed reminiscence, she had ended her life recalling Billy's summer idyll on Long Island and his pretty (or so the story went), much-loved girl who had died; she had sought a remedy for him, even as she went about securing her own soul.

BILLY DID RETURN to the Long Island house, in the summer of 1975. It was early July and my father and I met him at the train station in East Hampton. I was on a break between summer semesters at college. Having, perhaps, inherited my grandmother's distaste for too much of a good thing, I had decided to get through college in the shortest time possible and had taken courses during every summer and winter break. I was due to finish that December, a year and a half ahead of time.

Since my grandmother's death, my father had spent two weeks every summer at the Long Island house and then rented it back to Mr. West, the man he still referred to as "my mother's tenant," for the rest of the year. The understanding was that when my father was ready to retire in another eight or ten years, he would sell our house in Rosedale and move here permanently. The joke was that Mr. West would then return to his wife and three sons, whom he had deserted a dozen years before.

My own mother had died of lung cancer in the spring of '73. The solitary life my father now led could still, at times, strike my heart (my arms, my shoulders, the pit of my stomach) with an unbearable weight, but each time we were together I saw, too, that the life suited him well enough. He had always had a tremendous capacity for accommodation and contentment, whether alone with a newspaper or at a dinner table filled with friends and family. I suppose his mother had taught him not to expect much from life and so it was easy enough for him to see each day as an endless parade of unexpected pleasures. She said it as a caution against excess, but my father said it with a kind of amazed gratitude: enough *was* as good as a feast.

I suppose there's not much sense in trying to measure the breadth and depth of your own parents' romance, the course and tenacity of their love. Your parents' or anybody else's, for that matter. I know an older couple who have so convinced their grown children of the charm and endurance of their passionate history—married young and poor, separated by war, reunited to become dedicated and hardworking young parents, loving partners in the building of a business, patient guardians of teenagers, payers of tuition, and finally (looking proudly into each other's eyes) grateful, rich, and still passionate retirees and grandparents—that their children have had nothing but disappointment and grief in their own love lives and now, in middle age, look at their aging and still smug progenitors with envy and despair.

My parents, I have to believe, had a marriage that ran the typical course from early infatuation to serious love to affection occasionally diminished by impatience and disagreement, bolstered by interdependence, fanned now and then by fondness, by humor. That they loved each other is a given, I suppose, although I suppose, too, that there were months, maybe years, when their love for one another might have disappeared altogether and their lives proceeded only out of habit or the failure to imagine any other alternative.

A good-enough, a typical kind of mid-twentieth-century marriage that suddenly blossomed into something else in the year she was dying. I hesitate to use the word about a time that was filled with so much pain, that was for me only awful, but I think it was during my mother's illness that my parents became passionate about one another. Their meeting, their courtship, their years raising children, every ordinary day they had spent together until then all became merely the running start they had taken to vault this moment. To sail, gracefully and in tandem, across the abyss.

It made it easier that they both believed in the simplest kind of afterlife—that my father could say to her, even in those last days, joking but without irony, "You're going to get tired of hearing from me. I'll be asking you for this that and the other thing twenty-four hours a day. *Jesus*, you'll be saying, here comes another prayer from Dennis." And my mother would reply, her voice hoarse with pain, "Jesus might advise you to take in a movie once in a while. Give your poor wife a rest. She's in heaven, after all."

It was a joke, but they believed it, and they believed, too, I think, that their love, their loyalty to one another, was no longer a matter of chance or happenstance but a condition of their existence no more voluntary or escapable than the pace of their blood, the influx of perception. There was, I thought, a perverse joy about their closeness in that year, as my father, for the first and only time in his life, turned his back on the scores of friends and relatives who had come to depend on him as they had once depended on his father and thought only of her. (Refusing even Billy's calls. Putting a pillow over the phone in our upstairs hallway before he went to bed and telling me to ignore the thing should I hear it ringing in the middle of the night.) There was, in their anticipation of what was to come, a queer self-satisfaction. It was clear now that they would love each other until the last moment of her life—hadn't that been the goal from the beginning? They would love each other even beyond the days they had lived together; was there any greater triumph?

At eighteen, I was not so sure. At eighteen, I wanted only a mother who would be there in the flesh to see me graduate and get married and have children of my own. Who could keep my father from living the rest of his life alone, nagging his dead wife with a thousand daily prayers.

ON THE MORNING BILLY ARRIVED, my father and I had our usual breakfast on the front-porch steps. We were careful in those days to do everything in a usual way. It was different when I visited him at home, when he had his job to go to and I had my room and my friends, enough vestiges, for both of us, of our lives as they were before my mother died to help us through an hour or two without missing her. But out on Long Island our being alone together served first and foremost to remind us of her absence and we clung to routine (or I clung to what I was certain was my father's routine when I was gone) as if it had been prescribed.

Every morning he would wake at seven and do Army-issue calisthenics either in his room or out on the back porch. He would shower and dress and then go to the kitchen to get breakfast. I would get up when I heard him put the kettle on. By the time I was showered and dressed, the cereal would be poured and the juice squeezed and the tray ready to be taken outside, where we would sit on the front steps if the weather was fine so I could dry my hair in the sun.

The property was not much, but at that time of the year the weeds and brambles that edged the front lawn were full of Queen Anne's lace and black-eyed Susans and the honeysuckle along the side yard was lush. Across our mostly untraveled street there was a vacant field, also a tangle of weeds and wildflowers, that held at its center the crumbling cinder-block foundation for a house that was never built. Beyond that, there were some trees, the bay, the blue sky.

The grass at my feet was as green as it would get and the sandy soil was already warmed by the sun. I leaned back against the step, resisted flicking off the piece of cracked green paint at my elbow (my father was on the step above me, watching). I tilted my head back to catch the sun on my face, recognizing as I did the perpetual hope of a sun-shot transformation that certain young men might notice when I returned to school next week—the tan, the sun-streaked hair, the slimming effects of a daily swim...

When I opened my eyes again it was to the sound of a car pulling into our gravel driveway. It pulled in only far enough to get its rear bumper out of the road, and even the way its engine died and the driver's door opened seemed tentative. Slowly, Mr. West climbed out and walked toward us, looking all the while like a man on the verge of retreat. He was lanky, older than my father, I thought, but muscular and well tanned. He carried a cigarette cupped in his palm and held close to his thigh, and this made him seem even more furtive and cautious as he approached. I had met him only two or three times since my childhood, once down at Montauk, where he kept his boat, once on the street in Amagansett, although the matchbooks and magazines and mementos he'd left in the house each year made me feel I knew him better. He was, as my father liked to say, a Bonacker, a real Bonacker; a colloquialism that for my father meant Mr. West was a hick.

My father called good morning even before Mr. West had quite reached us, and when he touched his dark captain's hat and apologized for interrupting our breakfast, my father cried, "Not at all, not at all," jovial, friendly, sitting on the top step with his cereal bowl and spoon like Old King Cole. "What can I do for you?"

Mr. West pointed to the back of the property, to the clapboard garage where each year he stored his spare clothes and personal things for the two weeks of my father's vacation. "There are a few odds and ends I need to get at," he said politely. "If you don't mind." And my father waved his spoon. "No, no, no, of course not, go right ahead. No need to ask. Have you got your key?"

Mr. West nodded, holding up a ring of them in the palm of his hand.

"Then go right ahead. Take your time." Ever the benevolent landlord.

But as Mr. West crossed the side yard and unlocked and opened the wide door and began to rummage through his things (we heard him whistling, mumbling to himself), my father sat stiffly, uneasily, without sipping his tea or finishing his cereal or saying a word,

60

more tenant himself than landed gentry. The house and property still more his mother's tenant's than our own.

And then a sudden blast of music came from the car at the end of the driveway, a sudden zipping riff of talk and static, violin, rock. Both my father and I looked over, but I know I saw him first, through the sunlight and shadow that played across the windshield: a boy in the front passenger seat, leaning to adjust the radio. As he sat up again, he put his arm out through the open window to tap the car's roof. But then he stopped and suddenly raised his hand, the fingers spread, a dark band, braided leather, slipping down his wrist, in a gesture that seemed first and foremost to say: No harm. I raised my hand in the same way.

And there it was: our greeting. Our own children, in that first eternity, must have pricked up their ears.

"One of his boys," my father said. Cody or John or Matt, I knew from the names penciled on the back of the pantry door. Matt the tallest in 1967. "He's staying with his wife."

It was my father's belief that Mr. West would not have left his wife and three sons in 1964 if on the day he stormed out of their house in Amagansett my grandmother had not been there offering a furnished rental at a year-round, reasonable rate. What he would have done, what he should have done, my father claimed, was to storm out of his house, drive to the IGA, pick up a six-pack, drink it on his boat, which was then in dry dock in Three Mile Harbor, fall asleep, and then crawl home the next morning, hungover and remorseful and chilled to the bone. But what changed this scenario, changed forever the lives of Mr. and Mrs. West and their three children, was the index card on which my grandmother had written *Year-round rental, reasonable, furnished,* and stuck to the bulletin board just inside the entrance to the store, the index card that Mr. West had grabbed on his way out, six-pack under his arm, setting the thumbtacks flying.

Whatever guilt my father felt about evicting Mr. West in eight or ten years' time when he sold our house in Rosedale and moved out to Long Island permanently was assuaged by his belief that as soon as he did so Mr. West would return to his wife and now-grown children.

The man emerged from the garage carrying a jacket and some loose papers under his arm. He called a thank you and got into his car and backed out slowly, his son turning toward the window only briefly as they passed the house again.

Inside, as was our routine, my father and I did the dishes and straightened up. We briefly debated what to do with the wine and beer in the refrigerator, the Scotch in the cupboard, and then my father, with a wave of his hand, said, "Let them be. It's up to him, not us." But then he added that it wouldn't hurt us to lay off the stuff ourselves until Billy was gone.

As was our routine, we drove to the A&P in

East Hampton to pick up the ingredients for tonight's dinner—something to grill outside and something sweet for dessert. Then we headed for the train station, twenty minutes early.

It was one of those perfect eastern Long Island days. It was mid-week and so the village had settled into that polished lull it always acquired in the time between Sunday night and Thursday afternoon, when the weekenders began to arrive again. The sky was a beautiful, oceangoing shade of blue, with perfect white puffs of clouds, and the geraniums and impatiens planted around the station-house were lush. There was the sweet smell of hay and grass in the air, a touch of salt ocean. On the platform, I leaned to look down the tracks and saw the place, flocked by dark green trees, where the earth curved and merged the two black lines of tracks: *infinity*. How could anyone who had seen the illustration in grammar-school textbooks fail to think of the word?

A woman joined us on the platform, a tall woman in a thin dress, a bouquet of wildflowers held in the crook of her arm. And then two young men, tanned and sockless and dressed in expensive shades of pale yellow and pink. Then three girls in tennis whites and gold jewelry, another textbook illustration, but this time the caption would have read *Hamptons Debutantes*.

I wore cutoffs and sandals and a university T-shirt, my father a well-worn polyester polo shirt and gray gabardine suit pants, a beige base-ball cap stained at the bill and around the sweat-band, so that I suppose our illustration would be marked *Natives of Queens*.

"He'll notice a big difference," my father was saying about Billy. "After thirty years." And then: "He sure as hell better be sober."

"So what if he's not?" I asked. "Now that he's made this pledge. He goes straight to hell?"

My father glanced at me, seeing the apos-tate that I was. (Seeing, too, I suppose, his mother's one-cornered smile.) "I don't know," he said, to spare himself my sarcasm. We had long ago given up arguing about the niceties of our Church.

We felt the change in the air before we heard it confirmed by the far-off whistle of the train. Now all of us on the platform became attentive. Those at the back stepped forward, those at the edge stepped back. There was another blast of the whistle and then the black engine blotting out the light. There was the screeching of the brakes until, in what might have been mistaken for silence, the train came to a full rest before us, panting, it seemed, huge. We heard the conductor's voice, saw the shape of him moving past the windows. Another swung out of the middle car and looked up and down the platform as if he had arrived in an uncertain and hostile envi-ronment. Then he let go of the handrail and stepped out, turning to assist the passengers who had already gathered behind him.

Billy descended sideways, his black satchel coming first, black shoes and white socks and a Southern gentleman's pale blue seersucker suit. He smiled and waved and then placed his suitcase on the ground and waited for us to meet him.

He was taller than my father, but slightly stooped. He'd been thin all his life and the heaviness, the bloatedness, that age and alcohol had brought to his frame seemed irrelevant somehow; he still held himself like a thin man. You would still describe him as such. His dark hair was combed straight back from his forehead, still marked by the impression of his wet toothcomb. He wore the rimless glasses that you once saw only on priests and nuns, and his blue eyes were pale gray, nearly pearl. He smiled a little as he waited for us to approach him, touched his red tie, as elegant as a pope, but then, just as my father put out his hand and said, "Hey, Googenheimer," a wicked humor tumbled into his face. He grinned, they both grinned, shaking hands, laughing even, although neither had said any more than that yet. His cheeks and nose were bright pink with broken capillaries and spider veins, marks of his dissipation, sure, but, on Billy, subtly charming, almost intentionally so—like a touch of rouge and powder on a handsome actor's face.

"How was the trip?" my father was saying, laughing still as if in anticipation of a punch line.

"Behind me now," Billy said, grinning.

He took my hand, his was cold, and I gave him a quick kiss on the cheek, which was cold, too, and still smelling of Ivory soap and Sensen.

As the train pulled out again, he waved to someone inside—"Barney Callaghan's son," he told my father. "Can you imagine? A conductor on the Long Island Railroad." He turned to me and winked. "The children," he said, "are taking over the world." His face was all brightness, small white teeth, blue eyes, pink cheeks, and red lips, flashing lenses catching the changing light.

At the car, we put Billy's suitcase in the trunk—glimpse of my father's tackle box and fishing pole and the green army blanket dusted with sand.

My father offered lunch at the restaurant across the street, and Billy glanced at the place over his shoulder, nodding as if it was something he remembered. The intersection at that hour was nearly empty, and the sudden stillness that followed the departure of every train made the sunlight seem anticipatory, somehow: Dodge City at noon, a showdown pending.

"It's all the same," Billy said, even as the midday stillness began to fray around the edges: a light changing somewhere, cars once more headed our way.

"No, it's different," my father said. "It's not like the country anymore, more like any other suburb. We'll go for a drive, you'll see."

Inside the restaurant, the air was frosty

and dark, and although nearly every table was taken, there was a hush about the place. I shivered as I sat down, and rubbed my bare arms. Billy leaned toward me. "I'll tell you what's happening," he whispered. He held up one finger, lecturing. His lips were remarkably smooth. His eyes red-rimmed but clear. "Everybody here's been complaining about the heat all summer long and now they can't bring themselves to complain about the cold." He sat back a little, a smile working at the corner of his mouth. "Doesn't that tell you something about getting your heart's desire?" Then he motioned to the waiter. "Do you think you can adjust the air a bit?" he said softly, with just a touch of a brogue, a souvenir, no doubt, of his trip to Ireland.

"We're working on it," the waiter said, exasperated.

When he walked away, Billy pushed out his chair, stood, and then made a great show of swinging out of his suit jacket and draping it gallantly over my shoulders, saying to the people around us who had lifted their eyes to him, "A bit chilly in here, isn't it? Don't you think?" Getting each one to agree. Forming a union, it seemed. "Well, see now, you brought a sweater," he said to the older lady right beside us. "You're the clever one." The jacket smelled of Old Spice and the Long Island Railroad. Shivering, I pulled it over my elbows and felt as I did a small square weight in one pocket—a breviary or a flask.

By the time the waiter came to take our

orders, Billy had learned that the old lady with the sweater had lived out here since 1952 and wouldn't leave the place for a winter in Florida for all the tea in China. And that her companion, who had spent her childhood in Sag Harbor, felt much the same, although she still had her home in Yonkers.

"Well, I haven't been out here for nearly thirty years," he told them. The way he said it, this might have been his childhood home as well. The women were sufficiently sympathetic. Sufficiently puzzled. "My wife enjoys the Rockaways, you see, or used to, anyway, before it changed," he went on. "She likes a place with a boardwalk. And you know how it is, one summer passes and then another and you find yourself saying, 'Next year, let's go out there.' It's the prettiest spot on earth as far as I'm concerned, but you know how it is, suddenly it's been thirty years, even though it seems like yesterday."

As he spoke, he rolled up his shirtsleeves— his pale forearms were sandy with the remnants of a winter psoriasis—took a fountain pen from his breast pocket, and began to scribble a note on the corner of his paper place mat, all the while seeming to give the ladies beside us his undivided attention. He folded the place mat in half, then in quarters, and then folded a neat triangle at the top and tucked it inside. He wrote a quick address on the white front—Father somebody or other, it seemed, Albany, New York. He slipped a finger into the breast pocket of his shirt, extracted a single stamp, licked it, and put it in the corner. He placed the envelope at the edge of our table as if a courier might momentarily snatch it away.

"Oh, it's changed out here," the woman with the sweater told him. "It's not like it was in the forties."

"It is in my dreams," Billy told them. "Just the same." He winked, ran his hand through his hair. "But then again, so am I."

"Oh, aren't we all?" the sweater lady and her friend both said at once.

Billy smiled at them with something like gratitude, as if he could not imagine being seated beside two more pleasant and perceptive women. He raised his water glass. "God bless dreams," he said, and the ladies returned his toast. If there were shoes to be had, I suspect he could have sold them a dozen.

When the waiter brought our sandwiches he looked at the empty space before Billy with some perplexity and then quickly shifted the extra place mat at our table to Billy's place. Throughout the letter writing and the simultaneous conversation with the ladies, my father had been sitting back, grinning, watching his cousin be himself and delighting in it—there was no other word—delighting in him. I glimpsed for the first time what it must have cost my father, during all those years of my childhood when Billy was banned from our home until he could show up sober, those same years when my father's voice would wake us all in the middle of the night, as he shouted into the phone, "Billy, you're killing

69

yourself" or, more tempered but more desperate as well, "Just let me know where you are, Billy. Just tell me where you are."

I moved my elbow against the weight in Billy's jacket. If it was a flask, it was empty. If it was a breviary, it was rather thin.

"So how's everyone?" my father asked, leaning forward to lift his sandwich.

Billy launched into a familiar litany: his sister Rosie's kids (Holy Cross and Katherine Gibbs, Queensborough Community and the telephone company) and Kate's kids (Regis Fordham Notre Dame Marymount Chase Manhattan) and his mother at eighty, who still liked her nightcap. And who he had seen from the old neighborhood and the office and who had invited them out to Breezy Point next weekend and did you hear Kate's husband is now CFO of the entire organization, which means another addition to their house in Rye, which is already big enough for anybody, if you ask him, so he said to her, Why not take some of that money and feed the poor rather than redoing a house that's already well done. It's not like she's happy with her life or ever has been, if you know what I mean. She told him she could very well feed the poor and put a new guest wing on her house at the same time, which only goes to show she's not only missed the point of charity but become as addicted to spending money as her husband is to making it.

"And how was Ireland?" my father asked.

"Cold," Billy said, shaking his head as if the

weather were a moral deficit. "And wet. A miserable place to quit drinking."

My father smiled, indulgent. "But you quit." It was not a question.

"I signed on," Billy said, nodding. "And the day after I signed on I got a car and drove out to County Wicklow. All by myself. To Clonmel."

"And how was that?" my father asked—I have to say he asked it casually.

Slowly, Billy put his sandwich on his plate and sat back, his fingers touching the edge of the table. "Eva runs a gas station there," he said. "With her husband. She has four kids." He paused. "Eva does."

My father was stirring his iced tea with a long spoon. He nodded, carefully lifting the spoon and placing it on the tiny plate beneath his glass. He touched the lemon wedge beside it. "I knew that," he said.

Billy raised his eyebrows and smiled a little. His teeth were perfectly straight and even. Dentures, I remembered my mother telling me once, courtesy of Uncle Sam. "She told me you did," he said.

My father fiddled with the spoon. Had I asked earlier in the conversation who Billy Sheehy was or Marge Tierney or Eddie Schmidt or Tony D'Agostino I might have been inclined to inquire here about Eva and her gas station and her four kids. But the chicken salad had walnuts in it that I was thinking I really could have done without and it was easy enough to guess that Eva was someone from the neighborhood, from the company, from my grand-father's sprawling legacy of immigrants and immigrants' children. Someone Billy might send place-mat letters to.

"I did know," my father said. "I'm sorry to say."

And Billy blew some air from between his lips and shook his head and glanced at the cold ceiling above us. Then he winked at me. "When you were christened," he said, "your father drove us over to the church from your house. Your mother, God rest her soul, stayed at home—women did that in those days, didn't they"—to my father—"missed out on their own babies' christenings to stay home and get things ready for the party?"

"They were supposed to still be in con-finement," my father said, and then, acknowl-edging the truth: "But they were usually getting things ready for the party."

"So your aunt was holding you," Billy went on, "your mom's sister Louise, and she and I went on in with the others while your father here parked the car. You were brand-new to that parish, weren't you, Dennis? To St. Clare's?"

I saw my father beginning to grin, anticipating what was to come. "We'd just bought the house the month before."

Billy turned back to me. "Well, he must have gotten confused parking, because he took longer than we thought he would, and next thing you know, we're all standing at the baptismal font, waiting for him. And in he comes, at a run, and when he sees us standing up there with the priest he does a little leap to get to us—I guess he thought we were going ahead without him—and splat, lands right on his face at our feet."

My father was grinning now, looking at his lap, shaking his head.

"I've heard this," I tried to say, but Billy went on.

"Well, everybody says, Good Lord, and when the priest bends down to help him, your father looks up all red in the face and says, 'I'm just so loaded.'"

"With happiness!" my father said now. "I meant to say, I'm just so loaded with happiness..."

Billy shook his finger at him. "Yeah, but what you said and what everyone heard was 'I'm so loaded.'" To me again, his eyes suddenly wet with tears, although only my father was laughing. "And just a week later I go into a diner up on Linden Boulevard and there's the priest who did the baptism—what was his name, Dennis, he was an older man?"

My father shook his head to show he couldn't recall. "I should remember," he said. "He gave me such a talking-to when the christening was over."

"Anyway, there he is in this diner and he comes over to me and he asks, 'How's that unfortunate brother of yours?'—he thought we were brothers—and I told him, 'Still full of the same stuff, I'm afraid.'" And now Billy, too, began to laugh, a deep, quiet but irrepressible laugh, his eyes shining with their unshed tears. "'Still full of it,' I said." He glanced at my father. "Not exactly a lie, you might say. More a matter of interpretation."

My father bowed his head again, as if to concede something, but when he looked up his smile showed a shadow being lifted. "All right," he said, as if he were ready to stand corrected. "All right." As if he believed he was being forgiven.

WE TOOK HIM on the usual big-home tour through the estates of East Hampton and he seemed to remember every one of them from his single summer here after the war. One he identified as the Appleton residence—he had bought a postcard of it way back when. Mosler, Eastman, Bouvier. His favorite was a place on the edge of the beach, above a potato field. "Where's Pudding Hill Lane?" he asked, and my father turned down it for him, driving slowly. "They called these their cottages," Billy said at one point, turning to me in the back seat. "Yes." I nodded as if the irony of it was still interesting. We had the windows open and Billy had one arm raised, holding on to the roof; the other hand was in the left, empty pocket of his jacket.

"Well, it's still beautiful," he said as we headed back to the village and the little house. "Nothing's changed."

"Just us," my father said, but Billy had begun to recite slowly, softly, like a man humming a tune to himself, letting the words get caught in the breeze from the window. "'I will arise and go now, and go to Innisfree...'" It was a matter of some pride to my father, to Billy's friends and family in general, that he had carried a volume of Yeats with him all through the war. Not that my father, or most of his family, read the poems themselves; more that Billy's interest absolved them from any interest of their own. When my generation of cousins began to come back from college with copies of Ginsberg and Ferlinghetti and Sylvia Plath, our parents could sniff, "Oh, poetry, sure. Billy Lynch loves that Irish poet, Yeats (or Yeets)"—with a proud nonchalance that seemed to hint that the poet was a friend of a friend. "'And I shall have some peace there,'" Billy said.

At the house I quickly changed into my bathing suit and headed out for my daily, transforming swim, stepping past the two of them on the front steps, short glasses of lemonade in their hands and *Time* magazine on my father's knee: an article about Nixon, poor man (they were saying), poor hounded man, caught in his tangle of lies. Billy had left his jacket and tie in the guest bedroom.

The bay was about a mile and a half away, through streets that were, as my father had said, becoming more and more suburban. As he'd pointed out each time we'd walked this route together, thirty years ago there was hardly a house between ours and the bay, and the road that was tarred now was mostly dirt then. He and Billy himself that first summer they were back from overseas had widened part of it with the scythe Mr. Holtzman had lent them.

Now there were as many houses, as many cars on the tarred road as you might find in any of Long Island's greener suburbs. And although most of the houses here, with their leanto carports and decorative lobster pots, with nautical flags and badminton sets in sandy tree-shaded yards, were clearly summer homes, beach cottages in the less ironic sense of the word, there were a number as well that had pale aluminum siding and custom-made drapes in bay windows and full two-car garages, as sturdy and suburban and dull as any in Rosedale or Franklin Square. Places for year-round living, for six o'clock dinners of macaroni and cheese and hurried mornings of getting to work and meeting the school bus. Suburban sprawl overtaking summer romance, as far as I could see. The chances for any of us living that rare two weeks in high summer, in a wild place by the sea, a hiatus, as Billy and my father had called it after the war, diminishing and diminishing.

When I heard a car behind me, I moved to the dusty edge of the road, as I'd gotten into the habit of doing on this walk. I shot an angry look over my shoulder when I felt the warmth of its engine on the back of my legs. It was, after all, my life coming at me, my future that was threatening to run me down—who wouldn't give it a dirty look?

I slowed further, even stepped onto the

sandy edge of the road, into the tall weeds and the grass. Finally, I turned. It was Mr. West's car and Matthew or Cody or John was driving, leaning across the front seat to call out the window and offer a ride.

He (Matthew, you) was due to meet a friend at the lobster dock in twenty minutes, so we were spared the memory of a first conversation on the same sunny bay beach where Billy met Eva in those first weeks he was home from the war. We sat in the car instead, the broad front seat. There was the scent of stale cigarettes and old joints and the sweet smell of the beach towel I held on my lap. You were tan and wore the leather band around your right wrist. Just out of Stony Brook. Worked a charter fishing boat all summer. Wanted to own one of your own. Wanted to see the West Coast. Never went into the city, didn't like it. Couldn't imagine living in a place like Rosedale, going to college way up in Buffalo. A Bonacker, a real Bonacker. But your mouth was wry and your eyes dark brown. I suspected you would age into your father's face exactly, but without the furtive brows. You ducked your head when you laughed, like someone who has flubbed his lines onstage, someone needing to correct himself.

We agreed to go out that night. Walking back from the bay—I'd stayed longer than usual, accruing benefits, I thought—I wondered if my father would be offended. I knew what my mother would have said: a date was for her my primary social obligation and superseded all other claims. Even in her final days she insisted I go out if someone asked me. "Go," she had said, frowning as if she could not believe my hesitation, as if to say, Haven't I taught you anything? When she couldn't speak, she merely waved her hand, sweeping me out: *go.*

They were sitting on lawn chairs now, my father and Billy, on the sparse grass in front of the house. As I came down the road, my father was leaning forward, his forearms on his knees, his head bent, listening like a diligent priest. Billy was leaning forward, too, but with his arms folded across his chest and his back straight. They both looked up when my sandal hit the gravel driveway, but they were too lost, it seemed—in conversation? in the past? in recrimination?—to fully notice or recognize me until I was almost beside them. Or close enough to see that my father was shaking his head, ever so slightly, refusing, refusing something that Billy wanted him to take. And that Billy, holding himself carefully, speaking slowly, softly, even as he turned to smile at me, had already had quite a bit to drink.

O F THE (LET'S FACE IT) half dozen or so basic versions of the Irish physiognomy, they had two of them: Billy thin-faced with black hair and pale blue eyes behind his rimless glasses; Dennis with broad cheeks, eternally flushed, and dark eyes and fair hair that had only begun to thin under his combat helmet, somewhere, he claimed, in northern France. One every inch the poet or the scholar, the other a perfect young cop or barman. The aesthete priest and the jolly chaplain.

But in fact they had both gone to the RCA Institute before the war and had left steady jobs at Con Ed to enlist. In July 1945, they both had plans to return there in the fall, or as soon as the Long Island house was finished, as soon as they were ready to end this hiatus— they called it that—between their lives as they were and whatever it was their lives were to become.

Their charge had been to make the place livable again after nearly a decade of abandonment. To update the plumbing and the electrical, chase out the mice and the wasps, repair or replace whatever parts of the floor or the ceiling, the windows or the doors needed repair or replacement. The directive had come from Holtzman, the shoe salesman, as if an afterthought, over dinner the second night Dennis was home (although it was not home to him, it was the salesman's house, even though he sat at his mother's dining-room table). He offered the project as if in a burst of inspiration, even said something like "Here's an idea for you boys..." although Dennis knew that in his kit in an upstairs bedroom (not his room, although the bed was the one he had slept in as a child) he had the letter his mother had sent him, the laundry list of reasons to remarry. He knew by the anxious glance Holtzman shot her, even as he pretended to be inspired, that the project had been his mother's idea all along.

On the afternoon of their arrival, they parked the car in the rutted and overgrown driveway and in shirtsleeves and fedoras and army boots cut through the knee-high grass and the weeds with the scythe and the clippers Holtzman had lent them. City-bred, they made quite a show of it, testing their arms and the heat and their resolve, and sending the tall grass, the bees and grasshoppers and zithering beetles every which way as they made a good path across the sandy soil to the three peeling steps at the front door. They pulled the screen off its hinges with the first tug.

The key Holtzman had given them was attached to a chain that was attached to a metal shoehorn engraved with the name and the address of his Jamaica Avenue store. It was only this, this awkward key chain, that made them fumble a bit. The door itself opened easily, the way it would in a movie or a dream, as if the lock hadn't been real at all, or as if the hinges had been well oiled. The place was musty and warm and you could see dust motes in the sunlight that came through the kitchen window as clearly as you could see the sink and the stove and the sagging gray couch.

Now the vague thoughts Dennis had been having about every place he'd been to since his return from overseas took form and he said to Billy, "This has been here," as if Billy would know what he meant. What he meant was, this house has been here, just like this, all the while he had been locked in the adventure and tedium of the war. This had been here, just as it was (like the Chrysler Building, his mother's new home, the Jamaica Avenue El), all the while and at each and every moment he had been away.

"Since the twenties, I suppose," Billy said, not getting it.

"Forever," Dennis told him.

But Billy got it later, after they'd found a restaurant in East Hampton for dinner and then, because neither of them had been here before and because the charm of the village gave them the sense that the roads that led from it offered something more, they toured the place in Holtzman's car. It had all been here. The elegant trees that lined the broad streets, the great green lawns that grew, even as they were slowly passing, greener and deeper in the twilight so you could almost make yourself believe that night was seeping in through their roots, not moving across the sky above them. The houses—when had they ever seen such houses, how was it they hadn't known they were out here? Grand and complex palaces, *cottages* wood-shingled or white, with gazebos in their gardens and great pillared porches that curved like bows and widow's walks and gabled attic rooms from which you could probably glimpse both the silver spires of the city and the black ocean edge of the earth.

They moaned to see the darkened places that had not yet been opened for the season— "No one even there"—and whispered, "Take a look at that," when one was lit like a steamship from stem to stern. But what killed them, what really killed them, were the houses that looked out over the ocean, that had for their front or back yards a dark lush carpet of beautifully mown grass and then, running down from the other side, as if front and back had been built on different planets, magnificent dunes, sea grass, white beach and sea.

"Leave me there when I'm dead," Billy said of one of them—a large house on a wide lawn with a starry backdrop of sky that even in near darkness seemed to contain the reflected sound and sparkle of the ocean. "Prop me up on the porch with a pitcher of martinis and a plate of oysters on the half shell and I'll be at peace for all eternity. Amen."

They made their way home in darkness, under the thick leaves along Main Street and out toward the sandier and less elegant regions of the Springs and Three Mile Harbor. They made several wrong turns and even in the driveway sat squinting at the little house for a few minutes before they decided it was the right place, after all.

They agreed to sleep in the car that night, since the mattresses were mildewed and the mice well ensconced. With GI resourcefulness they hung T-shirts over the opened windows and secured the edges with electrical tape in order to keep out most of the bugs.

They smoked for half an hour, Dennis in the front seat, Billy in back. "I never knew," Billy said at one point, his glasses in his hand, his hand resting on his forehead, "I never knew what it was like out here." It was what he would write on his postcards tomorrow, creating artifacts. "Isn't that something? I had no idea those places were out here."

"It's something," Dennis said. "Bridie was here once," he added. "She came out to Southampton with someone. She said it was really something."

"It is," Billy said. He paused. "It almost makes you wonder what else you don't know about yet."

Dennis frowned for a moment and then said, "Plenty," with a laugh. But although Billy looked the part he was no poet or scholar and could not explain: what else did he not know about yet that would strike him as the village tonight had struck him—strike him in that very first moment of apprehending, of seeing and smelling and tasting, as something he could not, from that moment on, get enough of and could never ever again live without.

83

By the end of their first week they had a routine and a sufficient knowledge of the roads to find the dump and the bay beach, the cheaper restaurants and the hardware stores. They did the heaviest work early in the morning and then ducked inside before noon to wire and paint and plaster. Around four or five, when the sunlight began to edge from white to yellow, they took their towels from the clothesline they had rigged between two trees out back and walked with them draped around their necks the mile and a half to the bay. They cleared a shortcut with Holtzman's scythe. The beach there was rocky at the shoreline, littered with shells, but the water was warmer than the ocean, and since neither of them was much of a swimmer, they both welcomed the chance to just float and dive and touch their toes to the bottom at will.

Some nights they stopped into a bar off the Springs road. They both drank too much the first and second time, but only Billy, engaged in long conversation with the bartender and an ugly old Bonacker who could not hear enough about the war, drank too much the third and fourth.

Billy drunk, in those days, was charming and sentimental. He spoke quietly, one hand in his pocket and the other around his glass, his glass more often than not pressed to his heart. There was tremendous affection in Billy's eyes, or at least they held a tremendous offer of affection, a tremendous willingness to find whomever he was talking to bright and witty and better than most. Dennis came to believe in those days that you could measure a person's vanity simply by watching how long it took him to catch on to the fact that Billy hadn't recognized his inherent and long-underappreciated charm, he'd drawn it out with his own great expectations or simply imagined it, whole cloth.

They talked about the war: the characters in their divisions, Midwesterners always the crudest, didn't you notice, something to do with living around farm animals, no doubt; the officers good and bad, the morning just before they returned, when a group coming out of first mess claimed they were serving cake for breakfast, which turned out to be only bread, fresh bread. The tar-paper shack Dennis and two other fellows had constructed, warmer than the tents, the Pilsen Hilton. Their luck in avoiding the Pacific. Their quests for souvenirs. Patton and Ike and F.D.R., the lying old smoothy. The kids begging chocolate and chewing gum. The French girls, all of them beautiful, one coming to Switching Central in Metz, where Billy was operating near the end, to ask if a message could be sent to her fiancé, another GI gone north. She said she even knew his code name, Vampire, which made two or three of the other boys laugh out loud. She was a dark-haired girl with great big dark eyes. She wore a white handkerchief knotted around her neck, as lovely as diamonds. The message she asked Billy to send was simply: "I am still here."

THEIR SHOULDERS AND ARMS and the backs of their necks burned and freckled and peeled, and after dinner each evening they walked through the village with toothpicks in their mouths or drove past the great houses on the surrounding streets, noticing the changes in them, how they looked in the rain, in clear twilight, how well they bore even the oppressive air of the hotter days and marveling, marveling still, that this Eden was here, at the other end of the same island on which they had spent their lives.

One afternoon just before VJ Day a family was spread across a blanket on the widest crescent of bay beach—at least they thought it was a family as they approached from the road. But as they dropped their towels and bent to unlace their already loosely laced boots, to slip off the socks they wore under them and the pants they wore over their swim trunks, they quickly changed their assessment. Six children, the oldest no more than nine, and two women, girls, actually, who were not old enough to be mothers to them all.

They nodded a greeting to the girls and the children as they made their way to the water and then, swimming out with as much form as they had ever shown for as much distance as they dared to go, floated a bit under the paling sky, glancing as they did, in subtle, sidelong glances, at the group on the shore, at the

86

girls especially, one standing now at the water's edge, a pail and shovel in her hand and two little ones at her feet. The other, only a little plumper, on the blanket still and wearing an old-fashioned swim cap over her curly hair that from the water's distance—at least for Billy, whose glasses were in his pants pocket on the sand—seemed like an aura of royal-blue light.

Five of the children were knee-deep in the water now, dipping their outspread hands just as the one girl was instructing them to do, fingers splayed like starfish, washing off the sand. Then one of the children, the tallest boy, stepped out of the water with his splayed hands held high, as if he were a surgeon, as if the sand might leap up at any minute and cover them again and called, "Eva," toward the blanket, "Eva," although it was impossible to tell if he meant the girl in the swim cap or the sixth child, who sat beside her, because at that moment a huge black touring car pulled up from the road and in a sudden gathering of pails and shovels and shells and picnic baskets and cover-ups and blankets— a sudden momentum that died the minute everything was off the sand and they made, in incredibly slow motion, the trek from beach to car—they were gone.

The two swam a little closer, to a shallower, more comfortable distance from the shore, and then climbed out of the water completely. They reached their towels and in an economy of terry cloth that they had learned in the service dried face and arms and shoulders with one end, chest and legs with the other, and then sat on the dry middle on the sand to smoke a cigarette and then, flicking their feet with one sock and then the other, put on socks and boots for the walk home.

The road was hot and Dennis had both his pants and his towel draped over his shoulders to protect his latest burn. He could feel as he walked the salt drying on his legs and on his face and arms. He could see a line of it on the pale hair of his cousin's calf.

They were virgins, both of them. Before the war, all the girls they'd known had seemed to be another cousin's schoolmate or the daughter of an aunt's best friend, and while desire had presented itself often enough, the tight quarters and the rigorous decorum of that time and place had failed to offer opportunity for more than an accidental brush or a chaste kiss. And later, when opportunity did abound, when they were handsome in their uniforms and perfectly fit, they were only weeks or days away from shipping out and the looming possibility of their own deaths made even the desire to commit, at this late date, that kind of mortal sin seem as foolish and as fleeting as the mad longing to hurl yourself, willy-nilly, from some great height—the parachute jump at Coney Island, for instance, or the observation deck of the Empire State Building—or to raise your head from the mud during a live ammo drill at boot camp, just because you had the urge.

They had bruised girls' lips with kisses then, had learned the pleasure of encircling a waist or running a hand along a stockinged leg, of feeling a heartbeat behind a breast, but the Paulist Fathers had gotten them at an early age and they had studied heaven and hell long before they knew that at the top of a stocking there was only bare flesh, and boys they had known from the basketball court or the K. of C. had already gone over and lost their lives. And even in Manhattan, at midnight, in uniform and as drunk as the girls on their knees, they saw through the bold music and the laughter and the smoky air their foreshortened lives, the nearness of eternity, and so always rode the subway home alone, reeling and laughing and helped by the hands of innumerable smiling strangers, to sleep it off under their mother's own roof.

THE NEXT AFTERNOON the two girls and their six charges were there again, the thinner one in the same dark blue bathing suit that cut squarely across the top of her thighs in the front but in the back relented a little and followed the sweet lines of her bottom; the other in yet another swim cap, a pale yellow one this time, a halo now as Billy squinted at her from across the sand. They had a beach umbrella with them today, green with yellow stripes, and in its shade they had both a lunch hamper and a wicker laundry basket.

The children were in the water already when the two of them arrived, the younger ones equipped today with red and blue inner tubes, and so it was easy enough, after they had shed their boots and their socks and their khaki pants, to nod at the ladies once more and then to say to the children as they walked past them into the gently lapping surf, "The water's very wet today, don't you think?"

There was a pause of children's stares.

Billy winked. "It wasn't quite as wet yesterday, was it?"

The four children gazed at them, four towheads with blue-green eyes and a red bandage of sun across each nose. "No," one of them, the tallest girl, said. "It couldn't be."

"Sure," Billy told them. He rubbed some water between thumb and forefinger as if he were feeling cloth. "And one day last week it was hardly wet at all."

"Didn't need a towel," Dennis said.

"Didn't need a towel," Billy agreed. "Went in for half an hour and came out dry as a bone."

The older girl was still looking at them skeptically, but the younger ones had begun to giggle, the laughter bobbing up to their throats much as they were bobbing inside their swim tubes. "No," they said. "You're making that up."

"It's the truth," Dennis said indignantly, and then Billy pointed to the smallest girl, who, because she could not touch the bottom, moved with more abandon as she laughed.

"Look at this little one here," Billy said. "She looks like a buoy."

Dennis shook his head gravely. "No, she's a girl."

The little one looked to her bigger sister and the sister said, "She's a girl."

"But she looks like a buoy," Billy said again. "A buoy, a buoy." He pointed out to the bay, to the black buoys that dotted the horizon until the children saw what he meant and began shouting, "A buoy, a boo-eee, one of those."

But Dennis continued to shake his head. "How could she be a boy with all that hair piled up on top of her head? You're a girl, aren't you?"

And the little one, uncertain of the joke but delighted by the attention, merely giggled and bobbed and let the other three cry for her, "Yes, she's a girl, but he means a buoy, a buoy."

The commotion had the desired effect (blessed, blessed children) and slowly, the young woman in the navy-blue suit sauntered toward the water with a toddler on her hip, a smile beginning, Dennis was certain, if she would only raise that coyly bent head.

This she did as she entered the water and with her free hand splashed some of it on the baby's plump leg. "Hello," she said, meeting their eyes just long enough to show that hers were gray and darkly lashed.

"Hello," they said, one after the other, with as much gallantry and graciousness as they could, being bare-chested and thigh-high in water. Had they been wearing hats, they would have tipped them.

"Isn't the water wet today, Mary?" the older girl asked.

91

Mary continued to sweep up water languidly with her fingertips and to brush it onto the child's legs. "Yes, isn't it?" she said. The poor child looking down into the bay with something nearing terror, clinging to her shoulder and the neck of her suit, pulling it down just that much to show an inch of pure white flesh just below a delicate suntan. "Wetter than yesterday, I think," she said.

And there it was.

"You're Irish," Dennis said, and Billy asked, "Where from?" at the ready with the information that his own father was from Cork and his mother Donegal.

She was from a place in County Wicklow, although she'd been over here since before the war. Since before Jonathan, the oldest boy, who was now stretched out under the umbrella with a magazine and an apple, was born. And of course, looking up at Jonathan on the blanket, they could not help but see the other girl, too (although Billy saw her as a mirage of smeared color, pink legs and a dark suit, pink shoulders and arms and face, and a yellow cap like a low flame, a mirage that perhaps only wild hope and great imagination could form into a solid woman).

"That's Eva, my sister," Mary said. "She's only visiting. She's on her way home."

The family they worked for had a place on Park Avenue and a house in East Hampton and money, Dennis gathered, that poured down like sunlight. The man of the house had spent the war in Washington, D.C., but not so much of it that the babies ever stopped coming, all six of them born in the past decade, and the seventh, the newest, now asleep in the wicker basket.

"It was really too much for me," Mary said. "So I asked if my sister could come for the summer. She'd been with a family in Chicago. She'll be going home in the fall."

Billy squinted and nodded and stirred the water around him with his hands. It might have been quicksand, he seemed, at the moment, so mired in it. It was not that Mary herself wasn't pretty enough, with her gray eyes and her dark hair and her boyish and direct way, but Dennis already had the greater part in the conversation and she herself seemed to like it that way. And he wanted to swear no allegiance until he had considered both options carefully, and he sensed, perhaps because she was still a blur of colored light, that the girl on the blanket was the one for him.

But how to get to her? How to end this conversation here (he and Dennis, after all, hadn't even swum yet) and get up on the shore and near enough to the blanket where she sat in the partial shade of the umbrella to say, "Well, hello, Eva."

And then the infant in the basket began to cry. At first he thought it was the cry of a gull and he looked toward the sky, but then he saw her kneeling beside the basket and lifting the child—another blur—to her shoulder, then standing, rocking, beginning to pace. The other children were oblivious to the crying, as

93

no doubt they had to be in a family where year after year another baby arrives to bump them that much further into adulthood, but Mary and Dennis were oblivious, too, talking now, just the two of them, about certain lucky investors who had done nothing but profit from the war.

Billy walked past them, through the water and over the rocky edge of the shore. He had not swum and so only his trunks and legs were wet and even his hands seemed to dry as he made his way toward her. The baby was crying full blast now, hot and sleepy and desperate against her shoulder. She had a hand behind its head and was hushing and clucking, but as soon as he was close enough to see her better, he knew she'd had her eyes on him all along. The boy with the magazine turned his slim back to them, as befit a magnate's son.

She smiled ruefully. The blossom of curly hair above her forehead was dark, dark red, and the yellow cap that hid the rest of it had been partially knocked back, a dishevelment that made what at a distance was the illusion of an aura, a halo, seem, close up, only childish and adorable. Her eyes were brown, her cheeks smooth and broad, and because her teeth were crooked her mouth was crooked, too. She was shorter than her sister and indeed plumper. And the shoulder the poor babe was wetting with saliva and tears was whiter than the sand, scattered with dark beauty marks as delicate as distant stars.

"Can I take him?" Billy said, holding out his hands. He stood at the edge of the blanket, darkening the sand with the water from his suit.

"If I can just get him his bottle," she said—her accent, too, was plumper than her sister's, and there was a tremble in it, a kind of panic, set off, no doubt, by the child's insistent misery.

"I'll take him," he said.

If he had been more self-conscious, it wouldn't have worked. Or if he had been more calculating. If, when she handed him the screaming child he had noticed the movement of her breasts, the size of her waist, the shape of her legs and her thighs as she quickly turned to the lunch hamper to find the bottle of milk, the child would have stiffened in his arms and screamed all the more and he would have been forced to hand him back to her and perhaps even, awkwardly, make his defeated way back to the water, matters far worse for his interference.

But the child was as light as a feather in his hands and the lightness took his breath away. The baby wore a seersucker sunsuit that left his tiny arms and shoulders bare, and Billy covered these with a cupped palm as he rested the child against his chest. The flesh was as sweetly warm as if the hand of God had just formed it. He blew softly across the child's downy hair and closed his eyes to say, "Now now, little fellow. Now now."

The child was lighter than the sun-warmed air. The miracle of it, for him, was the perfection of the tiny head and spine, ear and hand. The miracle was that the child quieted immediately in Billy's arms, placed his cheek to Billy's heart, and heaved one deep and restful sigh even before she had turned from the cooler with the bottle of milk in her hand.

"Will you look at that now?" she said, showing her crooked smile, her flashing eyes. "You must have a way with children."

And he could see from the start (her eyes were not so much brown but a kind of mahogany, the exact color of her hair) that there was nothing she more admired in a man.

"Have you got lots of brothers and sisters?"

What better way to begin? He held the child and they talked together until the wet sand at his feet had dried again, and when the child next woke she handed him the bottle and he lowered himself and the baby onto the blanket, under the umbrella's shade, and fed him there while the other children ran up and back and Dennis and Mary, now standing at the edge of the water, talked and talked.

When did he fall in love with her? Probably it was the day before, before she had even come clearly into his view. But that afternoon he fell in love with the rest of his life, and that was better still. The days ahead when he would come to the beach here and the child he held, the children who ran to them, wet and trembling, would be theirs and when the flesh of her arms and her throat and her sweet breasts would be as familiar to him as his own.

It was there, that life, that future. It had been

there all along. He simply hadn't known it until now, or had the capacity to imagine just a month ago that something like this might be his. That this golden future, this Eden, had been part of the same life he'd been living all along. Wasn't that something? He hadn't known until now that it was there.

They met again the next afternoon and the next. Dennis and Billy began to quit work a bit earlier each day, and at times it was nearly dusk before they left their boots on the steps by the front door.

The Mr. and Mrs.—or so the girls called their employers—were in Washington for the week, and so it was easy enough for them to tell the driver not to come until six or so, then seven. The children were glad to be out late and to have their supper at the shore, with the candy Billy brought them for dessert.

At night the boys still made their slow circuit of the stately homes, but now with a keener interest and intent, to discover the house the girls lived in. Although they tried gentle questioning for the first few afternoons ("You're not in one of those places on the beach, are you?"), it was only by direct inquiry that they learned which house it was exactly and then were rewarded that same night with the sight of Eva, glimpsed through the only opening in the high hedge that until now had made the house uninteresting, crossing the front path, barefoot, and going up the steps to the porch.

Late in August, a Tuesday night, they met

the girls at the house itself. It was nine o'clock. The Mr. and Mrs. had said the girls could go out, but only after the children were asleep, and the girls told them to come around to the back and knock at the kitchen door.

At deep blue twilight they passed through the village and down the now-familiar streets. They were newly showered and shaved and they wore the white shirts they had washed out in the morning and left to dry in the sun all day long and then ironed themselves, with an ancient, secondhand Proctor-Silex, on a towel under a pillowcase spread out on the kitchen table. They turned in, as they had been instructed, past the tall hedge, and the crackle of their slow wheels on the gravel drive was enough to set their nerves drumming, the way the fanfare did in the moment before a curtain was raised on a stage.

They parked, and now locusts and the hush of the ocean filled the air along with the odor of honeysuckle and salt water. There was a line of windows across the back of the house and each of these was warmly lit, and on the nearest side a simple set of steps led from the driveway to a darkened door.

These they climbed, whispering, "Is it here?" and peering in before they knocked to a small square hallway lit by a rectangle of curtain-filtered light from the room beyond. There were the familiar shovels and pails, the swim tubes and the hamper. They heard Mary's voice, and then the inside door was pulled open and there she was in a pale dress, opening the door to let them in.

"We'll need another minute," she said. "There's a mutiny in progress."

The room they followed her into was huge—easily as large as the apartment where Dennis had been raised. A kitchen with a table as big as a bus and an icebox that could have housed a short family. The room was softly lit now and quiet, but it was possible to imagine the chaos there must have been just an hour or two before. You saw it in the two wooden high chairs, still slightly askew, at the far end of the table, in the five empty milk bottles lined neatly on the metal drying board, the scattered children's books and crayons and paper airplanes on the window seat at the far end of the room. You smelled it in the pleasant odor of dishwashing soap and coffee and the lingering scent of some kind of roast.

Eva sat at the near end of the table, her back to them, and as she turned at their entrance they saw she had Sally, the five-year-old, on her lap. Eva, too, wore a dress. It had capped sleeves and a rounded neck and there was nothing more beautiful than the way she turned in her chair and smiled up at them over the little girl's head. There was a glass of milk and a half-eaten cookie on the table before them.

"All in bed but this one," Mary said.

"Oh, but she's going now, isn't she?" Eva whispered, leaning around to see the little girl's face. "Now that the boys are here."

She was a bony little angel in her thin cotton nightgown and her braid. A sprite. And too small, Dennis thought, to be at home in a house

99

this huge. But she nodded and said yes, clearly exhausted, and put her feet to the familiar linoleum.

"'Down by the salley gardens,'" Billy said in a light brogue as Eva stood and took the little girl's hand, "'my love and I did meet...'"

The child smiled up at him, recognizing the poem he had recited to her before, on the beach. "'She passed the salley gardens with little snow-white feet.'" He put his hand to his heart, emoting. "'She bid me take love easy, as the leaves grow on the tree; But I, being young and foolish, with her would not agree.'" He winked at Eva over the little girl's head. "'She bid me take life easy, as the grass grows on the weirs; But I was young and foolish, and now am full of tears...'"

"Say good night to the gentlemen," Mary told her, and Sally whispered good night and waved shyly.

"Good night, dear," they both said, and then watched as Eva led her down a darkened hallway, lit at its far end by the lights in other rooms, and then up the back staircase.

Had he been a poet or a scholar, Billy might have remarked how, in any house, children asleep in far rooms add a sweetness to the air. But he would save the remark for Eva alone, when the children and the house were theirs.

SINCE IT WAS TOO LATE for supper, they went into Southampton, to a place Dennis remembered Bridie mentioning—a bartender there the brother of a friend from Woodside. But the bartender this night was a stranger, although an amiable one—another GI who'd been lucky enough to watch the war from an air base in England. He'd seen Glenn Miller there, just before he boarded the plane he disappeared on. And married a girl from Cornwall, who hadn't joined him yet but was already saying in her letters how much she was going to miss bloody England.

Mary and Eva clucked their tongues. Poor girl.

The bar was cool and dark and it gleamed in sundry places like a jewel; like a jewel it caught light along its polished surfaces, in its brass rail, in the mirror that ran its length and the various glasses and bottles that lined the heavy, stately counter across its back. There was only another couple at a table in the corner and the four of them, until the door opened and a single young man walked in. He sat opposite them, at the far end of the bar, and because the bartender was in the middle of a funny story about a crazed airman and one unloaded bomb, the man sat unserved for a good while, until Dennis, when the story was finished, pointed and nodded.

The bartender wiped a tear of laughter from his eye, threw the bar rag over his shoulder, and turned toward the new man, and then, just as abruptly, pulled the rag down and began slowly to polish an empty foot of bar.

"But I was sorry to miss seeing Paris," he said. "That's my one big regret about the war." He moved in front of them again. "We had this one fellow," he said. "Another pilot." He began to lean his elbow toward the bar, to launch another story, and Dennis, thinking he was either nearsighted or lazy, pointed again and said, "There's a man who's been waiting."

Still leaning down, the bartender looked over his shoulder toward the man, and the man— he was no older than themselves—lifted his hand and raised a finger to indicate he was there, as if he were in a crowd of patrons and not alone at the end of a mostly deserted room.

The bartender turned back to them. "This guy went to Harvard, this pilot I'm talking about, but he was a nice guy just the same, regular. And he comes up to me one morning and he says..."

Now Billy, beginning to feel parched in sympathy for the man (although his own glass had twice and quite generously been refilled), interrupted to say, "I think there's a man who needs a drink."

This time the bartender didn't turn around, just bowed his head and smiled a bit—he was a good-looking guy with a strong chin and thick hair—and picked up his story again.

The girls exchanged a look of both surprise and concern, and then Eva looked at Billy in a way he imagined he would someday find familiar, looking for him to explain. While the bartender continued with his story, the man sat, impassively, his hands folded one upon the other on the bar, and then, without a single look of impatience or anger or disgust, only perhaps a single deep breath, a defeated movement of his shoulders, he swung off the barstool and pushed out the door.

The boy from Harvard, it seemed, would have flown the bartender to Paris after the liberation, as a wedding present, if he'd survived the war.

He straightened up again. "This is my round." But Dennis put his hand over his glass and pointed to the place where the man had been.

"What is he, a boozer?"

The bartender turned casually, the cocktail shaker in his hand. He seemed unaware until then that the man had gone, and still maddeningly indifferent to having lost a customer. He shook his head, selecting rye for the girls' old-fashioneds. "We don't serve Jews," he said, as neatly as he poured the drink and placed it on the bar before them.

THEY WERE GRATEFUL to get outside, and more grateful still to get back into the salesman's car and return to the dark and elegant roads of East Hampton. "Well, I think it's a shame," Mary said from the front seat. "Good Lord, what did you boys fight for anyway? Has he read about the camps? What was the war all about—that poor man."

And the other three shook their heads, yes, poor man, but unwilling to let the shame of it, the sluggish, sickening sense of false hope and false promise, invade their idyll in this lovely place.

Billy leaned down toward Eva's lap, pointing

out her window. "Look there," he said. "That one. That's my idea of heaven."

They parked at the Coast Guard beach, and the girls sat together on the bumper while the boys found driftwood and built a small fire. While they were gathered around it, the beach became vast and black, and the thud of the invisible ocean, even with its predictable rhythm, seemed relentlessly startling.

They each put an arm around their girl's shoulders, and then Dennis lifted the dimming flashlight and asked Mary to take a walk with him down to the shore. Billy and Eva watched the swaying beam as it moved through the dark and then disappeared over the seawall.

Eva had her shoes off and her white toes were partially buried in the sand. She had her knees raised under her skirt, the skirt's hem pulled down around her ankles. She leaned forward when the other two had gone, moving out of his arm to stare at the burning wood and say, "When I was a child, I used to pretend I was a little person caught down there, inside the fire. A lost soul." She moved a finger to trace an imaginary path. "I'd see myself running, up one log and down the other, to escape the flames."

She turned to him, the firelight on her cheek and her bare arms. "I was certain I was going to hell and I thought it was a good way of practicing—you know, planning how I'd manage in there, how I'd outsmart the devil."

He laughed. Her eyes were marvelous.

"What made you think you weren't going to heaven?"

She pulled down the corner of her crooked mouth. "Don't all children think they're going to hell?"

He shook his head. "All children think they're going to be saints—probably martyrs. I did."

"Well then," she said, raising her head so that for a minute he thought she was addressing someone else, perhaps Dennis and Mary returning, some third person out there in the darkness. "There's the difference between you and me."

Kissing her was like inhaling the essence of some vague but powerful alcohol. He recalled his poetry: like taking the wine breath but not the whole wine. He knew it was the literal commingling of her whiskey and his gin, of the smoke from the fire and the sea spray that was too fine to dampen their skin but that had made a delicate veil for her soft hair, one that broke as he moved his fingers through it, perhaps too roughly. But he knew it was something else, too, something that could not be distilled from its parts; that was the dark flavor of desire, but a desire for something he couldn't give a word to—for happiness, sure, for sense, for children—for life itself to be as sweet as certain words could make it seem.

"I wish you would marry me," he told her, surprising himself not because he had broached the subject but because he had not said, "You will."

"Oh, Billy," she whispered, and laughed, straightening his glasses and then, coyly, taking them off completely. "End of September and I'm back home."

Now the darkness around her, and the firelight itself, had softened—even the threatening bang of the ocean had dimmed. "But you'll come back," he said.

She held the glasses between them, against her heart. "It costs a lot of money to go back and forth," she said.

"Then stay," he told her. "Can't you just stay?"

She shook her head. "My parents are there," she said.

"But your sister is here."

"And three more over there."

"Then send for them. Send for your parents, too."

"Oh sure," she said with a laugh.

"I mean it. That's how my father's family did it. Dennis's father came over first and then brought over his six brothers and his sister, and Lord knows how many more."

Her head was bent low now; she was tracing his glasses with a finger, holding them in her lap. "I have to go back," she said. "They're expecting me."

He could see the line of her parted hair, her scalp so white against the rich darkness. "I'll send for you," he told her. "Can I do that? You go home for a while, and as soon as I save the money I'll send for you. I'll bring you back. Can I do that?"

She shook her head only slightly and, with her chin still lowered, whispered, "There's still my family."

"I'll send for them, too," he said, and because he heard her laugh a little, perhaps saw her smile, he added, laughing as well, "I'll send for them all, your parents and your sisters and the next-door neighbors if you want me to. Does your town have a pastor—I'll send for him. A milkman? Him too." She was laughing now. "Is there a baker you're particularly fond of? Any nuns? Cousins? We'll bring them over. We'll bring them all over." It was what his life had held for him all along.

Laughing, she raised her shining eyes, her dark brows that nearly ran together above them and proved, as far as he was concerned, that Nature in her overprotectiveness understood what a glorious pair of eyes She had created. "You're planning to rob a bank or two, are you?"

"Sure," he said. He took her face in his hands, but even this close he couldn't tell if it was firelight or tears that made her eyes shine so, or maybe his own muddled vision. He pulled her to him, but carefully this time. There was a vast darkness beyond them and the indifferent pounding of the sea, and adrift in the same world that held their fine future there was accident and disappointment, a sickening sense of false hope and false promise that required all of God's grace to keep at bay.

Fifty yards away, the dimming flashlight lit a yellowed inch of sea foam and then rolled a little toward the ocean with the water's retreat. The next wave crashed with such a sound it might have been the great iron door of perdition closing behind him. But Dennis hardly flinched.

He would have something to tell the priest at St. Philomena's on Saturday.

TWO WEEKS LATER, Holtzman and his mother came down by train to assess the boys' progress and, for the shoe salesman's sake, to get some idea of just when they might return to the city and their real jobs. Holtzman was a generous man in his way, and he appeared to love his petite wife to distraction, but while half a century of bachelorhood had made him more than ready to indulge her, it had also made him wary. A nation's gratitude was all well and good, but it, like his, was not to be taken advantage of, and should not be expected, he told his wife at the Jamaica station, to outlast the first gesture. The gesture had been made, they had had their hiatus on Long Island. Uncle Sam might be offering twelve for twelve, but he him-self put more stock in a young man's finan-cial independence.

And yet the sight of the restored little house elated him. Billy acted as tour guide, and as he pointed out each improvement they had made, Mr. Holtzman congratulated them both for their skillful way with plaster and paint and fresh wood. He patted his heart with forefinger and thumb—it was a gesture of his that always made Dennis think of someone feeding coins into a machine—and told them how, fifteen years before, he had bought the house on impulse, after seeing an ad in the nether reaches of the newspaper. He'd had no idea then what he'd do with it, he said, he only knew it was a good price, an incredible price, as much as the woman who sold it to him— daughter of the now-bankrupt builder—might once have paid for a new dress. Less. He touched his heart. He only knew that he shouldn't pass it up, just as you wouldn't pass up a dime you saw on the sidewalk, even if you had a mason jar filled with them at home. Just as you wouldn't pass a pile of junk at the curb if you saw something, a chair, a table, a three-legged telephone stand, that was usable and whole. (Which explained, Dennis thought, the one in the hallway of the Jamaica house.) She was throwing the house away; he picked it up.

Dennis's mother, in the meantime, strolled through the tiny rooms as if she'd expected no less than smooth walls and fresh paint and new fixtures in the tiny bath. "We're going to have to do something about this furniture if we're going to rent next season," she told her husband, and Holtzman said, "Sure," in a way that even Dennis could tell—and he hardly knew the man—meant he had no intention of renting at all.

They drove to the bay, passing as they did the newly risen frame of another bungalow. "I think this place is going to get popular," Billy told him. "Long Island's going to start booming, Mr. Holtzman," he said. "You're lucky to have your foot in the door." And Holtzman nodded, fed some more coins to his heart. So well pleased with himself that Dennis couldn't help but say, glancing into the rearview mirror, "There're two sides to lucky, aren't there? There's the guy who picks up the dime and the guy who drops it, isn't there?"

But Holtzman wasn't the sort to imagine himself into anyone else's life. "You boys did a fine job," he said again, as if a compliment was what Dennis was fishing for.

At the beach, they watched him hop awkwardly over the shells and rocks that edged the water and then dive into the bay. Was there another GI in America, Dennis wondered, who had returned from the war to find that a fat German had married his mother?

His mother sat beside him on the blanket he had spread out for her, the wool field blanket he had carried across Europe. She watched her husband from under a straw hat and behind dark glasses, inscrutable.

The day was warm and humidly overcast. Mary and Eva were at a Firemen's Fair with the children. They wouldn't see them today—which he was beginning to think was just as well. Billy was standing at the foot of the blanket, still wearing his T-shirt and pants and his boots, staring out at the water. He had not said Eva's name since they had met his mother and Holtzman at the station, which was either a remarkable display of restraint or a devastating string of opportunityless hours. Either

110

way, Dennis thought, that, too, was just as well.

He had learned at an early age to be careful about what he brought his mother—odd paintings or dreams, fanciful plans—not because she had no interest in him (he was her only child and she was in her way an adoring mother), but because in an instant, he knew, she could show him that the painting was unintelligible, the dream nonsense, the plans intemperate or illogical, or fatally incomplete. She would not do so cruelly or blindly or with any sense of mean-spiritedness, but rather in the same careful and loving way another mother might tell a child that the aspirin was not candy and the laundry bleach not fruit punch.

Growing up, Dennis knew that whenever his father left the kitchen table or walked out of the room, he had only to glance at his mother to learn that whatever story the man had just told them was a lie, an exaggeration, a rehearsal for or a rehash of a story he would tell or had told someone else—the passengers in his car or the men in the saloon or whoever happened to be living in their parlor. Dennis had only to glance at his mother to learn that the man, for all the people in New York City who worshipped him, was flawed, difficult, full of too many other people's lives and not enough of their own, of her own.

What his mother would make of Billy's rabid infatuation he could only guess, but his sense was that it would grow thin under her steady gaze, become a childish delusion, perhaps even to Billy himself. She would, he knew, put it into perspective for him, remind him that it was summer and he'd just returned from the war; that this girl, this Eva, was a stranger, after all, with plans of her own, back to her own country in another few weeks and, when you came right down to it, on fifty a week from Con Ed (minus train fare and clothing and the rent he'd have to pay his poor mother), how likely was it that he'd be sending for her anytime soon? His mother would, Dennis knew, open Billy's eyes for him, diminish things.

But of course two hours without Eva's name crossing his lips was far more than Billy could stand.

He sat heavily at the foot of the blanket and began to unlace his boots. "Where did they say they were going today?" he asked Dennis over his shoulder. "Montauk?"

Dennis glanced at his mother, who had inclined her head toward them ever so slightly.

"A Firemen's Fair," Dennis said.

Billy nodded and smiled. "The children will love that, won't they. Let's hope Mary and Eva can keep up."

Now his mother turned her face, the blind eyes of her dark glasses, fully toward him. Love, Dennis thought, had made Billy not rude but insidious. He knew the discourtesy of this private exchange—the violation of that primary, schoolboy rule of social intercourse, "Is there something you'd like to share with the class?"—would force Dennis's hand. Force him to explain.

"Some children we met here at the beach,"

he told her. "Seven of them, steps and stairs. They come here every afternoon with their nursemaids so they can paddle in the bay. They have a house in the village, but they like to come here because one of the little girls..."

"Sally," Billy added, unable to resist. He was in love with all of them.

"Sally," Dennis continued, "is terrified of the waves."

His mother smiled a little under her dark glasses. She was sitting erectly on the blanket, holding one knee. Her skin was ivory white and downy and scattered with pale freckles. In the shade of her hat she could have been twenty.

"They have a fabulous house," Billy went on, the opportunity here at last. "Nearly a mansion, and they just use it in the summer. Pudding Hill Lane is the name of the street. Like something from a nursery rhyme, don't you think? Seven children in a house on Pudding Hill Lane."

"You've been there?" his mother said pleasantly. Billy blushed from his throat to the roots of his hair—no, from his waist to the roots of his hair; even his white T-shirt seemed to turn pink. "We've taken the girls out," he said. "The nursemaids, what, Dennis, two, three times now?"

"About that," Dennis said, and pulled his own shirt up over his head. "Are you going to swim?" he asked Billy, cutting short a sentence that began "They're Irish girls..." Billy still had his glasses on and so had vision enough to catch Dennis's look.

"All right," he said, reluctantly pulling off his shirt, reluctantly closing the marvelous door that for a moment had allowed him to say Eva, Sally, Mary, Pudding Hill Lane...

As they waded into the water Dennis said softly, "Don't tell her any more about the girls."

Billy looked at him with innocent, myopic eyes. "All right," he said, and then could not help but add, "Guilt must be a terrible thing."

Dennis felt the reproach but laughed. It was, after all, Billy's sweet romance he had thought to preserve.

"Guilt is glorious," Dennis told him with a wink. "When it's well earned." And then dove into the same salt water Holtzman was floating in—making, when you thought about it, a fine stew.

HIS MOTHER ALWAYS IRONED Holtzman's shirt first, down in the basement of the Jamaica house, on an ironing board she set up once, in April of '45, and never took down again. She washed their shirts by hand in the sink down there and then ironed them the next morning. Holtzman's first, she said, because he was, after all, her husband, the owner of this spacious house, sponsor of the feast. Her son's second, because the iron would be hotter by then and so make a neater collar. Loyalty, to blood or to water, being a complicated thing for his mother.

The routine they fell into after he and Billy returned from Long Island that summer was a balancing act. She'd be in the kitchen when Dennis came down in the morning, making his coffee and buttering his toast, but she'd never eat anything herself. She'd wait for Holtzman. Instead, she'd lean against the counter and watch her son, assessing: the cut of his suit, the knot in his tie, the prospects for his future. Although at that time in her life she had held only two jobs herself—one in a bakery in Brooklyn, one in the mailroom of the gas company—she had a considered opinion about what the workaday world could do to you, and it wasn't a very high opinion, either, despite her Protestant blood.

In part, she objected to the monotony of nine-to-five, the tedium, the hours and days you ended up wishing away, swinging from one Saturday morning to another like a monkey at the zoo. In part, it was the anonymity: Forget what dreams you'd dreamt the night before, forget the adoring eye that beheld you over breakfast, or even the grief that had been wringing out your soul all night long, because the way she saw it, once you boarded the subway or the bus or joined the crawling stream of automobiles or found your space in the revolving door, the elevator, behind the desk or the counter or the machine, you became what you really were—you became, when you got right down to it, what you really were: one of the so many million, just one more.

As a boy, Dennis had been made to recite "The Village Blacksmith" for every guest and boarder and drinking partner his father brought to the house. He would stand in the middle of the parlor or, in summer, when the place was stifling with immigrants and heat, in the middle of a circle of them up on the roof, and emote: "Under a spreading chestnut tree..."

Whenever he reached the lines

Each morning sees some task begin,
Each evening sees it close;
Something attempted, something done,
Has earned a night's repose.

his old dad's eyes would fill with tears—a full stanza behind the tears that had already sprung to the eyes of every other Irishman in the room as soon as he figured out that the blacksmith's wife was dead—and when the poem was finished, those were the lines his father would ask him to repeat.

Dennis had only to glance at his mother to learn that she found no charm in the words, that it sounded to her like monotony. A slow march to an unremarkable end.

The job at Edison, in fact, had been a gift to his dying father from Bart Carroll and Uncle Jim, who already worked there, back in '37, when Dennis was eighteen. "The greatest city in the world will always need electricity," his father had said, well pleased, his face under the hospital lights already a death's-head. The death's-door smell of ether. The other visitors around him—brothers, cousins, friends—had agreed. "Dennis will do all right," they'd said, touching his shoulder, patting his back, turning him a bit so he would not see the way his father drew up his knees under the thin sheets, so he would not see his father, who had loved life, being pulled from it, writhing, by a miserable death.

"Any one of the utilities would be a safe bet," they told him, turning him away. "But you can't do better than Edison, Dennis. There's security, if you stick with them. Stick with the company and you'll be fine."

At home, his mother said, Cooper Union, City College, the RCA Institute if electricity's what you're interested in. A public-speaking course then. The service, officer's training. Something else. Something more.

He had humored her, sitting through night classes when he could, joining the Army in '41, telling her, to her consternation, that there wasn't much he wanted in the long run. That when he got right down to it, he was happy enough with what he had.

Now, on these mornings after he and Billy had returned from their hiatus on Long Island, she watched him get ready to go to the office, forever ordinary, as far as she was concerned, forever out of uniform and in suits that she thought could have been better tailored (although his shirt was well pressed). She watched him eat his breakfast, adjust his hat in the mirror in the hall, lift his briefcase and his umbrella, and head out to the bus that would take him to the subway that would take him to the office, precisely as she knew he would be doing for the next forty years, and she would not be able to disguise her regret. He could see it in her face as she watched from the front window: good-natured son, loyal employee like his father, one of the so many million. Just one more.

Holtzman would come down the stairs as Dennis went out the door, and he'd always take his time saying good morning to her and putting on his hat and his coat, making sure that Dennis was a good three or four blocks ahead of him before he himself set out to pick up his morning paper at the corner store. If the bus was late, Dennis would see him there, tossing a nickel into the cigar box where Dennis had just tossed his. They'd both raise their respective copies, intent on three-inch headlines and at the ready with an expression of complete surprise (Well, hello, didn't see you) should either one of them acknowledge the other, which of course neither one of them ever did.

Back at the mansion, Dennis knew, his mother would have the eggs boiling and a plate of sliced bread set out on the stove. When Holtzman came in, he would pin each piece to a long fork and toast it perfectly over the open flame of the gas burner. He did the same for Dennis on weekends. Dennis imagined that it had been the bane of the man's long bachelorhood: having no one for whom to demonstrate this technique.

("And you ask me," my father said, "if I think Danny Lynch is a lonely soul.")

Every morning, Holtzman and his mother sat catty-corner at the old kitchen table where Dennis had once done his homework, where his father had once sat, recited, sung, put his forehead to the bare wood when the night had been long and the sun too quick to rise. Sitting catty-corner, Holtzman and his mother talked about money: investments they had made, bills that were owed, profit from the store, and the wholesale price of shoes. Every once in a while Holtzman would reach under the table to pat her knee or she would touch his hand, still talking, so that anyone watching from behind the kitchen's thick-paned windows would think they'd been pledging love for half an hour over their cooling eggs, not

119

determining the limits of their inventory.

She was a continual marvel to Holtzman, as far as Dennis could see, this tiny woman who had arrived so unexpectedly into his late middle age. She seemed to think of him as the embodiment of good sense, practicality, relief, the soundest investment she had ever made.

When they had eaten, he would take the paper and a second cup of coffee into the living room or, more discreetly, up the stairs to the hall bath, while she did the dishes and then went down to the basement to start the wash. It always gave her enormous pleasure to consider how her marriage had brought her not merely a house but a basement. A basement all her own. It struck her as a great luxury not to have to maneuver around the baby carriages and footlockers and the deplorable armchairs of a dozen neighbors but to be able to sail, unimpeded, from stair to washtub to clothesline and ironing board—which she had set up in April of 1945, when she first moved in, and would never be required to take down again.

Of course, Holtzman's basement wasn't empty, but what it contained was mostly hers—her footlockers and garment bags and end tables. As she had said in her letters to Dennis overseas, Holtzman was terribly reasonable about her things, insisting that since she was the one giving up her apartment (her home, he'd called it), then she should not give up her furniture as well. It hadn't taken much to accommodate it all: his house had three

times as many rooms as the apartment, and
what became redundant, his dining room and
kitchen set, for instance, a number of lamps,
a bed, he had generously allowed her to offer
to her late husband's relatives. With the war
ending, there were plenty of takers among
the various cousins, even among those who
hadn't found homes of their own yet, or even
spouses. Holtzman's old kitchen chairs, for
instance, ended up in Mary Lynch's bedroom in Astoria, piled in a column against the
wall for what must have been at least three years,
maybe four: a monument to hope her father,
Uncle Jim, used to call it, until Mary met
Jack Casey just in time (she was nearing thirty
herself) and the chairs became kitchen chairs
once again.

For Dennis's mother, these excess bits of furniture not only established her new role as bene-
factress (she, who for so long, throughout
her first marriage, in fact, and well before, had
been supplicant); they also paid off a debt. She
was, to a great extent, beholden to her first husband's people, who had supported her so
generously during the period of his illness
and her widowhood and especially in the
years after Dennis joined the service. And
throughout those years, try as she might to pay
them back, or even to temper their generosity
with the insistence that her widow's pension
was sufficient, her needs few, they would
only hold up their hands and respond with some
long and often exaggerated tale of what self-
less and bighearted miracle "her Daniel" had

once done for them, tales that would more often than not end with tears and a "God bless his soul," or a "We won't see another one like him again," until she, Sheila Lynch, the impoverished widow with the soldier son, would find herself brewing them a cup of tea or pouring out a drop of vermouth or putting an arm across their shoulders to whisper, "There there."

My father would say this much for his mother: she never distanced herself from her first husband's family after she married Holtzman. As much as she might have liked to.

In the basement, she would plug in the iron and pause to see if the lights would flicker—they did, something to ask Dennis about. She'd fill her sprinkler bottle at the sink and take the shirts from the line and iron them: her husband's and then her son's.

HE HAD BEEN, WITHOUT question, Holy Father to the entire clan, her Daniel. Forty-four years old when she met him, with a shock of dark hair falling down into his homely face. Holy Father to the world, if it had let him.

The story went that she had been living at the time off Nostrand Avenue in a small and airless apartment that belonged to her Great-uncle Robert and Aunty Eileen, his dour wife. They didn't want her there—she had seen the man bite his lip when she reached for a second piece of toast and grip the table, as if he might at any minute leap up to stay her hand if she poured more than a splash of milk into her oatmeal. But their only son had left for Europe and news of his empty bedroom reached Washington Heights, where she had been living with another, younger aunt and uncle, sharing a bed with an eight-year-old cousin—a boy with limbs of lead and the odor of a wet overcoat.

Aunty Eileen had resisted the idea of some sixteen-year-old girl occupying her son's room (drilling the scent of her hair into his pillow, scattering undergarments, bleeding onto his mattress—she thought of everything, that woman) and relented only after she swore never to dress or undress in the son's room. She was instead directed to leave her bags in a corner of the pantry and to change her clothes there before her uncle was up in the morning and after he went to bed at night. This she did willingly—her cousin's wide feather bed, all to herself, was such a luxury—and seeing her up and all ready for school just as he was shuffling into the kitchen must have given her uncle an inspiration.

She wasn't there long when he announced that he'd found a little something for her to do. A couple he knew, countrymen of his, had a bakery on DeKalb, and since the wife was troubled with back problems, they could use a girl to come in first thing in the morning to set out the breads and the cakes. He never said how much she would be paid and she understood without asking that whatever money she made would go straight to him. Her uncle knew that it had been her parents' dying wish that she stay in school, and he himself had enrolled her at Manual Training the very day she left Washington Heights, but the morning job was a nice way of offsetting what the care of her would cost him without compromising whatever reluctant pact he had made with the dead.

The day before she was to start, she went by the place after school. Only the baker's wife, Mrs. Dixon, was there, but she was rosy-cheeked and merry and cried out when she saw her, "Oh, but you're a wee little thing!"

It was like a fairy tale, that first morning. The streets were wet and dark, full of reflections. Somewhat ominous, sure, so early in the morning that it was nighttime still, but also full of promise, adventure. When she came into the empty shop it was warm and dimly lit and full of the scent of baking bread.

All the light came from the back, where the ovens were, but there was enough light to see by, and she found the cap and coat she was to wear folded neatly on the counter. She thought of the elves and the shoemaker. She covered her hair and slipped into the smock. Yesterday, when Mrs. Dixon had showed it to her, it had buckled over her shoes. Now it was hemmed to just the right length, ten inches above her ankles.

Hesitantly, but ready to begin, she peered into the light of the back room. She felt the heat of the stove like a warm hand on her face, and then she saw the baker sitting on a

124

stool beside one of the wooden tables. His shoes and his pant legs beneath his apron were covered with flour; his shoulders were slumped and he had his hand around the glass that was resting on the table beside him. He was a dark-haired man with black brows and a broad, flushed face.

He looked up at her from under those brows and then waved his free hand and said, not unkindly, "Well, come in, come in. I'm not going to bite you."

She stepped in. The wooden floor seemed soft and it, too, was covered with flour. On another huge table just opposite the great cast-iron stove there was a sheet of scones not yet baked and a wicker basket full of small brown loaves.

"My wife showed you what to do?" he asked.

She nodded. "Yes," she said, but there was little voice in it.

She had to rise up on her tiptoes to get a good grip on the basket and then nearly crashed into the doorframe as she carried it out, feeling him watching her. When she returned, he was standing, slipping the sheet of scones into the oven; another sheet, golden brown and redolent, was on the wide table. He looked at her over his shoulder as he closed the oven door. "You're a little bit of a thing, aren't you?" he said pleasantly, friendlier than he'd been before.

They were standing together in the narrow space between the oven and the table, and the empty basket in her hands made the space seem narrower still. He suddenly reached out and pulled at her earlobe with a floured hand. "A wee thing," he said. He wasn't much bigger, really only a head taller, than she, but his chest was broad and had begun to press against the basket and her arm. He tugged at a strand of hair near her temple, poked at her cap. By now she could smell the drink on his breath but didn't know enough then to recognize it for what it was.

"A wee baby doll in her dress," he said, and pulled at the collar of her smock. He chucked her chin. She only grinned, blushing. He was old enough and she was young enough; she believed he was playing with her the way you would play with a young child, admiring her, making friends.

He told her to take the empty basket to the kneading table. She was grateful to be free of that tight space, free of his attention. She could feel her face begin to cool.

He was on her so fast she thought for a moment that the lights had gone out. He had her head in the crook of his arm and so startled her that he caught her opened mouth with his own and she could hear the click of their front teeth. It was not a kiss, it was all teeth and wet bone, and she could feel the low laughter in his chest in the moment before he released her. Laughing still, he turned casually back to his work.

Out in the shop, she dropped half the scones and had to wipe them off on her new smock.

She rubbed her mouth with the sleeve. In the back, he had begun to sing. Pieces of folk songs and of lullabies. Some of the songs her own father had sung—a beautiful maiden much loved by a young boy going off to war, a sea captain bound for his last voyage, kissing his wife at the garden gate. When she returned with the empty tray, he merely glanced at her over his shoulder, his mouth now gently shaped for his tune. He had a good voice, soft and sweet, although the words gave him some trouble.

When she left the shop that morning, the sun was up and the street, newly washed, smelled like the coming spring. The world was populated again, with people whom she might, in time, come to know. On the way, she met a plump girl from her class, Alma, who was delighted to accept the bag of warm scones Mrs. Dixon had pressed upon her as she left the store. "I don't like them," she told Alma by way of explanation. "Never did."

She lived the next year not so much in a nightmare as on the verge of one. Because there was no telling. Days would go by and he wouldn't touch her. Then there would be a jolly morning: he might be singing, icing a cake, and in an instant he'd have her by the throat. Or worse, she'd come in to find him morose, mostly silent, hardly moving from his stool. She'd keep her eye on him then, avoid him whenever she could—even taking things out of the oven herself, which Mrs. Dixon told her never to do, so she would not have to disturb him.

Sometimes it would work, and she'd slip out of the shop at eight o'clock like a fish released to a stream. Sometimes he would raise his heavy brows and say her name again and again—"Shee-la, Shee-la"—wagging his great head, until she had come close enough for him to grab her wrist or her skirt or her sleeve and aim his murderous yellow teeth toward her breasts. Sometimes he would just appear behind her and take hold of her hair. He'd back her up against the alley door or press her into a wall.

("A filthy, dirty man," she said, telling the tale. This would have been in their kitchen in Woodside at the crumb-scattered table, just Dennis and his mother alone in the apartment now. Dennis just beginning his career with Con Ed. What was lucky, she'd said, was that the man was a drinker, or else who knows how far he might have gone. "A man can't, you know," she'd said. "After too many drinks. I don't suppose your father ever told you.")

Child that she still was, she began devising rituals that might protect her, or at least predict for her how the morning would run. If she could walk from her uncle's building to the bakery without lifting her eyes, he wouldn't touch her that day. If she saw the street sweeper's cart at the corner, he would.

Then there came a morning when she handed Alma her bag of treats and Alma said, "I'm going to miss these."

She had a job, at an office building downtown. Her father had put her onto it. She was leaving school at the end of the week. Two hours later Sheila herself sat in front of the man Alma had described. He was a balding man with a mustache and a bow tie and an old-fashioned high collar. The cubicle he met her in was small, with one window wide-open to let in the breeze. He began by talking a little about the war and the patriotism of American youth and asked if anyone near and dear to her was over there, carrying her picture.

She said no. Had she leaned any farther back in her chair she'd have been out the window herself.

He gave her the job, no doubt because he thought she was a serious and steady young woman bound for spinsterhood. She didn't go back to the bakery. She didn't finish school either. She knew this part of it would have been a blow to her parents, who had been mad for education, but in the nearly half dozen years since they had both—one within four months of the other—taken sick and died (her mother not taking nearly so long to go about it, hurrying to join him, someone had said), she had received very little aid from them and even less comfort. At twelve she had imagined two hovering angels to guide her for the rest of her life, but she had since lived too many desolate nights in rooms where she was not wanted and did not belong, eaten too many bitter meals, every bite and every sip counted and resented. She had tasted Mr. Dixon's breath, smelled the sharp, lingering scent of his saliva on her cheeks and lips even as she bowed her head and asked them to deliver her. Had they lived, she knew, they would have been sorry to see her leaving school, but they hadn't and that was all.

("That was all," she had said in the tiny kitchen in Woodside, in the middle of her dark fairy tale. Something else his God-fearing, ghost-hearing, saint-loving father hadn't told him: they hadn't lived and that was all.)

Her uncle frowned to disappoint his friend, but since she would turn her salary over to him, he was reconciled.

On a Monday morning, she joined Alma on the train. She figured she had pulled herself from the edge of hell, and even if the job proved dull (which it did) and Alma, without her daily bakery bribe, disloyal (she did not), there was the luxury, anyway, of this gray purgatory.

At Borough Hall, she followed her friend's wide rump up the steps of the streetcar. Eclipsed by the great expanse of black gabardine that was Alma, she heard his brogue first, that loud and laughing voice. And then, climbing aboard, she got her first glimpse of his homely, happy face.

WHEN SHE WENT UPSTAIRS again, Holtzman would have opened the window and sprayed the bathroom with cologne. She'd give him his pressed shirt and hang Dennis's in his room. (Another luxury her marriage had brought her: closets to store things in, closets to step into.) When Holtzman was dressed and ready, he would find her again and kiss her goodbye.

He would always have the newspaper under his arm and, without fail, it seemed, a shoebox. He was daily finding new shoes for her in her size (it was, after all, the way he'd wooed her), and more often than not she found them lacking—a harder sell as a wife, my father said, than she had ever been as a customer.

Holtzman took the bus to the store in those days, and as soon as he was gone she would put on a housedress and wrap her hair in a duster and clean. You have to understand what the house meant to her, a woman who had spent so much of her adolescence as a guest in already overburdened households, sleeping on the edge of beds, keeping her clothes in a box out in the pantry or the hallway. Who had spent her first married life in one- and two-bedroom apartments that also served as permanent way stations for an endless string of penniless Irish immigrants.

He was a character. This was the word the passengers on the trolley said to one another, or so the story went: men in straw hats and bowlers (in those days), women in their dark office costumes. They'd lean toward one another in their seats, smiling over something he'd said or, more likely, cried out. "Isn't he a character?"

"Is it spats you're wearing today, Mr. Ellsworth?" he might ask the frail old gentleman who had just, cautiously, seated himself. "Aren't they handsome? Now, if you die in those today, you know, the undertaker will be dancing in them tomorrow."

Mr. Ellsworth would grin, "Oh, I won't die today, Mr. Lynch,"—the passengers all around them smiling in anticipation as if they were watching a couple of vaudeville comedians—"not until I hear what happened to Paddy at Asbury Park."

Daniel would lift his cap and brush back that shock of thick dark hair. "Jaysus," he'd tell them, "there's a tale."

He was a legend—at least in that part of Brooklyn at that hour of the day. He talked constantly, pointing out as he did some fellow on the street, or a cop he knew, or a building that was a part of another story. Eventually, the talk always came around to Paddy—and sometimes Paddy was a brother and sometimes Paddy was a cousin and sometimes an uncle or a friend. Paddy making the crossing and Paddy on Ellis Island and Paddy taking the wrong train to Pittsburgh or Vermont.

"Paddy's in Philadelphia. My brother put him onto a job there, making cre-aam cheese, of all things. He's staying with some relations who have a cat as big as a suitcase, and when Paddy comes home the first day at the factory, he smells for all the world like a six-foot bottle of milk..."

There were passengers who waited on the street, letting other cars pass, in order to board Daniel's. Others who timed their commutes simply to be able to ride with him.

Sheila began to do the same. Not because she cared for his stories—too many of them, she said, were either impossible or absurd—

and not because he called her by name or tickled her fancy each day with some sly running joke (old Mr. Ellsworth had made it through another night, and sweet-faced and asthmatic Mrs. Timoney, always huffing and puffing, was being sought by the police, and Saul, a hunchbacked office boy, was a colonel just back from the front, even fat Alma, who carried an umbrella no matter the weather, was a prognosticator of disastrous storms—"Tornadoes today, miss?" "Is there a typhoon in the air?"). She waited for his car because she silenced him.

Her life had slipped into its tedious routine. Out of the son's bed by dawn (and always with a shudder to recall what other early mornings had brought) and a quick wash and dress in the tiny space of the pantry. Breakfast for herself and her aunt and uncle and then the washing up, the walk to the train. In the mailroom she was corraled like a horse with an unending number of envelopes and packages, twenty minutes for lunch, ten for coffee...one of the many million, just one more.

But once or twice a day, if she caught the right car, she was a rarity, a sphinx. She was watched for. She silenced him.

He who had something to say to everyone could only stammer and blush as she walked by, could only say, "Good day, miss," and not even that if she looked him straight in the eye. The other passengers saw it, even Alma saw it, and the initial surprise it had engendered

133

gave way to curiosity and then a sympathetic awe. He was in love with her, they whispered, had to be. And she giving him nothing in return, not even the time of day. In that odd moment of silence that always followed her boarding, she was the one who had everybody's attention, not Daniel.

And that was what she couldn't get enough of—after the life she had led. To be noticed, to be singled out. To be recognized as someone unlike any other.

It was midsummer the morning his car pulled in, but he was not on it. There was a general backing down the stairs. "Where's Daniel?" someone asked, debating whether to go forward or to wait.

"Out today," the strange man said.

Resignedly, they boarded, and just as they were seated, Daniel himself swung up into the car, looking ridiculous in a brown suit and a straw hat with a green-and-yellow-striped band. He was flushed and breathless.

The other passengers greeted him as if he were a returning hero, but he ducked his head shyly and took the seat just behind her.

"Any hurricanes?" he asked Alma, but with unutterable sadness, as if he had just been gutted of all humor and all resolve. She giggled and squeezed her arms together, turning in her seat to see him. "Not yet," she said.

His brown eyes were on the back of Sheila's neck.

"Your day on the town, Daniel?" a passenger asked him.

"You might say that." But nothing more for them. Not this day.

"Out and about with Paddy?" a woman asked from across the aisle.

"No," he said softly. "Not me."

When she got up to leave the car, she turned to him—what a lost soul he seemed, in his brown suit and his good hat. She saw that whatever it was he had imagined he would say or do had been washed out of all possibility, just the way the color was washed from his face.

The next day, he was himself again, although he reddened even before she passed him. His cousin Paddy was getting married, he told them. Lucky man. To a redhead, no less. Not very big, but with a fine face. He was having some trouble with the ring, however—he's thick, is Paddy—with the size of the ring, and so he took a two-cent washer and a ham bone down to the jeweler...

Everyone's eyes going to her as he spoke. She watching only the street: a girl unlike any other.

In September, the women in the office were warned that they might have to make way for the returning veterans. On a Friday night in October she came home to find Mr. and Mrs. Dixon in the living room, him with his suit on and his hair slicked back as if he had come courting, her heavier than she had been, her moon face hanging wider and lower than usual over its cushion of soft chins. When she went into her bedroom to take off her hat, she saw that the mattress had been

135

stripped, the pillows and blankets heaped across the opened window.

The son was coming home (on Aunty Eileen's yellow face, joy looked like a stomach disorder) and she would have to find another place for herself. The Dixons had a little extra room in their apartment above the store—tiny, Mrs. Dixon said, but neat—and with a child on the way (Mrs. Dixon touched her wide waist) they would need someone to help them full-time. So it could all work out very nicely.

Over dinner, Mr. Dixon moved his black little teeth to say, "You're not eating."

And Uncle Robert laughed and said she usually ate plenty.

On the trolley car that Monday, she followed Alma's swaying backside up the stairs and then said, "Hello, Daniel," with an angel's smile. "How are you today?" There was a pause (she was certain) and then, from somewhere in the car, a smattering of applause.

"I'm fine, thank you, miss," Daniel said. "It's a lovely day, isn't it?"

"Yes, it is," she told him, although it was cold and damp with a spitting rain. "Just lovely." Passing old Mr. Ellsworth in his seat, she swore she saw a tear in his eye. Not dead yet, after all.

The rest of the story went that on her second morning as a young bride she stepped out of her bedroom and found two characters asleep on the living-room floor. They wore mis-matched parts of dirty suits and used their battered satchels for pillows and they slept with their hands tucked between their thighs, like hobos. There was a warm, barnyard odor in the air.

She stepped back, startled, and bumped into Daniel ("your dad," she said in the kitchen in Woodside when the word alone was enough to make Dennis's heart ache with his own loss), who was right behind her. "Who are they?" she had asked.

"Paddy" was the answer.

She claimed she never again had the place all to herself and would not have it to herself until Dennis went off to Fort Dix.

She never had his attention all to herself again, either, my father said, not even when he was dying and the parade of Paddys in and out of the ward where he lay so impressed all the nurses that one of them had asked—or so he'd heard told—Is he a politician?

But now she had this sturdy house, all brick, three bedrooms upstairs and a full basement and foot after foot of baseboard to dust and floor to polish. A tiny garage out back, a small yard with a tree, a front hedge. You could say it was the influence of her tidy German husband that transformed her from the indifferent housekeeper she had been while Dennis was growing up into the cleaning dervish she became as Mrs. Holtzman, but the more likely explanation seemed to be that cleaning Holtzman's house was her way of pacing off her acreage, tallying her assets, running her hands through her pile of gold doubloons. There was a laundry list of reasons why she had married again and not one of them had anything to do with love, but with enough space (when you came right down to it), enough base-board and yard and empty room, enough heat in the winter and sufficient windows to open for a cross breeze in summer, love was an easy thing to do without.

For some of us, anyway.

IN THOSE DAYS, Billy was at Irving Place, too—and it wasn't unusual for Dennis to run into him in the morning, on the subway or out on the street. Strangers watching them in those days would have thought they were long-lost comrades-in-arms, a couple of ex-GIs, maybe brothers, who had not seen each other since before the invasion. Dennis would catch a glimpse of light off Billy's glasses and shove his way through the standing com-muters in his car to shout, "Hey, Bill!" Or he'd hear his own name out on the street and turn to see Billy bobbing through the traffic, heading toward him. "How are you?" "How's things?" Shaking hands and slapping their fresh newspapers on each other's back. "Good to see you."

It would take an act of will to picture him now as he was then: to put aside every image that had come in between, including that dark, stiffly bloated remnant of his face that was Billy in death, and remember him clearly: thin and handsome in those days, the dipped brim of his fedora over the blue eyes and the rimless glasses, a nick of dried blood on his smooth cheek, a red blush from the cold. A lingering scent of the church he had just come from on his overcoat, and a taste of the Eucharist still on his breath as they stood together in the crowded subway car, hand over hand on the same white pole, exchanging shouted bits of news or falling into silence as the train rattled and screeched and tried to knock them off their feet. As glad for each other's company as if they'd long been deprived of it.

("The way your brothers used to be," my father said. In their teens and early twenties, when a buddy or two would come by the house and they'd all stand in the living room for a few minutes before they went out, grinning, knocking shoulders, laughing at everything because the world that just moments before had seemed the source of only aggravation and concern had suddenly become easy and diverting, theirs for the taking. "'Pity the girls,' I used to tell your mother when they'd gone"—tires screeching out of the driveway and the furniture they had dwarfed beginning to crawl out of the corners again. "'Pity the poor girls,'" as my parents went back to their newspapers or Friday-night TV shows and tried to keep the smell of the boys' aftershave in their nostrils, because they could not, as they would have preferred, stand out in the street to look after the taillights. "'The girls,' your mother would always say, 'can take care of themselves.'")

The daily Masses were a new thing with Billy, and tied up with Eva no doubt, although the relatives thought it had something to do with the war. He would not have been the first in the neighborhood to have come back with a new need for religion, a new sense that only the daily, formal petition for mercy would get them through the rest of their lives.

But what Billy was asking for in those days was not mercy, or maybe it was mercy of another kind. The mercy of time. He needed time— weeks at work and bits of his salary tucked away and saved—but he needed to stop time as well. He needed the world to hold its breath for a while; for all affections, all hopes, all plans for the future to stop in their tracks for a while, to remain as they were, all across the city. For all of us to be true to our own intentions.

The church itself would have obliged: the good sound of the familiar Latin, the same women every morning saying their beads, the red sanctuary lamp, and the candles beneath the statues of the Virgin and St. Joseph, steadfast and true.

Even old Father Roche, an insomniac who said the six o'clock Mass every morning, because, Billy knew from his own days as an altar boy, he would be sound asleep in the sacristy by eight. Unchanging.

And yet: from his sister Kate's bedroom at any hour of the night there came her husband's hushed and angry voice, and more often than not when Billy left for Mass she would be on the couch in the living room with Danny, her baby, in her arms. She would be crying softly.

"Are you all right?" Billy would whisper, awkwardly, embarrassed for her.

She would wave him away. "I'm fine."

The poor child, nearly two but wrapped like an infant against the drafts, wide-eyed, watching them both.

On the drainboard in the kitchen, shades of his father when he was alive, there would be a bottle of gin and an empty glass, his mother's antidote for a widow's long nights.

After Mass, on the platform at the Woodside station, among the pressing crowd of strangers headed toward the train, Billy would hear his name called out and turn. Or, walking toward the office, he'd see a hat on a head and above a pair of shoulders that he would recognize as Dennis's. They'd slap each other with their newspapers and grin madly at the not-at-all-unlikely happenstance of meeting. "How are you?" "What's up?" "How's Mary?" "What do you hear from Eva?" "Eva's fine, had a letter on Tuesday." At last and the first of the day: "Eva's fine." Even the mention of her name, the shouting of it over the subway's roar, an act of courage, a reaffirmation of faith.

THESE WERE THE DAYS when everyone they knew was getting married or having babies. When it was not unusual for the hat to be passed around the office two or three times a day, a big diamond glittering on the finger of the girl who handed out the card and the pen.

"Is this for you?" Dennis would always kid her before he signed. "Come on, when is it going to be for you?"

She was a pretty blonde, round-faced and small-mouthed. A great white smile that had a kind of bonus in it: the electric click of snapped gum. She was engaged to her high-school sweetheart, who was still in the Navy.

"What do you want to marry a sailor for?" he'd ask her as he signed his name to the card. "Who's going to be the Sunshine Girl when you leave?"

She'd grin (snap, snap) and lean over to take the card and the pen from his hand. "I want to marry a sailor," she'd say. "So I'm not the Sunshine Girl when I'm sixty-three."

Claire Donavan was her name. From Brooklyn via Stenography.

That fall and all through the winter and spring they visited more churches and synagogues than Dennis could have imagined—following hand-printed maps or hastily copied instructions, riding the subway in good suits or driving with Billy or Danny or Mike, or with his mother and Holtzman in the old car. Or crowded into a taxi with a group from the office, dry-mouthed and laughing over what they couldn't remember about the night before. There was always the smell of bay rum and Vitalis and Chanel. The hangover breaking up like dark ice in the fall sunlight or a bracing winter rain, or in the triumph of finding St. Charles Borromeo in Brooklyn or Faith United Methodist in Hastings or Beth El in Little Neck,

142

Queens, with twenty minutes—time for a quick cup of coffee—to spare.

And then the stepping inside, resisting the habit, in the Protestant churches, of reaching for the holy-water font (although, more often than not, they blessed themselves anyway, the ushers in their morning suits smiling to see it: with a face like that how could he do otherwise?), and slipping the yarmulke on in the synagogues, self-conscious but game (the jokes in the Yiddish accent would come later), the point of the ceremony, of their gathering like this in their best clothes and their polished shoes being everywhere the same.

For Billy, it was sustenance. Even the churches and synagogues themselves provided sustenance: crowded among apartment buildings or brownstones, sitting among trees or parking lots, appearing as you climbed up out of the subway or made the last of a dozen wrong turns through suburban streets or flipped the map upside down and looked through the windshield to say, "It should be here." The number and variety of them sustained him. The sense that in every town, up to the Bronx and out to Staten Island and even far into New Jersey, the need for faith, for that which was steadfast and true, had given rise to these holy places. These cathedrals and sanctuaries and catering-hall altars before which Grace from Stenography might stand, or Jack from Service or Peggy Lynch, Uncle Mike's pretty daughter, or her sister Rosemary, who was not the pretty one, or Tommy from the neighborhood or cousin Ted (straight as an arrow in his morning suit, you had to hand it to him, considering how comatose with drink he'd been the night before). Stand and say, "This will not change."

On Sunday evenings while Dennis was going into Manhattan to meet Mary (taking the subway when he had resolved to sin no more, Holtzman's car when just one more was the current resolution), Billy wrote to Eva. Still in his suit pants and the clean shirt he'd worn to Mass. His mother—God help her, she was a miserable cook—would be toughening up a roast in the oven and cooking the color out of Brussels sprouts and green beans (figuring that flavor was not inherent in the vegetables themselves but acquired after long simmering when they were doused in their serving bowls with butter and salt). Rosie and Mac, her husband, would be at his mother's or the movies, Kate down to Uncle Ted's with the baby so her husband could study.

"Dear Eva," he would write, and no doubt he could have filled a page with it, the way he loved to repeat her name: "Hello, Eva. How are you, Eva?"

He told her how he spent his days, writing as well as he could, but being careful, too, he said, not to go on too long about ordinary things. He knew better than to say everything he felt. But he also knew that the listing of too many ordinary details was worse. To say what he felt would have been to stifle with one sentence a thousand others. But to say only what he'd done would be like describing a city that blocked out the sun.

He must have thought of the girl in Metz— "I am still here"—because surely it was all he meant to write to Eva, every Sunday as his mother put out her wedding china and Mac and Rosemary bustled in and Kate returned with the baby to timidly knock on her own bedroom door. As somewhere some church rang a distant bell and a bus spit exhaust on the boulevard and Mary took Dennis's arm as they crossed Park, headed toward Lexington and a bar-and-grill owned by an Irishman who'd been brought over by his father. As the water struck the sand that led to the great house on the hill that Billy and Eva would marvel at again, together, his idea of heaven, before returning to their idyll in Holtzman's little place, an idyll that would begin whenever the money he was putting away each week, which was increasing itself incrementally, even now, over at East River Savings, had grown sufficient enough to bring her back.

Unwavering faith: This will not change. I am still here.

But the money was slow in growing.

There were all the wedding presents, after all, the baby gifts and bachelor parties and the office collections and cab fares and cleaning bills. There was the money he gave Kate when she needed a lift after a night of the baby crying and Peter, her scholar of a husband, shouting about the exam he had to take the next day, the studying he'd not yet done. There was the money he lent his cousin Ted when he smashed his car on Queens Boulevard—so his new wife wouldn't know—and the money he gave his mother when she broke her bridge. There was the special collection for Father Roche's fiftieth year as a priest.

"You're more like my father than my father was," Dennis told him one night at Quinlan's when he was crying in his beer that he would not have the boat fare by summer, much as he tried.

"In this family," Billy said, his glass to his heart, "you couldn't say a kinder word."

Danny Lynch raised his own drink. "Amen to that," he said, ever the keeper of the flame.

IN THOSE DAYS, Dennis had his territory on the Lower East Side, from Broadway to the river, Houston to Canal, shops full of Jewish and Chinese merchants, streets littered with bums. The bums would pull themselves out of doorways when they saw him coming, rise from the edges of curbs to say, "We're moving, Officer, we're moving"—as if any round-faced Irishman in a topcoat and a hat had to be a cop. They'd salute like old soldiers, or hunch their shoulders and cower like serfs in the Middle Ages, like men who more than once had felt a nightstick crack upon their backs. "We're moving, Detective." Dennis would raise a fist at them, touch his overcoat as if he indeed carried a pistol and a badge. "You'd better move, fellows. And keep moving." Drunks, bums, booze hounds.

What you thought of, in those days, when someone said alcoholic.

Four steps down and into a dingy little shop that he'd remembered being closed up even before the war. The door propped open with flattened cardboard boxes, not for air— it was a cold gray day—but light, since the power hadn't been turned on. There was a narrow counter filled with haphazard piles of shirt boxes, another dozen or so large containers filling all but a thin passageway through the store. There was a barrel spilling straw, an odor of old damp brick and roach powder. He rapped on the counter and called out, and a man appeared from the back. A small, short man in a wool jacket that was too big for him and a fur hat that was too small. His hands were bare and he held them together. They were bright white in the gray place and he rubbed them together because it was cold, of course, but the effect, with his hooked nose and his stooped shoulders, made Dennis think "Shylock."

"Edison," he said, warily, because he knew this was a guy who would not take anything he said at face value. The man moved his head like a turtle, getting a better look at him in the gloom of the store. "You the Edison man?"

Dennis put his hand out to introduce himself and saw that the man was missing the middle three fingers of his right hand, and the tips of the last three on his left. He was a

Polish Jew, not long in New York. A tailor, he said, before the war, and without indicating his hands gave a vaudevillian shrug. Now a shopkeeper, ladies' and children's apparel. Or anyway, as soon as he had the power he would be.

As Dennis had predicted, the man didn't want to hear anything he said, and end of next week was too long for him to wait. He was not an old man, not as old as he'd first appeared, but he seemed shrunken inside his big coat and he had a lousy set of dentures that slipped as he spoke and made his breath stale.

"Mr. Lynch," he said—once he got hold of Dennis's name he was like a dog with a bone—"consider my situation."

"Mr. Leibowitz," Dennis told him, "consider your wiring. Consider your shop going up in smoke."

The man pretended to be resigned. He looked around the place as if all his struggle, through the war, through the camps, through the long crossing over, had come to this cold pathetic end. He shook his head, as if he was familiar with this, this mundane disappointment delivered by this mundane, earnest, broad-faced man, a disappointment as pervasive and as terrible as the world's more famous evils. He shrugged and then suddenly turned and gently took Dennis's hand, holding his wrist in the space between his pinky and thumb on the left. He drilled a folded bill into Dennis's palm with his right.

"Anything you can do," Mr. Leibowitz said.

Dennis objected and tried to hand the money back, but the man turned away, waving his gaped hand beside his ear, swatting at the words. He might have said, "It can't hurt."

The folded bill was still in his pocket when he got back to the office. He rode the elevator up with Claire Donavan and three other girls, just back from lunch, their fur collars smelling of perfume and cigarette smoke, their bright lipstick fresh and the powder on their cheeks and noses like a dusting of sugar.

"You're quiet, Mr. Lynch," Claire Donavan said into his ear as they watched the lights moving behind the numbers for each floor.

"I'm praying for a power failure, Miss Donavan," he said, moving only his eyes to look at her, her bright white smile and the gum cracking like sparks behind it. Peppermint. Sugar. Lilac perfume. The war was far enough behind them now: bread was bread once again, not cake. He had a hankering for cake.

Billy got on at twelve. "Dennis!" he said, and Dennis said, "Billy boy," as if he'd spent the morning looking for him. They nearly shook hands. But the eyes of the four women were on them, on Billy more accurately. He was the only one of them not wearing a hat and a coat, and it made him seem finer, somehow, in his gray suit and white shirt and simple tie—the way a priest all in black can seem the more elegant in the midst of brightly colored wedding guests.

"You've been out in the field?" Billy asked softly.

"Till just now," Dennis said.

When they got to their floor, the girls stepped out, but Dennis pinched Billy's sleeve and made him stay on.

"Who is he?" they heard before the door closed on them again, and Claire Donavan answered, "Cousins."

Dennis reached into his pocket and pulled out the folded bill. He was surprised to see it was a ten. He handed it to Billy. "Put this in your happily-ever-after fund."

Billy looked at it sheepishly. "Where's it from?"

The elevator stopped and Dennis pushed another button for a higher floor. He told him. He said he was going to put it into the poor box at St. Brigid's but the door was locked. "I think the bums have been coming in and stealing the Communion wine."

"Catholic bums," Billy said.

Dennis nodded. "The worst kind. So take it and put it in your happily-ever-after fund."

Still, Billy hesitated. He told Dennis to put it in the collection basket on Sunday. Dennis said he'd have it spent by Sunday. Billy said, Spend it. Dennis said he had a rich mother, he didn't need to spend it. Finally, he pushed the money into Billy's palm as Mr. Leibowitz had done to him. He said when the time came, when Eva was back here and they were snug in their little cottage in East Hampton, Billy could buy all their baby clothes from Mr. Leibowitz.

"Will it ever happen?" Billy said wistfully, even as he folded the money into his pocket.

Dennis said, "I don't see why it shouldn't." Although, in truth, he saw: indistinctly as yet and as if from the corner of his eye. Think of those ruined, ragged men in the street, Billy among them, in the unimaginable future. Think of Leibowitz's butchered hands. Think of the promises he had made to Mary at moments when the girl had every right to believe him. When, for as long as it took, he managed to believe himself. With so many other forces at work in the world, brutal, sly, deceiving, unstoppable forces, what could be more foolish than staking your life on an ephemeral feeling, no more than an idea, really, a fancy, the culmination of which is a clumsy bit of nakedness, a few minutes of animal grunting and bumping, a momentary obliteration of thought, of conscience?

Indistinctly, and as if from the corner of his eye, he saw what Billy's fine dream, Billy's faith, was going to come to. But he also saw, in his own (his own father's) romantic heart, that its consummation would become a small redemption for them all.

HOLTZMAN'S HEAD WAS HUGE when you came upon him from behind, in the dim back corner of his shoe store, bent over his inventory sheets and fresh from the barber's, so the only way of telling where his neck stopped and his head began was the seemingly arbitrary place where a shadow of tiny hairs began to sprout from that Germanic column of red-and-purple flesh.

The stockroom smelled of shoe leather and cardboard and, as Dennis came closer, dill pickles and mustard. The overhead lights were remarkably dim; the only brightness came from the single gooseneck lamp that sat on his desk. His sandwich in its wax-paper nest rested on the corner of the desk, just outside the circle of light, and when Dennis saw Holtzman's fat hand reach for it and lift it to his mouth, he knew for certain that the man still hadn't heard him come in and that if he cleared his throat and called Holtzman's name or came a few steps farther and touched his shoulder, he would startle the old Kraut, perhaps send that plug of ham on rye with butter and mustard right into his esophagus.

So Dennis paused, long enough to see Holtzman return the sandwich to the desk, long enough to see that it was chewed and swallowed (he turned an inventory sheet over and sighed and lifted a finger to his mouth to dislodge something from between cheek and gum). Long enough, too, to reconsider what he was doing and to turn around, get back on the train, get back to work. Let Billy's sweet romance follow its own course.

But the road to hell...and Dennis said, "Excuse me, Mr. Holtzman. I'm sorry to interrupt."

The man turned, his big head like an old buffalo's, peering over his flank. And then, when he saw it was Dennis behind him, he swiveled his chair around and wiped his mouth and began to stand.

Dennis held out a hand. "Don't get up," he said, although Holtzman was already standing, already saying, "Dennis," and then, "Is everything all right?" the chubby hand to the heart, the heart lacking even the courage to let him say, "Is your mother all right?"

Dennis knew then that he'd had the right idea, coming here, to him.

Holtzman offered him the metal chair beside his desk. "Please, sit," he said after Dennis had assured him that his mother was fine, that he had only come to ask a favor. Even in that dim light, Dennis saw two things pass in quick succession over the man's face: one was the relief that there was no bad news. Second, the sudden suspicion that he was about to be asked for money.

Which Dennis, did, of course, and without too much beating around the bush. He said he wanted to borrow five hundred dollars to give to Billy so he could send for his girl and her mother by summer, find an apartment for them all, and get on with his life. He said Billy would be glad to work in the store on the weekend so that the money would be an advance against salary, not a flat-out loan, and that Billy, and he, would be sure all of it was paid back in a timely manner, with interest.

He said he was certain that Billy would eventually save what he needed himself, without anyone else's help, but it could take him another year, and a year was a long time for a young girl to wait all alone on the other side of the ocean.

"You met her," Dennis said. "Last summer. On Long Island. Outside St. Philomena's."

Holtzman nodded. "A pretty girl," he said, and already Dennis could see that he was forming an argument against him: prettiness was a virtue. She would wait for Billy to earn the money himself.

Dennis nodded. "Pretty enough," he said, countering what he hadn't spoken. "But for Billy, the moon and stars encircle her head. I don't know that he can wait."

Holtzman shrugged a little, touching thumb and forefinger to his chest. Dennis saw his eyes glance longingly at his thick sandwich.

"Eat, please," he said. "Don't let me stop you."

Eagerly, Holtzman took hold of the sandwich, sending, as he did, another longing glance toward his inventory sheet. Dennis began to wonder if he should have gone to his mother instead. But he'd been certain that his chances with Holtzman were better. The man had, after all, given up what had seemed a comfortable and complacent bachelorhood to take on a penniless wife and her grown son; he had opened his home to them, his cottage on Long Island; he had moved his ancestral furniture to the basement or distributed it to her relations in order to accommodate her secondhand junk. He had readjusted his morning routine, rewritten his will, instituted what was called a "family discount" at his store (which was essentially 20 percent off for anyone who was identified as part of Daniel Lynch's sprawling legacy), and increased his own grocery bill by at least 50 percent. He had complicated his life. All because a tiny woman had entered his shoe store looking for size fours. All because she had placed her stockinged foot in the palm of his hand.

He had, according to Billy's mother, who was there, wept copiously, gratefully, as he recited his wedding vows in the dim front room of the rectory.

Holtzman took another bite of sandwich, passed his tongue over his teeth, chewed, put the napkin to his thin lips. He never had managed to look Dennis straight in the eye. *My mother's husband.* Finally, he said, "I'm not a wealthy man."

Dennis nodded, murmuring like a priest. He understood that, he said.

"I'm not made of money," he said. Dennis understood that, too. "It's an awful lot of money," he added while Dennis continued to nod. "I don't know that I have access to that much money myself."

Dennis pursed his lips sympathetically. He was always struck by the irony of it. His father's wealth, which was purely figurative, had always been boldly proclaimed. Holtzman's, a literal fact, was relentlessly denied.

"The business is still recovering from the war years," he said. "Long-time customers came in and told me that they wouldn't shop here anymore because of what went on in Europe.

There was leather rationing, you know. I had these damn corduroy shoes to sell. I lost a lot of business."

He looked at the big sandwich in his hand, seemed to consider whether or not it contradicted his lean-times story, bit into it anyway.

"Billy might be an asset, then," Dennis told him as he chewed. "It might impress your customers to know you're helping out a former GI."

Holtzman considered this, seemed to like it, but then shrugged it off lest Dennis begin to think he had an advantage.

"He's a good-looking guy," Dennis went on. "Soft-spoken. People like him. Women like him."

Holtzman shrugged again as if to say Dennis didn't understand the shoe business.

"If you would think of it as an investment, not a loan."

"It's a lot of money," Holtzman said.

"It's what I figure he really needs."

"And when would he be in here? Just Saturdays?"

"Isn't Saturday your busiest day?"

Holtzman shook his head. "He'll take a long time to earn back five hundred dollars just working on Saturdays."

"He'll be paying you off from his salary at Edison, too," Dennis said. "And I'll be helping him out."

Holtzman put the sandwich down, daintily wiped his fingertips and then his mouth.

Turned a little in his chair, as if, Dennis thought, he was about to dismiss him. But then he said, working that tongue into his cheeks, looking over his papers, "I'm thinking of staying open Thursday nights. Gimbel's does it."

"Billy could be here Thursday nights," Dennis said. "Billy could be here by 5:30 easy."

Holtzman sucked his teeth again, turned to another inventory sheet on the desk before him. It was clear he was becoming more and more interested as he feigned growing indifference. Not nearly as sly as he believed himself to be. "What does he know about shoes?" he said.

Dennis laughed. "How much is there to know?" and then quickly amended it. "Smitty can show him what he needs, I'm sure."

Holtzman looked up from his desk. "He's willing to do this?"

Dennis grinned. He hadn't mentioned any of this to Billy yet. "Are you kidding?" he said. "He's dying to do this. He's nuts about this girl. It'll be nearly a year. He's dying to see her."

Casually Holtzman leaned down to slide out the bottom drawer of his desk. "I'll give him a dollar an hour to begin. Thursdays till nine. Saturday nine to six. Twelve-fifty a week. Fifty dollars a month." He lifted a heavy check ledger from the drawer, tossed it onto his desk. Flipped it open. "He adds whatever he can from his regular salary once a month."

"What kind of interest do you want?" Dennis said.

Holtzman waved the pen he had lifted. "This is family," he said. And then he added as he wrote, exacting another kind of payment, "You boys will never have any money if you spend everything you make before it's earned." He might have been talking to a child.

Dennis felt the warmth in his cheeks. "This is an advance, Mr. Holtzman," he reminded him. "Billy will earn it."

Holtzman lifted his head to give Dennis a shrewd look—a skin-deep look if there ever was one. "But first he'll spend it," he said.

BILLY WAS AT HIS DESK when Dennis got back to the office. He put the check in front of him. "Here you go," he said, and understood for the first time why it was that his father had bankrupted himself and estranged his wife and filled their tiny apartment with far-flung relatives from the other side: simply to know this power, this expansiveness. Simply to be able to say, as he said to Billy that day in the office on Irving Place, "Here you go." Here's your life.

Full of himself, and of Billy's sweet, blushing gratitude, he decided that day, too, that he would marry Mary when Eva came. Make a good confession for a change, say yes and mean it, rather than have it turn into another instant sin when the priest behind the dark screen asked him if he planned to marry this girl he was having his way with. He'd give her a ring on the day Billy married Eva. Find them a place of their own. Get his life started. Why not? He could afford it, he had a rich mother. Why not? Bread was what you wanted over the long haul, when you got right down to it. When you got right down to it, you wouldn't want a lifetime of cake. And it would make for a fine summer.

BILLY WIRED THE MONEY to Eva in April and in his next letter asked her to send him her shoe size and the sizes of her younger sisters so he could pick up something for them at the store. This she did, including in her last note to him a folded sheet of butcher paper that contained a tracing of her right foot and each right foot of her three younger siblings. She said she knew that shoe sizes were different in the States and thought this was the best way to be sure of a good fit. She said, too, that she was making this letter a short one—she wanted to catch the postman—and would write more later. She said she was busy making plans.

In the shoe store that Saturday morning, Billy spread the brown paper out on the counter so Smitty, Mr. Holtzman's assistant, could determine each size. Smitty advised oxfords for the sisters, and by lunchtime Billy himself had selected a pair of tan-and-white spectators for Eva. He had sold a pair to a woman that morning, a young woman who had come in intending only to get her old father fitted with a pair of wingtips. The shoes had made even her thick ankles seem elegant and sporty.

The same girl returned twice that summer, once more with her father, once with a talkative girl friend who did all the trying on and buying. This was the summer that Billy, holding his breath, was going through the mail his mother had left out on the sideboard each evening and finding nothing, as he told them down at Quinlan's, nothing at all from Eva. The same summer that Dennis had begun to keep a tally of all the simple things a Brooklyn-born girl knew that an Irish-born girl had to have explained to her.

Like the prohibition against a girl calling a fellow on the telephone. On a Sunday afternoon in late September of 1946, Holtzman told Dennis there was a young lady on the phone and with a disapproving shake of his head handed him the receiver. Dennis sat beside the three-legged telephone table Holtzman had once retrieved from a pile of junk at someone else's curb. An hour later he met Mary at the service entrance of her building, on Seventieth Street, just off Park. He was thinking that if she was expecting a child, then he would, of course, marry her immediately, and tell himself that it was the hand of God (his father consulting) moving him toward a future that he only understood now he never honestly wanted. A future in which his own bad luck was the other side of Claire Donavan's sailor's opportunity.

But what Mary had to tell him was all about Eva.

This was the same week that Maeve, trying to orchestrate her own fate, came into the store by herself. It was a Thursday night, just beginning to get dark, and Smitty was working alone. By way of making conversation, he told her that he wasn't sure if he'd lost his young

161

assistant or not. Mr. Holtzman had simply told him this morning that Billy wouldn't be in tonight. "We'll have to see if he shows up on Saturday morning," Smitty told her, releasing her heel and allowing her to place her foot on the ground and wiggle her toes a bit, leaning over her lap to look at the new shoes and to tell him, finally (no surprise here), that perhaps she wasn't that fond of them, after all.

Gently holding her ankle, he removed the new shoe and returned it to its box. To save her more embarrassment (she was already blushing to the hairline) he didn't even offer to show her another pair. He simply said as he slipped her foot back into the tan-and-white spectators—well worn now and out of season—that there were always new styles coming in. She should stop by again sometime.

He pushed his footstool aside and held out his hand to help her up, thus lending her—it was a favor he did for every female customer—a moment of regal grace as she stood.

"Try us again," he said gently.

He was a dapper little man with thinning hair and a dark mustache. She was twenty-eight or so, in a brown tweed three-quarter-length coat and a gray skirt and shoes that should have been retired after Labor Day. She had combed her hair into fluffy curls that just brushed her shoulders, and her lipstick was fresh enough to have left a mark on her front tooth. Smitty had been selling shoes for twenty-five years, ten at A&S, fifteen with Holtzman. He was married with no children and, at this stage of the game, little love, but he had memory enough to know what it had cost her, walking in all by herself, no preoccupying old man or bold girl friend to hide behind. He asked Dennis later if it didn't seem to him to be the exact way of the world that the very night she decided to take the risk, to throw the dice or spin the wheel and see just what might come out of being by herself in the shoe store with Billy, the two of them (with any luck) all alone, would be the very night, the first so far, that Billy didn't show up.

Smitty thought to tell her as he walked her to the door that there was a girl over in Ireland who had his diamond ring, but who could heap that kind of humiliation on anyone? There was no time for it anyway, because once she had gotten through the obligatory trying on of just one pair, once she had discovered that Billy was not, indeed, in there, she was out the door. Perhaps believing that the time saved on this fruitless visit could be added to the next when, surely, by the law of averages if nothing else, she would not miss him again.

It was the very next morning when Holtzman came in that Smitty learned the reason for Billy's absence: his fiancée in Ireland had passed away. Pneumonia. It was just like the man to mention the news only after it had had some effect on the running of the store. Holtzman himself, and Billy, it seemed, had known since Monday or Tuesday.

"He won't be back working here, then," Smitty said. "With no wedding to save for."

But Holtzman shook his head. "He'll be back." He patted down a hiccup, touching his heart, the gesture making him appear to be soothing himself, reassuring himself. He liked Billy, knew the ladies liked him as well. Business was booming. "He just wanted last night off. He'll be here Saturday. He'll stay on."

Confirming what Smitty had begun to suspect, watching Holtzman carefully record Billy's hours but never seeing a pay envelope pass between them: Billy was working off a debt.

"What a blow for him, poor fellow," Smitty said.

Holtzman turned his hand back and forth, as if there were a number of ways to look at the situation. "Life goes on," he said.

As promised, Billy was in the store again that Saturday morning, paler perhaps, perhaps thinner. Maybe a new puffiness around his eyes, a whiff of alcohol on his breath. "I'm sorry for your loss," Smitty said, and Billy gripped his arm just above the wrist and said, "Thank you, Mr. Smith. I wish you had met her," before his voice broke. There was such perfect trust, such perfect helplessness in Billy's brief touch (Smitty had felt something like it only once before when he'd given his arm to a blind woman on the subway stairs), that Smitty, although he barely came to Billy's shoulder, immediately placed his hand under Billy's elbow, as if to offer more support. "He was at odd ends," Smitty told Dennis when Dennis next came by the store. "I've always said that it's the ones who are always joking who feel

164

things more deeply than the rest of us. It's something I've always said."

Smitty began, in the next months and years, to step back whenever a young woman came into the store while Billy was there, certain that sooner or later, the urge to live being what it was (he winked when he said this to Dennis, as close as he could come to indicating that he was talking about sex), the grief would pass and one of the young women who came in would catch his eye.

When Maeve returned sometime in January with her shuffling old father once more in tow, Smitty ducked into the stockroom until Billy was finished with his current customer, and when he peeked out onto the floor he saw that Billy had the old man's shoe off and was trying to get him measured—the man grumbling all the while, the girl cajoling. Billy patiently lifting the man's thick foot onto the wooden measure and watching it slide off again.

"He's a piece of work," Smitty said when Billy stepped into the stockroom to pull the man's size.

"You can smell the beer on him," Billy told him. "He must have had a quart with his corn flakes."

There was a bit of business with the shoehorn: the old man making an awkward circuit of the store with the silver shoehorn still stuck into his heel, up under his pant leg, and Billy going after him in a loping, stoop-shouldered run, trying to retrieve it. The girl watching, beginning to smile. Billy catching her eye and smiling as well. A start.

But of course it was the old man he befriended first, Maeve standing by like some storybook princess awaiting her fate as Billy discovered that the old man's family on his mother's side was from Mallow as well and that he himself had more than once ridden on the streetcar in Brooklyn with that storytelling Irishman everyone was so fond of—that was your uncle, was it? There was the war to discuss and the Yankees and the Dodgers. The radio sermons of Bishop Sheen. The inconvenience, for a man his age and with his stomach problems, of the midnight fast before Sunday Mass and the people he'd known, over the years, who had worked for Con Ed, had worked two jobs the way Billy was doing, had worked for the NYPD, as he himself had done. "When Maeve, my girl here," indicating her downcast eyes and the parted brown hair, "was eight years old, her mother passed away on us"—and you can imagine the boundless sympathy in Billy's blue eyes, boundless and unhesitating and, best of all, untempered by the count of intervening years, the years since that everyone else the old man knew handed to him like a shot of diluted whiskey, a cup of tepid tea, as if the time passed since her dying was a kind of comfort. Billy, of course, understood that there was no comfort, not when the love you'd felt had been fierce, and true.

They sat almost knee to knee, Billy on his footstool, the box of new shoes in his lap. The old man in the worn red-leather chair, his hands on the cool steel of the armrests and the tears springing to his eyes—always red-rimmed and rheumy—the handkerchief going to the nose—always swollen and cherry-red—as he repeated the story of his wife's life, his own insult and devotion, while Billy, with all the patience, all the time in the world, listened with the attentiveness of an avid apprentice, an admiring acolyte, listened as if he were receiving instruction, if even then he needed any instruction, in the perseverance of grief.

Looking on, Maeve saw her father's future with this kind and attentive young man before she had the courage to imagine her own. Or rather, being nun-taught, lives-of-the-saints—saturated (the quiet, handmaiden saints who, if they had not chosen the better part, were freed by their bustling about with food and drink and dishes from ever having to form a sentence, or even a clear thought, about how they loved Him and why), she saw that only through her father's life, which was all the life she had planned to know, would he gain any part in hers.

MAEVE'S, OF COURSE, was not an unusual case. "Unusual for your generation now," as my father put it, "but not for ours." The girl child wedded to the widowed father. Speaking of Maeve, my father had once said that

167

although the joke is always the Irishman, the Irish bachelor, ever faithful to his dear mother, take a look at an unmarried Irishwoman's attachment to her old dad if you want to see something truly ferocious. It was, I suppose, the very image I'd fought against myself, in the years after my own mother died, when I went off to Canisius instead of staying at home and going to St. John's or Queens or Malloy, when I took only short breaks during the summer so that my father would know I had a life of my own, despite him, despite the weight that hit my heart stomach chest bones every time I thought of him alone, waking alone, going off to the office, shopping, eating, coming into the house at 4 A.M. after getting one of Maeve's calls, after getting Billy off the floor or out of his car or into the hospital, if that's what was needed. Even when I married Matt and we headed for Seattle. Lives of our own, we said. Self-sacrifice having been recognized as a delusion by then, not a virtue. Self-consciousness more the vogue.

Maeve was only eight when her mother died—my father getting the story in her tiny kitchen, over all those cups of tea and slivers of cake she had served him after they'd gotten Billy into bed, over all those nights she had summoned him. There had been another child, an older sister, who died of lead poisoning when Maeve was very small. A policeman's daughter, Maeve had gotten some sense early on of the precariousness of life, the risk taken by simply walking out the apartment door. Her mother, all false courage, touched her father's back, the hem of his coat, as he went out, saving the intake of breath, the sign of the cross, for the moment she saw him gain the street. Anything might happen, and did, and Maeve felt the heavy weight of her grieving father's hand on her shoulder. He might have shipped her off to female relatives, but he managed instead to trade in his beat for a desk job so he could stay alive for her. The nuns at her school were more than happy to take the child in for as many hours as he needed them to, and Maeve spoke often—or as often as she spoke of anything—of the pleasant afternoons she had spent in the tiny courtyard of the convent beside her school (vine-covered walls, a single oak, a statue of St. Francis above a concrete birdbath, one of the Virgin in the crook of the tree) or in its seldom-visited front room, where the silence was palpable, luxurious, punctuated as it was by the soft steps of the sisters going through the hall or up the stairs or stopping in to bring her a glass of ginger ale and some digestive biscuits on a saucer. There would be frost on the windows, her schoolwork spread before her on a narrow, lemon-scented desk, her handwriting, the lovely round perfection of it, her greatest vanity.

There was no question, when she finished school, of having to find a job—which made her the envy of most of her girl friends, who were struggling with stenography and switchboards, and getting to the subway by eight. There was no question, either, that she would join the nuns for good. She did the shopping and cleaned the house and cooked his meals. Lipstick was for weekends, a movie with the girls, a Saturday afternoon at the stores along Jamaica Avenue. Her father drank most evenings, but it was a man's right and, with a wife in her grave, his only solace. And when things got out of hand—when, in his cups, he growled at her or cursed her or waved his arms about as if her love and attention were cobwebs she'd draped around him—there were the nuns to go to, who would listen quietly and advise prayer, but also make sure that the pastor crooked his finger at the old man next time he and Maeve were at Mass. So she had the attention of men, too; her father when he was feeling fond of her and the priests when he was giving her trouble, and the butcher and the fellow at the newsstand, and even on occasion some boys she had known from school, not the best-looking ones, of course, the homely mostly, the bad-skinned and wet-palmed, the untalkative (which meant a long night of short questions and short answers for them both) who saw in her plainness, her lack of prospects, their own advantage. Billy she first laid eyes on as he leaned to place a pair of new shoes in Holtzman's window on Jamaica Avenue, his hand held over his heart to hold back his tie. He looked up and smiled, but she knew even then that he would have smiled at anyone.

Bringing her father to the store was her way of showing Billy her life in one sweeping glance. Bringing her girl friend was a flirtation with despair—if he fell in love with her talkative friend, Maeve would, at least, in her lifetime, know him. Walking in alone was a dream, but as it turned out, it was another girl's dream. She was the plain one with the father, the one who without him would have become a nun. She was the one who, having chosen this part, must stand steadily by as his future was formed for her.

No one gathered in Maeve's living room that evening could have recalled it either, not accurately anyway: how young they had been then. How much these things had mattered.

Mac, Rosemary's husband, who had once been as young himself (in the cramped apartment, in the childhood bed of his young bride), sat on the brocade-under-plastic-slipcovers couch, his shirtsleeves rolled up, his pant legs neatly tucked above the knee. He had assigned himself the task of cracking the walnuts that had been set out in a porcelain bowl on the coffee table and spreading the pieces of meat out on a paper napkin. He leaned over his work like a watchmaker. He had already walked down to the corner deli once for more rolls, and again for a bottle of ginger ale. He had stood on a chair to change a lightbulb in the kitchen and swept the wet walk with a broom from Billy's garage, and now he cracked walnuts as if to keep up with a relentless demand, although the pile he had accumulated had already begun to overflow the paper napkin.

Billy's sister Rosemary was moving back and forth from the kitchen to the living room, pausing at intervals to glance out the front windows, hoping to intercept any visitor—as she had intercepted us—who might ring the doorbell or knock on the door and disturb Maeve. There was another couple in the living room with Mac, next-door neighbors, and Kate was there, although still without her wealthy husband. Two women friends of Maeve's from the Legion of Mary had installed themselves in the kitchen.

An Indian couple from across the street stopped by with a covered dish, but couldn't be convinced to stay. Two men from Edison and their wives were just leaving as we walked in. Dan Lynch arrived by bus with a box of bakery cookies. He was changed out of his suit but looked that much more polished in a pressed sport shirt and tattersall pants. He took a seat in the living room as well and placed his teacup and saucer on his knee.

The narrow house was a gallery of Billy's life that evening—how could anyone help but think it? From the curb where we parked to the three brick steps to the cool hallway, dim as a church, that led past the living room and the staircase to the kitchen and the back yard where Shortchange, Billy's motley mutt, had begun to whine as soon as she heard my father's voice.

How could my father keep from thinking of it: the sight of Billy's car pulled up over the curb and the berm or left fishtailed out into the street, of the brick-edged gash above Billy's eye, the pale soles of his shoes as he sprawled in the dim hallway, of Maeve standing over her husband in her pink chenille robe: "If you can just get him under the arms, Dennis."

How could he help but think of her maddening calm on those nights when she went into the kitchen to put the kettle on after they'd managed to drag Billy into bed—the drunk hauled up the stairs and pulled out of his clothes, wounds dabbed at with a cotton ball soaked in peroxide, shoes wiped clean with a wet cloth and set out on the front steps to dry, just another housewifely task completed.

"Would you like a little sliver of cake with that, Dennis?"

(How could he help but think of my mother on those nights, at home, still healthy, sound asleep in their bed while he sat with Maeve and discussed a solution, a cure. Or of all the nights in the past decade when he came back to our house after Maeve had summoned him, and found himself there all alone.)

It had always been my father's contention that Maeve was as satisfied with the appearance of sobriety as she would have been with the sobriety itself, more so, actually, since real and permanent sobriety would have meant the end of these mad nights, these long days of nursing him and waiting for him, and then what would occupy her time?

From the phone that hung on the wall in the tiny kitchen, she would tell my father when he called, "Oh, Billy went up to bed already, Dennis. I'm sure he's asleep by now..." or "He just left to take Shortchange for a walk," letting an hour or two, or even the rest of the night, go by before she called him back to ask if he would please come over and get Billy out of the street or off the floor or, once, away from the door of her bedroom, where she had barricaded herself against him.

Or he might hang up, convinced she was lying (turning to my mother to say so), and suddenly the phone would ring while the receiver was still under his hand and there would be Billy's voice, a little breathless but still sober: "Just got in," the rattle of the leash behind him and the click of the dog's paws against the linoleum. "Let me just get her her biscuit."

Billy's voice over the telephone, this telephone: how could he help but think of it?

We'd been in the house only a few minutes, had walked only from curb to front hall and into the kitchen, when my father reached for the leash that hung from a hook by the back door and said he'd take the poor animal for a walk.

Upstairs, Maeve was resting. Rosemary and the two women from the Legion of Mary made it clear that she had insisted no one leave on her account—that everyone should stay, have a drink, eat up all the food. She had insisted that it was a comfort to her to have people in the house, but she needed half an hour or so to put her feet up, to rest her eyes in a darkened room. To take the measure, perhaps, of how she felt now that the ordeal was at long last over.

On the wall above the tiny kitchen table that was covered now with casserole dishes and foil-covered cake pans and bakery boxes, there were three red apples made of pressed wood, one with a smiling pressed-wood worm poking through it: remnants of a back-to-school promotion from Holtzman's shoe store.

In the living room, Dan Lynch was describing another funeral: the church full, the aisles full, the vestibule full, even the steps leading out into the street. It had rained that day, too, but the crowd at the cemetery was so thick that their umbrellas had made a solid canopy. And even if you weren't standing under it, you were so well flanked by other people that only the top of your head and your shoulders could get wet. And out of the crowd, in one silent moment as the coffin was lowered into the grave, Billy Sheehy's dad, all unrehearsed, began to sing. "Danny Boy," of course. A lovely tenor that almost sounded like a record being played, what with the raindrops on all the umbrellas. It nearly killed everybody, it was such a moment. And Dan Lynch had said to Dennis when it was over, both of them teenagers then, "Your father would have loved this." But Dennis pointed across the road to another, smaller group of mourners who were just leaving another grave. "My father would be wondering why we hadn't invited them over," he said.

Out in the street, a passerby had asked Dan Lynch's own mother if it was a politician they had buried—there were so many people. "My mother told him yes, but the best kind of politician, because he never ran for anything. He'd go out of his way to shake your hand, to see how you were doing. He would give you the shirt off his back if that's what you said you needed, but he wasn't running for anything and never had, so he was the best kind of politician." He nodded to put a fine point on it. "That's what she said. I'll never forget it. I thought that was very good."

"He was actually a streetcar conductor," Kate said to the couple from next door. "Over in Brooklyn." She was wealthy enough to be proud of the fact—to use it as a marker of how far she had brought her own branch of the family—while the couple themselves (two more Irish Americans, the man florid, the woman plump) seemed to indicate by their quick nods of approval and their generous "aahhs" that they themselves might have lied about it, said he was a supervisor with the Transit Authority, at least—add a promotion to his history even if he hadn't had one in life, what harm?

"He met Sheila on that trolley," Kate said, and to the neighbor couple: "Dennis's mother, our Aunt Sheila. There was a story that all the passengers on the trolley applauded when she first spoke to him."

"I remember," Dan Lynch said.

"She must have been all of seventeen or eighteen when she married him," Kate said.

"And he was well past forty," Rosemary added.

The two Legion of Mary ladies had come to stand beside her in the dining-room doorway. "It often happened that way in those days," the taller one said. It seemed to amount to a dispensation. "You know, the girls so young and the men middle-aged." She was gray-faced and confident. Even as she leaned casually against the wide doorframe she seemed ready to take over.

Mac was tapping another broken walnut shell into his thick palm. "So there's still hope for you, Danny boy," he said. "You may turn up with some sweet young thing on your arm even yet."

But Dan Lynch held up a hand. "I'm long past that possibility," he said, and laughed and blushed, and then quickly retrieved the teacup and saucer that were about to leave his knee.

Rosemary was turning away from us, into the darkened dining room behind her. "I think my Michael wants to follow in your footsteps, Danny," she said, calling as she went to the sideboard where the Waterford decanter and surrounding glasses were nearly obscured behind a dozen framed photographs. "I told him just the other day that his father and I are off to Florida in two more years." She came back into the living-room light, a picture in her hand. "So if he wants to wait until he's fifty to have children, he's going to miss out on two first-class babysitters."

Mac selected another walnut from the blue porcelain bowl. "He shouldn't be in any hurry," he said, looking over the tops of his glasses. "There's still time for all that."

"He's thirty-two years old!" Rosemary cried: it was the echo of an ongoing argument. "That's hardly too soon."

Her husband, putting pressure on the silver nutcracker, would not meet her eye.

She turned to the Legion ladies, handing them

the framed photograph. "This is Uncle Dan and Aunt Sheila," she said pleasantly. "On their wedding day."

The ladies looked and nodded and handed it to Dan Lynch to pass on to the neighbor couple. He paused to look at it, too, although among my father's relatives, the photo was as familiar as a crucifix or the portrait of the Sacred Heart, and as consistently displayed.

"He was a lovely man," Dan Lynch said as he passed the picture on.

There followed a pause that threatened to get awkward, all of us smiling slightly and looking at the floor. "And where did she meet her second husband?" the neighbor woman said softly into it.

Mac winked at her own husband. "These dames can't get enough of this stuff, can they?" he said.

And the man smiled and nodded. "Romance," he said, rolling his eyes.

Mac broke another walnut shell.

"Well, it's interesting," the neighbor lady objected, slapping her husband's knee, smiling.

"You have to talk about *something*," Rosemary said, not.

"In the shoe store." Kate spoke like an adult among bickering adolescents. "In Jamaica, the one where Billy used to work."

"Ah," the woman said, nodding. "Jamaica Avenue. It's Baker's now. Not that you'd want to go there now."

"Not if you're white," her husband said, and got Mac to agree with him.

"She met him during the war," Kate went on, keeping her nose above any onrush of working-class bigotry, "when she went in there looking for shoes."

"Same place Maeve met Billy," Rosemary added.

"There was a shrewd one," Dan Lynch said to the men. "That Holtzman." He counted off on his fingers, "A German," as if compiling a list of grievances, "owned his own shop, a big brick house in Jamaica, another out on Long Island, a third place down in Fort Lauderdale. He bought the Long Island house during the Depression, from some poor fool who thought Three Mile Harbor out there was going to be the next Coney Island. Holtzman paid practically nothing for it. Paid for it right out of his billfold, Billy said. Standing in the driveway of the place. Signed the deed on the hood of his car. Shrewd."

"Dennis has it now," Rosemary explained. "It's a nice little place."

"Dennis and Billy were the ones who fixed it up," Kate reminded them. "Right after the war."

In Maeve's own living room, on her brocade chairs and sofa, under the warm light of her lamps, no one who thought it would dare say, "Eva." Although Kate could not resist mentioning that Billy had never gone back out there, over the years. Except for that once, when he returned from Ireland. Back in 1975. She'd had a postcard from him.

"Maeve did, too," Rosemary said. She said

Maeve had a postcard upstairs, stuck in the corner of her mirror, from that trip as well. A picture of Home Sweet Home in East Hampton. She turned to the neighbor couple. "The house from the old song," she said. Billy had written something very sweet on the back. Beautiful wife or lovely girl. She couldn't remember the exact words now—it might have been something from one of his poems— but Maeve had kept the postcard and had shown it to her the other day, Tuesday, after they'd gotten word from Dennis that Billy was gone.

"Holtzman was another old bachelor," Kate said, cutting in. "He must have been near sixty when Sheila married him. And he hadn't been married before."

"That we know of." Dan Lynch smiled wickedly. "Billy said once that he wouldn't be surprised to learn that Holtzman had a flock of wives buried in the basement."

"No," Rosemary said, fighting the tears that the mention of Tuesday had brought. "Billy liked Mr. Holtzman. He always got along with him."

"Dennis didn't," Kate said.

Mac examined the last three walnuts in the dish. The lamplight showed the pale scalp beneath his thinning, graying hair. "Holtzman didn't marry Billy's mother," he said.

From the kitchen came the sound of the back door opening. Shortchange scurrying inside, my father's voice speaking to her, saying, "Hold on there, girl" and "Good dog." The ring of the leash. Water running in the sink and the dog bowl being placed on the linoleum.

"How did we ever get onto poor Mr. Holtzman?" Kate asked, and Dan Lynch said, "I was talking about Uncle Daniel—if ever there were two men more opposite."

We heard the clink of the cookie jar where the dog biscuits were kept and my father calling, "Here, girl."

"Well, they both married Aunt Sheila," Rosemary said, but Dan Lynch waved his hand: a meaningless connection.

"And they're all in heaven together," Kate said with a laugh. "There's that."

"I wouldn't be so sure," Dan Lynch murmured, winking at me. "You know what Our Lord said about a rich man getting into heaven." I saw him throw a glance at Kate, who deflected it nicely by leaning to reach for a shelled walnut and placing it elegantly on her tongue.

Rosemary turned to the Legion of Mary pair beside her to say, "I've often wondered how it works in heaven when there's a second marriage. I know it sounds silly, but you have to wonder—you know, who comes first."

"The first marriage is the binding one," the tall lady said with an easy expertise. Mac said, "Ha!" to his wife. "See that, you're stuck," just as Shortchange, in a post-walk ecstasy, came wriggling through the dining room and into the living room, all cool wet fur and wagging tail and snorting black nose. My father came in behind her, half a dog biscuit still in his hand, just as Maeve appeared in the other doorway, the one that opened onto the dim hall and the stairs. She wore a pale house-coat and was in stocking feet. She had her hand to her throat.

"Oh, Dennis," she said, squinting toward him as the dog made a quick circuit of the room, greeting everyone. She put her fingertips to the back of Dan Lynch's chair. "It's you."

With the excitement the dog brought in with her—the neighbor lady grabbed the arms of her chair and lifted her feet as Shortchange sniffed her ankles (Nice dog, nice dog), and Mac held out a walnut and Kate leaned down to say with puckered lips, "Hello, sweet-heart"—it seemed to take a minute for us all to hear what Maeve had said.

She said, "I thought it was Billy, coming in from a walk."

Dan Lynch struggled to his feet, awkwardly balancing his teacup, finally placing it on the coffee table, on top of the pile of walnuts, and all the while saying, "Have a seat, Maeve. Please, have a seat."

Shortchange wiggled toward her as she sat down, and Maeve lightly touched the dog's wet fur. "I thought it was Billy," Maeve said to my father. "You sounded so much like him."

A kind of pain swept my father's face. He was standing just outside the living-room doorway, still flushed from the walk, his shoulders still vaguely patterned with raindrops, his coat still holding a whiff of the green spring. "I'm sorry," he said.

Maeve shook her head, her hand now on her heart. "I thought it was Billy," she said a third time. Even the bit of lipstick she'd worn earlier in the day was gone and her simple housecoat was colorless, white and beige. She seemed as plain as a blank page.

She looked around the room, her eyes weak. "I was just getting up," she said. "I hadn't put the light on yet." Now she put her fingertips to her forehead and lowered her eyes. "I thought Billy was down here with the dog."

Beside me, the next-door-neighbor lady clucked her tongue and said, "Awww," with the sound of exaggerated sympathy you might offer a child. The Legion of Mary ladies both put their hands to their mouths. And then Maeve began to weep.

Clearly, this was the moment our presence here was meant to deflect. The moment we'd been waiting for, hoping against, staying around to have a drink and eat up all the food. But we were momentarily stunned by its arrival, unsure of what to do.

Maeve lowered her face into her own raised hand, the fingers splayed now from forehead to chin (the plain pearl ring), and let out a long, tremulous sigh that was meant perhaps to give her her composure but instead caught in her throat and formed another kind of sigh, terrible and unbidden. "I thought he was here," she said through it. "I thought he was right downstairs."

We stared for a few seconds and then suddenly—as if we had all been caught in that stilled interval between the first thunderclap and the first pelting drops of rain—we began to scurry, moving as though there were windows to close, laundry to be pulled in from the line.

Kate and Rosemary were immediately beside Maeve's chair, Kate with a hand on her shoulder, Rosemary patting her knee. The two Legion ladies hurried back to the kitchen, one to boil water, one to fetch a box of tissues. My father grabbed Shortchange by the collar and dragged her out of the room. The lady from next door stood, which seemed a cue for the rest of the men to scatter, as they did, heading for the kitchen just as my father came back through the dining room, where he paused by the sideboard to pour a glass of sherry from the Waterford decanter.

He stepped forward, holding the crystal sherry glass in two hands, but Rosemary waved it away. "She's already had quite a bit," she whispered. Kate reached out and took the glass from him anyway.

"I thought he was down here with the dog," Maeve was saying. "I thought it hadn't happened, after all. It was a dream. He was down here, just coming in." Her voice twisted a little, nearly vanished. "I thought I'd go down and put the kettle on."

Rosemary said, "There now," kindly enough, but meaning, too, enough of that. "There now."

Her sister leaned forward with the glass of sherry. "Take a little sip, Maeve," she said.

But Maeve raised her eyes to the two sisters, looking from one to the other, maybe looking for some trace of their brother's face, maybe only hoping for understanding. And then she looked beyond them to my father. "He's gone," she said to him alone. "Our Billy."

My father nodded. His eyes were dark and he held his lips together so tightly he might have been breaking the news all over again. "He is" was all he said, because even as he said it Maeve put her fingers to her lips and whispered, "I'm going to be sick."

Swiftly the neighbor lady grabbed the blue porcelain bowl, turned out the remaining walnuts, and handed it to Rosemary, who held it under Maeve's downy chin. "It's all right," she told her, shooting a deadly glance at her sister: there was the smell of sherry. "It's all right, dear."

"Poor girl," the neighbor lady said. The taller Legion lady had returned with the tissue box and was now pulling out tissues, one after the other, as if she were doling out an endless line of rope. She handed them one after the other to Kate, who was holding them beneath the bowl, piling them into Maeve's lap.

My father modestly stepped away.

An aluminum pot was produced from the kitchen, but Maeve, as Rosemary said, had nothing but the sherry in her stomach—hadn't eaten a bite since Tuesday—and so the sickness quickly passed. When it was over, Maeve sat back against the chair, her hands full of tissues, her face and throat blotched with red but deathly white underneath. "I'm so sorry," she said with her eyes closed. "I'm so ashamed."

Amid the women's cooing, the two sisters convinced her to stand and go upstairs to rinse her face and change her clothes, to make herself feel better. Maeve nodded, apologizing, coming back to herself, it seemed. Kate took her by the hand.

When the two of them were gone, we moved around the living room, sweeping up walnut shells and collecting teacups, straightening doilies and cushions. We could hear the men talking softly in the kitchen.

"The colored people have an expression," the shorter Legion lady began to say. "'No one's called home who isn't ready.'"

"She should have eaten something," the other said.

"It's good for her to cry," the neighbor lady told us. "Not to hold it all back. And what a shock for her, to think she heard him coming in like that."

The shorter one paused. She was stout, high-breasted like a wren. Wrenlike, she wore a beige sweater with a maroon-and-brown harlequin pattern across the front and brown stretch pants and tiny beige shoes. "I saw my husband three times after he died," she said softly. She held an empty teacup and saucer before her, in both hands. It made her look like a woman singing an aria. "In dreams, I mean. The first time he told me about that expression the colored people have. I'd never heard it before. The second time he was sitting right next to me, in church. There were lots of flowers and we were talking about how pretty they were. There was a huge snow-storm the day before his funeral"—turning to me to explain—"this was back in '78. And we hadn't had too many flowers there. It had bothered me a lot. That he hadn't had more flowers. But the dream put my mind at ease." She paused. There was a threat of tears in her voice. "The third time he just squeezed my hand and walked away." She took a deep breath, bending to pick up a crumpled napkin. "And that was it," she said. "I never have been able to dream his face again. I dream about him, but he's always in the next room, or he's got his back to me, or he's just gone out or is just about to come in. I never see him. There were those three times in the beginning and then no more."

Solemnly, authoritatively, sweeping a tissue over the surface of the coffee table, the taller Legion lady nodded and said, "I believe it's always three."

Rosemary agreed. "That's what they say."

There was a knock at the front door—three short raps that might have come from beneath a conjurer's table—and when my father opened it, we heard his soft voice saying, "Mon-signor." A single look went around the women in the room. You could feel the subject changing. Rosemary leaned over and turned on another light.

The priest came into the living room just as

the other three men came through the dining room to meet him. He shook hands all around. He was a heavy, scrubbed-looking man whose throat seemed to strain against his white collar just as his shoulders and broad chest seemed to strain against his black jacket and shirtfront. Even his shiny scalp looked taut against his skull. And yet, for all this, there was an air of tremendous ease about him as he shook hands all around like a politician (although he never ran for anything), making eye contact, Glad to see you, his palm warm and dry and encompassing. The taller Legion lady went to brew him his cup of tea and I was dispatched by my father to go upstairs and let Maeve know.

The stairs were carpeted, the same pale gray pile as in the living room. There was a wrought-iron rail, open to the hallway halfway up and then closed off by a wall. On the landing there was a round table draped with a pale blue cloth and covered with Hummel children, some of whom had black veins running across their legs and shoulders and through their necks, clearly places where they had been broken and then carefully repaired. Above this table was an oil portrait of the Christ Child that to the uninitiated would seem to be a portrait of a beautiful and dark-skinned prepubescent girl. A framed, cross-stitched copy of the Irish blessing and another of the prayer of St. Francis on the wall between the two bedrooms. The bathroom door at the head of the stairs was closed and I could hear water running behind it.

I glanced into Maeve's bedroom. Kate was sitting on the edge of the bed, on a lovely ice-blue satin quilt that still bore the mark of where Maeve must have been napping when she heard Billy coming in. She held a life-sized baby doll in her lap, cradling it.

"Monsignor's here," I said, and Kate looked up. "Good," she said. She lifted the doll. It was dressed in a white crocheted sweater and cap and a long, yellowing christening gown. A tiny blue medal on a scrap of pale blue ribbon was pinned to its collar. "This was Maeve's," she said. "This gown. She was christened in it."

She turned to place the doll where it belonged, in the center of the bed, between their two pillows. "Get this," Kate said, rearranging the doll's gown. "Maeve was just telling me that at the luncheon today Ted Lynch went on about an order of nuns that takes widows. He said he'd give her the name of the Mother House if she was interested." Kate rolled her eyes, blue eyes like Billy's. They seemed remarkably quick under the weight of her expensive eyeshadow. Her mouth had Billy's wry thinness. "Can you imagine?" she said. "An hour after a woman buries her husband, he's talking about her entering a convent? Can you imagine the gall?"

I shook my head. I had no trouble imagining it. "What did Maeve think?" I asked.

Kate waved her hand. Some of the makeup had settled into the creases around her eyes, the lines that framed her mouth. "Oh, you know

Maeve, she told him she'd think about it." She reached out to smooth the christening dress over the doll's tiny booties. "It's the idea of being alone now, of course, that's getting to her, but I said, 'Come on, when did Ted Lynch become this rabid Catholic?'" She glanced toward the door, lowered her voice. "It's one of the problems with these ex-alcoholics," she said. "They still have to be rabid about something."

She picked up the doll again. She seemed incapable of leaving it alone. "They should have had children," she said suddenly. "Billy and Maeve. They were both so fond of children."

Behind her, the closet door was opened, showing the empty arms and shoulders of Billy's suits and shirts, his shoes lined up on the floor. There were two windows in the far wall, both of them draped with pale blue chintz over white sheers. On the dresser between them was a photograph of Maeve and Billy coming down the aisle on their wedding day—Billy looking off to the side, acknowledging someone in a pew, it seemed, Maeve with her head down, her own smile nearly hidden. There was another, old-fashioned photograph of a pretty young woman in a high lace collar, Maeve's mother, surely, and another framed snapshot—in pre-Kodachrome color, the tones slightly off—of Maeve's redheaded father looking startled, immobile, in one of the living-room chairs. Billy's postcard from Long Island was stuck into the lower-left-hand corner of the mirror—Home Sweet Home.

"Not that it would have changed what happened, but it would be something for Maeve, now," Kate was saying. "To have a few children around." She smoothed the doll's gown, brushed at the bonnet, cradling it with what seemed half her attention, an old habit of motherhood. "You can't help but wonder— what's she got now?"

We heard the bathroom door opening at the end of the hall. "As if I should talk," Kate whispered. And then she put the doll back on the pillow. She said she'd tell Maeve the Monsignor was here.

DOWNSTAIRS, THE PRIEST HAD everyone in the living room laughing softly, teacups and saucers on their knees. The coffee table now held a plate of Dan Lynch's bakery cookies and another of small tea sandwiches, some ham and some cheese. Although he sat in one corner of the couch, legs crossed casually, thighs straining against the black fabric of his pants, elbow up over the plastic-covered armrest, the Monsignor was the center of everyone's attention. He had been recalling Billy. A Holy Name Society meeting and the speaker going on for so long about the significance of the Pascal feast that Billy had leaned over and whispered into the Monsignor's ear that the hind leg of the Lamb of God with a little mint jelly sounded good to him.

When Maeve descended the stairs a few minutes later, her sister-in-law behind her like a handmaiden, everyone stood as if for a meeting of dignitaries. Maeve put both her hands out for the priest and the priest stepped toward her easily, confidently, like an expert, a pro, like a slugger going to the plate or a surgeon to the operating table, a renowned attorney rising for his closing arguments. We all felt it, felt the tremendous sense of relief that we finally had among us someone who knew what he was doing.

She wore brown slacks and a white sweater now, but nice ones, only a step down from her funeral dress. Not ready yet, perhaps, to put on her everyday clothes, to let Billy's death begin to be something less than an occasion.

"How are you, Maeve, my dear?" the priest said, taking her hands (she still clutched a tissue in one of them) with perfect gentleness and sympathy and an understanding that was bolstered—you saw it in his physical ease, his lingering smile—by his utter faith that death was not what we believed it to be tonight, not at all. He apologized for not having made it to the funeral this morning, he'd been called to the hospital (another soul rising, he implied), but she had been in his prayers all day long. "How are you, then?" he said, and once again Maeve put a tissue to her eyes and began to cry.

This time, none of us stirred. We simply stood, watching, as he put his arm around her shoulder and led her to the couch and sat beside her, his large hand covering both her own. Slowly, we all took our seats. It occurred to me that we were like a defeated bucket brigade, our wet and empty buckets dangling from our arms as we watched the fire chief drown a blaze that only minutes before we had merely splashed at.

"I thought I heard him coming in," she said. "Earlier this evening." And he nodded, expert in these matters, letting her speak, tell him what she'd felt, lying down in their darkened room, drifting off a bit, hearing the back door open and the dog coming in and the sound of his voice, and getting up and coming down here as if their lives were merely going on. And then realizing that he was gone. "Gone, Father," she said. The terror of it struck her then. His life was over. Hers was not.

The priest nodded as she spoke. Everything in his face and his manner said he knew. He knew what she said, wanted to say, would say next. He had sat like this, his manner said, with so many other widows, so many times before. When he finally replied it was with an authority that superseded all our experience of Billy, superseded even Maeve's, my father's, his sisters' long years. He was like a physician carrying reports to a waiting family, suddenly more expert than any of them about the dying man. More expert, everything in the priest's gracious manner seemed to say, because only he understood that death was nothing that it seemed to be, to us, tonight.

"Not over, Maeve," he said softly, scolding her, but fondly, gently. "We are not abandoned, Maeve," he said. "You know that."

She bowed her head. Her tears, free-falling now, struck her lap, the back of his hand.

"Billy's life goes on, in Christ."

With her head still down, she said again, "I thought I heard him coming in."

The priest nodded politely. "I understand," he said.

"I thought he was here," she repeated.

He pursed his lips, biding his time, it seemed. "It was another shock," he said. "But think of the joy he's found today, Maeve," he added softly, smiling. "The old reprobate. Think of the peace. Gone to his rest, Maeve," he said, "with the hope of rising again. The promise of rising again, Maeve, in the fulfillment of time. Think of that, if you can."

Maeve lifted her head, but did not raise her eyes. You could see in the stubborn set of her jaw that it was not a figurative life that she wanted for Billy at this moment but a literal one, his literal presence, coming in with the dog as she dozed, opening the cookie jar where they kept the dog biscuits, hanging the chain on the hook by the back door. Their life together, even as it was, simply going on. It was the same literal presence the Legion lady had spoken of earlier, the literal presence, even in a dream, that contained the actual sound of his voice in her ear ("The colored people have an expression...") and the actual weight of him beside her, admiring the flowers, putting her mind at ease. She wanted the real pressure of his hand against hers.

"It's a terrible thing, Father," Maeve said

softly, her chin raised, her eyes cast down. "To come this far in life only to find that nothing you've felt has made any difference."

A sigh, quickly stifled, seemed to come from the women in the room. The priest raised his hand as if to quiet them.

"Listen to me," he said patiently, "listen now." He waited until she had raised her eyes, her expression showing him, showing us all, that she would not be convinced. "We could all tell ourselves tonight that we didn't do enough, Maeve. I had the thought myself when Dennis called me the other day and told me Billy was gone, and how they found him. I thought, Dear Lord, what could I have done? We could all of us say today that if we loved him it was a poor sort of love, or else his life wouldn't have ended as it did. But you know, if I said it to you, Maeve, if I said that I failed him, or if Dennis said it, or Father Jim, or Danny or Rose or Kate, if any one of Billy's friends said it, you'd be the first to tell us it wasn't true. And you'd mean it. And you'd be right. Billy succumbed to an illness we couldn't cure in time. It wasn't a failure of our affections, it was a triumph of the disease. That's the very thing you would tell any one of us and it's the thing you have to believe yourself. Of course, it mattered. Everything you felt, everything you did for Billy mattered, regardless of how it turned out." He bent his head a little to catch her downcast eyes. "I'm not kidding you about this, Maeve," he said. "I'm not making this up." He gripped both her hands in his, lifted them slightly. "You must believe this," he whispered.

She did not return his gaze. "I suppose I do," she said.

Rosemary stood in the doorway beside her husband, their shoulders nearly touching, their faces, both of them, drawn, as if they were accepting a reprimand. Kate sat in the chair beside the neighbor lady with her head bent, studying her polished nails, her diamond anniversary ring. The neighbor lady's husband had put his hand on her shoulder and was admiring, as were the two Legion ladies, admiring the man at his good work while Dan Lynch searched his pockets and then pulled out a large handkerchief and wiped both his eyes with it. He refolded the thing in some complex and elaborate pattern that reduced it to the size of a playing card and then wiped his eyes with it again. I turned to glance at my father, who stood just behind me, and saw some trace of the same look he had worn in the car today: that old annoyance, nearly trivialized by time. Or perhaps something troublesome, nearly healed. It was either the near-triumph of faith or the nearly liberating letting go of it. He looked down at me and nodded, as if I should attend to what the Monsignor was saying, as if his own experience, or age, excused him from the discourse, but I should attend.

Abruptly, before Maeve could say another word, the priest asked us all to say a Rosary with him, understanding (of course) that there was only so much more that could be said, that the repetitiveness of the prayers, the hushed drone of repeated, and by its numbing repetition, nearly wordless, supplication, was the only antidote, tonight, for Maeve's hopelessness. Rosemary began to get to her knees and he told her, good-naturedly, that he wasn't intending to kneel and would feel far more comfortable if she would simply get herself a chair. Chairs were carried in from the dining room and a kind of circle formed, although this was not the sort of Catholic gathering where anyone would think to join hands.

I T WAS THE SPRING of 1950 when Billy first came to Sunday supper—the old man issuing the invitation and Maeve in her nervousness dropping the whole bowl of steamed spinach onto the kitchen floor just as they were all about to sit down at the dining-room table. She scooped it back into the serving bowl—what else was there to do, there were only boiled potatoes and mashed turnips without it?—fighting with the dog all the while (Lucky was his name, her father would never be without a dog in the house, a mix-breed terrier always underfoot and mad for butter), unable to keep the animal's quick tongue from the spoon and the bowl and the spinach itself.

She put the bowl out on the table, the spinach still steaming, and watched Billy and her father help themselves and never said a word about it until years, absolutely years, later when she was serving Billy a bowl of boiled spinach with his dinner and suddenly couldn't help but laugh, and confess, and get Billy laughing about it, too. One night over dinner, not so very long ago. Billy sober because it was midday (they had liked having their Sunday dinner around three or four and then just a sandwich or something at around seven) and clean-shaven because he had gone to Mass with her that morning, and although he was only a week or two out of the VA and the fall he'd taken that had put him there, that time, was still evident from the fading yellow bruise on his forehead, although his face had grown thicker over the years, especially around the eyes and the chin, and his skin had begun to scale and peel and wear raw at his waistline and his wrists; although there was more silence between them, in those days, than talk, and she held in her memory, by then, a thousand and one moments she would never recount, things he had said to her, terrible things he had done, ways she had seen him (toothless, incoherent, half-clothed, bloodied, soiled, weeping) that she couldn't begin to tell, because even just putting it into words would kill her—a time, for instance (she will say it just this once), right before he went back to AA in '72, maybe the very thing that got him back to the meetings again, when she came down to the kitchen in the middle of the night and asked him to get himself to bed; she could see he was about to pass out and hoped he'd get himself up the stairs first. She leaned down to him at the table and said *Billy* into his ear (she knew enough to be firm with him, she knew that much), *Billy* (louder), and when he didn't budge, she turned away from him and started toward the stairs. "Dennis won't come, you know," she said from the hallway, talking to herself, as far as she was concerned. "He's got enough on his mind with Claire, he won't come even if you call him, Billy. Even Dennis has had enough of you. Even Dennis has troubles of his own." And the next thing she knew he had her by the throat. He was so much taller than she, and by then he had grown so heavy. His glasses were off. His face—well, it might have been a total stranger that had broken into the house. "Billy, you'll kill me," she'd said, clawing at his hand. And then he was weeping at her feet. And then he was unconscious on the floor and she had to call the couple next door because Dennis in those days had troubles of his own.

There was a rill of deep laughter from the men in the living room, but the women in the kitchen were silent.

Although, Maeve said softly, they'd had such a good laugh over the story of the spilled spinach that afternoon, a Sunday not long ago, that she saw again, for a minute (Oh, you know how it is), how handsome he was. Saw again those good looks that she had from the first been so taken with. She remembered again what it had done to her, to her nerves, to her beating heart, to have had Billy Lynch there, the boy from the shoe store, in the flesh, at her own table that first evening her father invited him to dinner.

"He was a handsome man," Bridie from the neighborhood said quietly.

In Maeve's kitchen, in Bayside, the day fading, the Monsignor gone off to make another call, and the women bustling about, putting together from the disparate supply of casseroles and cakes a nice little buffet, Maeve leaned over her milkless cup of weak tea and, smiling, said in her soft and patient voice that it wasn't until he was leaving their house that night, until he was right to the door with his coat on and his hat in his hands, that he asked her if she would like to go to the movies with him on Saturday. Naturally, she said she would, thinking of course, all the while— you know how it is—What will I wear? She had her best dress on, as it was, a gray wool with a slash of black velvet in the skirt.

When she went back into the living room, her dad was already asleep in his chair, and you know it was him she blamed, then, for the slight weave she had noticed in Billy's walk as he left their door and headed down the hallway toward the stairs that night—her father and his Jameson's saved for special occasions, such as visits from countrymen like yourself...So there was no one for her to tell, because she knew if she told him while she was pulling off his shoes and his pants, pouring him into his bed, it would be as good as talking to the wall. So she was nearly bursting with the news the next morning. But when she finally told him that Billy Lynch had asked her to the movies for Saturday night, her father merely sniffed and stirred his coffee and said, "No doubt he feels obliged." He said Billy had once been engaged, you know, just a few short years ago, to an Irish girl who died.

Rosemary quickly turned from the stove and said to us over her shoulder, "Oh, aren't men cruel?"

But Bridie from the old neighborhood, who

had arrived with her famous pound cake just as the Rosary was concluded, smiled kindly at Maeve and said, "I'm sure your dad meant no harm."

Maeve seemed inclined to leave the subject open to discussion. She had thought, she said, to buy herself something new for Saturday, but after her father said that she decided, Why bother? Any old skirt and sweater would probably do. They saw *All About Eve* and stopped at Horn & Hardart. She lit a candle in church that Sunday morning, but she didn't hold out much hope. And yet—the power of prayer—a week or two later, she was at the store and he asked her out again. And then her father asked him to dinner again, and soon they were seeing each other quite regularly. But she knew for certain that she and Billy were an item when they went over to Dennis and Claire's place for dinner one night—they'd only been married themselves a year or so—a nice little apartment off Prospect Park. Their first child ("your brother Danny") was just a few months old and Billy had held the sleeping infant against his chest throughout the meal, so that he had to eat with one hand. So that he had to ask her to lean over and help him cut his steak, which she did, of course, feeling him watching her. Even her father had to admit there was something more than obligation between them after that, Irish girl or no.

"For want of a shoe," the little Legion lady said softly. Everyone turned to her. "How does it go?" She touched the harlequin pattern across her breast. "For want of a shoe the horse was lost, for want of a horse, the rider was lost...How's it go?"

There was a moment of puzzled silence.

"For want of a rider," Bridie said helpfully, "the battle was lost..."

The rest of us hadn't stopped frowning.

"I mean, for Maeve," the Legion lady finally said, holding out her hand, and while we were all more or less convinced that she did not mean to say that for Maeve the battle, the kingdom was lost—although it might well be said—none of us had yet gotten her true meaning. "For Maeve it was just the opposite," she explained. "For want of a shoe, a boyfriend was found..."

The laughter was sudden and brief, crumbs shaken out of a dish towel. "Oh, I see," someone said. "Well, that's true."

Smiling, nodding, getting it (this is good for her, this kind of conversation—you could see all the women thinking it—this is just the kind of thing she needs), Maeve touched her teacup, the tea surely cold now, and said, leaning forward, "I'll tell you what I did."

We all smiled at her.

"I threw my father's shoe down the incinerator." Some color had returned to her cheek or, perhaps, was just returning as she spoke. "Not once but twice. If you can believe it. I said, 'Now, Dad, I don't know what's happened to the mate of your good shoes but we'd better get down to Holtzman's on Saturday or you'll have nothing to wear to church Sunday morning.'"

"Why in the world?" Kate asked. She had just returned from setting out the good silver on the dining-room table.

"Just to go in there," Bridie cried. "Just to have an excuse to go into the shoe store."

Maeve nodded. "Just to see Billy." Another bout of teariness passed briefly over her face—it was like the shadow of a small cloud moving over the earth—but was quickly gone. "I did it once, early on, before Billy and I had ever exchanged more than a few words, and then I did it again after our first date, because it had been a few months since poor Dad had come home minus a shoe—which he truly did often enough—and I got a little impatient. So I tossed another one down the incinerator, and good Lord, wouldn't you know it, we came back from Holtzman's that afternoon and there was Dad's shoe propped on the banister in the foyer. The super must have found it. It was still pretty new, so he must have thought it had fallen into the incinerator by accident and he put it out there for someone to claim it. I was certain my father would turn right around and take the new pair back to Billy, but when I said, 'Dad, your shoe,' he looked at me and said, 'It isn't,' very indignant. He wouldn't even look at it. He just marched up the stairs as if he didn't see it, refusing to admit anything. Here it was resurrected and he wouldn't have any part of it. The thing sat there for a good week or two and then disappeared altogether."

All the women were chuckling now, thinking of it, and how bright-eyed Maeve had become, telling the tale, and all without a drop of sherry in her bloodstream.

This was good for her. Good memories. And even if she'd given fate a push or two, wasn't it finally Billy's good luck that she'd shown up there, in the shoe store like that, so wild about him, so ready to give him her heart that surely it was a compensation of some sort for what he had lost, for the Irish girl. You could see Kate and Rosemary thinking it, the question answered: Maeve had known all along about the Irish girl, and still she had given Billy her heart. What was it the postcard had said? Lovely wife?

"Wasn't I terrible, though?" she asked us. "Throwing his shoes away like that?"

"You were determined," the neighbor lady said.

"The things we do when we're young," Rosemary said, shaking her head.

"When we're in love," the taller Legion lady added, although it was a leap even I couldn't make to imagine this gaunt and opinioned holy old woman as a girl in love.

"I told Ted Lynch about it," Maeve continued, "years ago, when he said the best thing I could do for Billy was to leave him. I told him how I'd thrown away those shoes. I wanted him to understand what I'd gone through to get him."

The women all nodded. Even a plain girl with

that kind of determination would be compensation enough for the beautiful Eva.

Suddenly Bridie, who was folding paper napkins, said softly, well, since we were telling tales, she'd tell one herself: Oh, what a crush she'd had on Billy Lynch when she was young. How many hours she had spent at her window waiting for him to walk by. Even up until the time she was dating Tim Schmidt, even after, she would have dropped anyone she knew to take up with Billy Lynch. "Except for Jim, of course." Jim was her husband.

"Oh, Bridie," Rosemary said, waving a crocheted pot holder. "Tell us something we don't already know."

"Really?" Bridie said softly, "You're kidding," but Kate had opened the casserole dish brought by the Indian couple and sniffed it and frowned as if to say not as bad as she expected. She held it under the tall Legion lady's nose. "Should we warm this up a bit?" she asked, and the tall Legion lady gave it the same kind of nasal inspection. "Sure," she said.

"It's some kind of chicken with rice," Kate said to Maeve, holding it under her nose as well. "I was afraid it would be something spicy."

"Oh no," Maeve said. "Lili's a wonderful cook." She turned to the neighbor lady. "They're fine people, aren't they?" And the lady agreed. "I have wonderful neighbors," Maeve said to us all. "I've been fortunate in that."

There was a moment of silent assent, and then the neighbor lady, sitting beside her at the small kitchen table, just under the particleboard apples, reached across and patted Maeve's hand. Maeve covered the lady's with her own.

"Monday night," Maeve said, and then corrected herself, "no, Tuesday morning, I called Dorothy here. When? one, two in the morning?"

"It was about two-twenty," Dorothy said softly.

"I didn't know," Maeve said. "I hadn't slept. There was a wind. Spring weather coming in is what Dorothy said. But it pulled at the windows. I usually dozed, waiting for Billy to come in. I usually said a Rosary and dozed, but not that night. I called Dorothy at about two in the morning. My hands were shaking, honestly, shaking like a leaf, and I asked her if she'd throw a coat on and come over."

"She didn't sound like herself," Dorothy told us. "She was frightened."

"And you said you were frightened, too, when you came in. Weren't you?"

Dorothy nodded. "Just crossing our driveways," she said. "There was something weird about the night. The wind and the warmish air."

"No doubt it was the hour, too," Kate said, being reasonable, it seemed.

"It was everything together," Dorothy said.

"We sat right here until when...seven or so?"

"Till John called."

"Till her husband called, at about seven. And then I walked her back across. It was raining by then, wasn't it, Dorothy? All that wind and then a cloudy morning anyway. Of course, Billy hadn't come in. John offered to call around for me. Even said he'd take the morning off to drive around a bit, but I didn't want him to trouble. It wasn't like it hadn't happened before, Billy not coming in."

"You said you'd let the police know," Dorothy said, and to the rest of us, "John made her promise to do that much. And to call Dennis. John said, Now, Maeve, Billy's a very sick man. He offered to call the VA himself, see if he was there. 'He's a very sick man,' John said."

"I said I'd call," Maeve told us. "I intended to. But when I got back to the house I did a few things first. I took a little bath. I washed out a few things."

"Billy's good shirt," Dorothy said.

Maeve nodded. "Billy's good white shirt."

"When she told me she'd washed out his good white shirt," Dorothy said to the rest of us, "I knew she knew. She knew he was gone. She'd known it all through the night."

"And then the hospital called," Maeve said. "About nine or so. And I called Dennis at Edison to ask if he could go down there. It was because he hadn't been admitted, see. They found him on the street, so somebody had to identify him." She looked at me. "Your poor father had to do it."

Kate said, "Everything's ready," and we all moved into the dining room, where the men were already waiting. Two or three of the women immediately began to urge Maeve to eat something. Maybe some of that nice chicken-and-rice thing, not too spicy. Maybe some of this ham. They followed her around the lace-covered table in the brightly lit dining room. Something substantial now, they said. Something easy on the stomach, too. Bridie's pound cake, of course. A pound of butter, the way it ought to be made. Old-fashioned ingredients being the best, when you came right down to it, because in the old days you really had to be of some substantial weight, women especially, in order to survive. Such as pioneer women in those covered wagons, or our own mothers making the crossing, although our mother was not a big woman and lived to eighty-three and Dennis's mother was just a wisp, too, and Uncle Ted's wife Aunty M.J.— the Lynch men apparently going for the smaller girls and Rosemary's daughter Jill with her tiny waist and you (me), too, although I see what little portions you've put on that plate, good for you, looking at you who would think you'd had two children, you must exercise, Kate does too, you should see the setup she's got in her basement, Jack La Lanne's, and so your husband's home with the little ones?—it'll be good for him, let him see what it's like with kids all day, right? men never understand until you ask them to do it and then they say, Well, the kids only act like this with me, it has to be much easier when *you're* with them, isn't that the truth? They're really thinking, You can't possibly put up with this day after day, can you? But it was so sweet of you to be here like this. Kevin and Daniel came in last night for the wake, but the girls are both up in New England, you know—both lawyers, have I told you? did you see the flowers they sent? They were fond of Billy, both of them. I know your father appreciates it, your being here with him. He and Billy were so close, like brothers, really—neither one of them having a brother of his own. And Dennis having to go down to the VA to identify Billy like that. What would Maeve have done, over the years, without your father to call on. He was the image of his own father in that, of Uncle Daniel. Always there for whoever needed him—what was it that you called him, Dan? A politician? Well, I don't know about that, but he did everything for my parents when they first came over. I'd call him a saint and I'm not just saying that. Not a good-looking man, your father was lucky to take after his mother's side of his family, but goodness poured out of him. I've never known anyone else quite like him. You would think he'd been put on this earth just to give the rest of us a hand, to give us some relief—isn't that just what a saint is? I remember people laughing, whenever I think of him, and I was sixteen when he died. Wherever he went he got people laughing, like Billy in a way, I suppose. Billy without his trouble. Your poor father losing his own dad at eighteen and his mother and his wife within a few years of one another and now Billy, too. I'm sure he's glad you came in. And tomorrow you'll go out to the Island with him? Good. Your husband will manage fine, don't worry about that. All young mothers think their kids can't survive without them, don't they? Didn't you? Soon enough you'll see. Next thing you know, they're all grown up and gone from home—isn't it the truth. Next thing you know, your house is empty again. Look at us, Bridie, Rose, Dorothy, Kate, how many kids altogether? Fifteen, good Lord, sixteen, sixteen kids altogether and not one of them left at home, right? Thank God for that, but see what I'm saying, see how fast it goes? But Kate's not going home tonight. No sense in her making that long drive back to Rye in the dark. Give Maeve some company, the first night and all. What's it doing outside? Can you see? It's been raining since Tuesday, hasn't it? Rain on a funeral day is supposed to mean a soul going straight to heaven. Did anyone bring the dog in? We should be going so Maeve can get some rest. Has she eaten a bite? Has she eaten anything? Her color's coming back anyway. It was just the sherry on an empty stomach. And the exhaustion, too, the poor girl. She'll be fine. Time heals and it's been a long haul. In many ways this will be a relief. God forgive me for saying so, she'll have some peace now.

While Rosemary and the Legion ladies cleaned up in the kitchen, Dorothy took Maeve's hands and asked her to please remember she was there, she and John were there, right next door, any time of the day or night, as always. "Thank you," Maeve said

212

softly, "thank you, dear," but in a way that seemed to indicate that she, too, was aware of how little need she would have, now, of aid and assistance in the middle of the night.

"Even if it's just a bad dream," Dorothy said. She glanced at her husband. "Even if it's just a strange noise or something you need right away from the store. An antacid or something. Just call us. Anything." She glanced at her husband again. "Even if you're just feeling lonely," she said, and then burst into blubbery tears—as much for herself, it seemed, and her own possible, probable long nights of widowhood as for Maeve's. The stocky husband she had just imagined into his grave put his fingers to her elbow and said, "Now, Mama," and Dorothy found a crumpled tissue in her pocket and waved it across her face. "I promised myself I wouldn't do this," she gasped.

But Maeve was smiling indulgently. She looked tired. The skin seemed to have thinned across her cheekbones, beneath her neck, and yet she seemed, too, to have found another source of strength, or composure, some last well of it that would see her through the final ceremonies of the day. "It's all right," she said. She briefly took the woman into her arms. "It's all right," she said again as they drew apart.

"He was a fine person," Dorothy was saying through her tears. "Without the drink. He was a sweet soul sober, Maeve. One of the best. Talking to him was like listening to poetry, wasn't it, John? Even when he was drinking, he was worth listening to. A smart man in his way. A sensitive man, Maeve, when you think about it. Maybe too sensitive for this world, if you know what I mean. A man with his fine feelings. The Lord made him as he was. There was no one to blame. You had your good years with him and that's what counts, doesn't it? Remember what you told us tonight about the spinach. And throwing away those shoes. Think of things like that."

Her husband was slowly drawing her out of the room, nodding goodbyes to everyone he passed. "Maeve's tired now," he told his wife. "Let Maeve get her rest."

"He was a sweet man," Dorothy was saying, on into the hallway. "If he hadn't taken to drink. What a shame he ever took a drink."

When they had gone, the Legion ladies stepped out of the kitchen, drying their hands on dish towels and slipping into their coats. They told Maeve what she had in the way of food in the kitchen. They'd be by first thing in the morning, they said, and no sooner were they out the door (bustling, in their plastic rain hats and short canvas raincoats, their caution in going sideways down the three wet brick steps the only physical indication of their age) than Mac turned to us all and asked, "Don't any of these holy women have homes and husbands of their own?"

Dan Lynch said, "Apparently not."

Bridie said, "Ah, but I do," putting her purse over her plump and freckled arm and taking her coat from the settee in the hallway,

214

which had begun to fill up with the odor of the wet night and the residual perfumes of the women's headscarves and spring jackets. "And my lady who looks after him will be charging me time and a half because I told her I'd only be here an hour or so," she looked at her watch, "And now it's been three."

"How is Jim?" Mac said soberly. Bridie waved a hand as if to show him there was no need for such solemnity. "He's doing all right, thank you," she said. "He doesn't always know me, that's the hard part. But as long as I can keep him home and keep him happy— things could be worse. He's more or less in his own little world." She shrugged. "Sometimes I envy him." She leaned to kiss Maeve, and then Rosemary and Kate. "God bless," she said to each of them, and then turning to us all: "I'm not going to make a speech. That was Billy's forte. The hard part's going to be going to the mailbox every day without hoping there's a note from him." To which everyone agreed, drawing in a breath as they nodded, as if they had not yet taken this into account but should have, would have, sooner or later. Bridie kissed me and my father and Mac, and with a "You, too, Danny," Dan Lynch.

"You'll be all right driving home?" my father said with his hand on her back.

"I'm fine." She shook her thick ring of keys. "I've got my siren and my Mace. I'm armed and ready. And it's not that late." My father said he would walk her to her car at least.

"She's a riot," Rosemary said when Bridie

was gone, clearly meaning something else.

"She's had a hard row to hoe," Kate said, directing her sister toward it. "Her girl with the drugs and Jim with Alzheimer's. And those babies she lost."

"And Tim Schmidt," Rosemary said, "in the war."

"She's a marvel," Maeve said, and Kate touched her shoulder and told her, "You, too, my girl."

Maeve laughed a little. "A marvel of what?" she said. Her shoulders seemed boneless.

"Of endurance," Kate said.

"Of patience," Rosemary added. "And loyalty."

Maeve smiled, dipping her head. It was clear that it pleased her, to have this much recognized and acknowledged. Her endurance, her patience, her long suffering. That same determination that had once made her throw her father's good shoes down the incinerator had made her a marvel at this, at being Billy's wife.

As Maeve took her leave of us herself, she paused on the stairs, her hand on the simple railing, and said to my father, "Thank you, especially, Dennis. I know how hard this has been for you." (Dan Lynch smiling sympathetically beside him, reserving his own tearful What about me? for another time, tomorrow night at Quinlan's, perhaps, with his cronies and a drink.) My father nodded. "Call if you need me," he said, repeating Dorothy's mistake, forgetting, as she had, that the mad nights were over.

216

For a moment the familiar weight struck me: I wondered how much lonelier my father's nights would be now, uninterrupted by crisis.

Billy's sisters, handmaidens still, followed her up the stairs, and a few minutes later Rosemary came down again to put her own coat on and gather up her husband. When Kate came down in her stocking feet to lock the door behind us, we followed Mac and Rosemary out. Dan Lynch, his jacket collar turned up and his feelings hurt by Maeve's last remark, began to walk to the bus stop in the light rain, under the orange streetlights, carrying the plastic grocery bag Rosemary had pressed on him, a supper or two's worth of leftovers. But my father called him back and said, almost impatiently, that he would of course drive him home. What did he think?

In the car, Dan straightened his collar and quickly recovered his good humor by asking us, Wasn't the Monsignor something? Wasn't he incredible? The embodiment of every good thing about the priesthood. He said he was certain there were plenty of fine rabbis and ministers, but there was something about a priest, a good priest, that those others couldn't match. A holiness. A closeness to God. "Don't you feel it the minute he walks into a room?" My father admitted he did. Dan twisted in his seat to see me. I admitted I did, too.

Well satisfied, he said, "It's a life lived on another plane, you see. A life that's all God, nothing else." He paused, but there was something false about the way he did, something theatrical. It seemed clear that everything he was about to say was well formed in his mind, well memorized, perhaps, a speech he had already worked out in every detail, that had, until now, lacked only an audience. "Think about it," he said. "A rabbi or a minister closes up his church or synagogue after a service and goes home to dinner with his wife and kids. He pays his bills," tapping his index finger on the car's dashboard, beating out the rhythm of an imaginary day, "does the grocery shopping, tosses a ball with his son, right? What's to distinguish him from anybody else, with any other kind of job? But a priest can take off his collar, play a round of golf, go to a ball game—he's still always different. It's a consecrated life, see, not just a consecrated profession. I mean, take the Pope, for instance, even non-Catholics are excited to meet him, aren't they? They know he's something special. Holy." He shook his head. "Now they're talking about changing things, but I hope they never do. It would be a mistake. We'll lose that, Dennis. The Church will lose the very thing that makes its priests a cut above."

I wondered if he meant celibacy.

"You're right," my father was saying. "Absolutely."

"I don't mean it isn't a sacrifice." I supposed he did. "It's a tremendous sacrifice. We had a young fellow, just out of the seminary, come to our parish a few years back, nice as could be, but he didn't last. He couldn't take it. Eventually he left and got himself married. So I know it's a sacrifice. But get rid of it and the priests will become just like everyone, wait and see. You'll do as well to confess to your barber."

My father was nodding, smiling, wondering, no doubt, as I was, about Dan Lynch's own single state. "Sure," he said.

"You can't have both eyes on heaven when there's a wife and a mortgage and new shoes for the kiddies to buy. It only stands to reason you can't."

"You're right," my father said. "I didn't."

"It only stands to reason," Dan Lynch said again. And then he turned a little, toward my father, lowered his voice just a bit, not enough to keep me from hearing him but to acknowledge, perhaps, that the company was mixed. "But I tell you, it gets my goat to hear the way people talk about it. It gets to me. You know, you can give up anything else these days, give up all kinds of foods to stay healthy, you know, salt, eggs. Or maybe give up sleep so you can be out jogging down the street at 6 A.M. You can give up an old wife for a new one, or a home life so you can run around the world like Henry Kissinger—oh sure, give up anything like that and it's just fine, it's just the ticket. But let the talk turn to Catholic priests and everybody's smiling behind their hands. Snickering. They're all out to make it something perverted. A man enters so fully into his faith that it changes the very fabric of his life, the very fabric, Dennis, do you see what I'm saying, and this society can't tolerate it. They want to see it as something bad. Our

Lord's okay as a story, you know, Christmas, Easter, something to talk about on a Sunday morning, but take it to heart, take Him to heart, have your belief change the very fabric of your life and oh ho"—he held his palm out toward the dashboard, shook it—"that's going too far for them. They've got to look for the dirt in it, not the glory. They say, It's an unnatural thing, giving that up, a man can't give *that* up, not for the sake of what's really only a pretty story."

"No one says that about the Pope," my father said, goading him, I thought.

"No, not about the Pope," Dan Lynch said, ever earnest. "Not in the papers, anyway. They're careful about that. He's a celebrity, after all. And he's a robust man. He skis, you know."

"Yes," my father said.

"But they'll say it readily enough about any ordinary priest, won't they? They can sense the holiness, but they don't understand it, so the first thing they want to do is mess it up a bit, kick some dirt on it, throw some sand on the fire. Sure, it's a great relief and comfort to the rest of us to find out no one's any better than we are, right? A man like the Monsignor walks into a room, and you know, it threatens some people."

"Sure," my father said, a touch of weariness in it. He'd had enough of Dan Lynch, I could tell.

Sensing this, not quite taking offense, Dan

Lynch crossed his arms in front of his chest and settled farther into his seat. He turned to look out the window, the wet dark streets lit by orange phosphorus. You could see by the way he turned back to my father, and paused, and looked, that he had struck on the thought some seconds before he said it. "Billy had something of that air about him, didn't he?" he asked softly. "That holiness, when he walked into a room. Don't you think?"

"Something of it," my father said, and then: "Look at this." There was an empty parking space right in front of Dan's building. "That's luck," he said as he pulled into it.

Dan Lynch reached down to gather up his plastic bag. He was flustered for a few seconds by his search for the door handle and then again by the unfastening of his seat belt, but when he was fully prepared for his leave-taking, he paused and said with a sigh, "It's the hardest night for Maeve, isn't it? The first night with Billy in his grave." He turned to the window. "It might as well rain." Beside us, his apartment building, pre-war Queens, six stories, dark brick, without cupola or awning or ornamentation of any kind, seemed as forlorn and hopeless as a penitentiary.

Dan Lynch cleared his throat. "Would you come in for a nightcap?" he asked. Without hesitation, my father turned off the engine and reached behind his seat for the club for the steering wheel.

"You don't mind?" he whispered to me as

we followed Dan Lynch across the sidewalk and up the barren path. "No," I said, my father's daughter, and stood beside him as we watched Dan Lynch let himself into his apartment building with his own key.

I N MY BOOK of Irish names," Dan Lynch said, "Maeve means 'the intoxicating one.'"

My father nodded. "There's an irony," he said.

"And Eva," Dan went on. "Eva, I suppose, would be some form of Eve. The first woman."

My father nodded again, slowly, his lips drawn a bit as if Dan Lynch had made a good point. As if in response to a good point, my father said, "There you go."

They both sipped their drinks—two fingers of Scotch in stubby glasses, plenty of ice. Serving them, Dan had poured three and then seemed taken aback when my father lifted the first and handed it to me. It might have been an aging bachelor's surprise to think that a woman—especially one he had known as a child—would accept anything stronger than sherry ("Would you rather a ginger ale?" he'd said), but it left me with the feeling that the glass had been meant for someone else. For Billy, perhaps. That I was sipping Billy's drink.

Dan Lynch's living room was dim—dim enough to make the double set of rain-spattered windows seem bright. The furniture was ancient: leather-topped desk where he had poured our drinks; claw-footed chairs, broad couch. Some of them his own mother's pieces, he said. Threadbare Oriental. There were neat stacks of *National Geographic* and *Time* and *U.S. News and World Report* piled against the bowed legs of every end table, and the tables themselves were piled with books, histories and biographies, from the Queensborough Public Library mostly. Winston Churchill and the Desert Fox, the War in the Pacific, D-Day, Guadalcanal, the *Enola Gay*, F.D.R., and Truman. There was a rattan magazine rack crowded with two weeks' worth of precisely folded newspapers. Today's *Daily News* as well as a *St. Anthony Messenger*—a cover story about celibacy and the priesthood—were on the coffee table between us.

There was the odor, especially when we'd first entered, of aftershave and the soap he had used in the shower he must have taken between the funeral lunch and the visit to Maeve's, but it was giving way now, as we sat, to the various scents—curry, onion, garlic—of some immigrant neighbor's late supper.

"Not to make too much of such things," Dan continued, seeming to believe suddenly that my father and I might do just that. "It's only something that occurred to me today, when Kate brought up that girl's name again: Eve—Eva. And when I got home, I looked up Maeve."

My father nodded again, shrugged a little as well, as if to say he would be careful. He would not make too much of such things.

"It's just that on a day like this," Dan Lynch said, "you find yourself looking at everything. In a new light, if you know what

I mean. You want to make some sense of it all."

"It's true," my father said.

Both men sat silently for a moment, cautious, it seemed, weighing words. Neither one of them would want to appear to be trying to say something profound—that was for the priest, of course—and both equally feared growing sentimental. And yet something needed to be said, on a night like this. There was the splatter of rain—like fingertips tapping against the windowpanes. The Scotch was mellow but with a bite. Each sip raised a kind of veil that was both a warmth across the cheeks and a welling in the eyes. A way of seeing, perhaps. Perhaps the very thing that Billy would have found so appealing, had the drink been his.

Not to make too much of such things.

"I never did meet her," Dan said. "That Irish girl. She was long gone back home by the time I was discharged. She was always just a story to me. You and Billy out there on Long Island that summer while I'm still getting eaten alive in the Pacific. Insect-proof fatigues, they told us." He smiled. "What a time that was." He turned to me. "Those A-bombs saved the lives of a lot of GIs, you know. Killed a lot of Japanese, sure. A lot of innocent people, too. But don't let the liberals kid you, none of them ever walked through a jungle sniffing for Japs. That's what we did, you know, sniffed for them. See if you could smell cigarette smoke or, you know, defecation. That's how you'd know they were there.

You couldn't see anything but lousy jungle. Those bombs kept an awful lot of GIs from dying in those jungles, you know. Those bombs let a lot of young guys go home in one piece."

I nodded. I recalled that Dan Lynch had once been known as a great letter writer, too, although his were always addressed to the editors of *Time* and *Newsweek,* the presidents of networks. I recalled that he was especially vigilant about slurs against Irish Americans and had once received a personally signed apology from Danny Kaye for a sketch he had done on TV about a drunken leprechaun. A one-man Irish-American anti-defamation league, my grandmother had called Dan Lynch at the time, out on Long Island that last summer when he'd come out for the day and brought the letter along. The rest of the Irish, she'd said, hear a slur against them and instead of being insulted get all guilty thinking that it's true. Kick a Jew in New York, she'd said, and one in Tel Aviv says "Ouch." But kick any Irishman and the rest of them shut their mouths and cover their backsides, thinking they're more deserving. Hadn't Danny Lynch, after all (when you got to the bottom of it), brought the letter in which Danny Kaye admitted all Irishmen were not drunks down to Quinlan's? hadn't he spread it out on the bar?

Dan shifted in his seat, recrossed his legs. "I remember meeting Maeve, though," he went on. "I remember the first time Billy brought her into Quinlan's. It was a Sunday afternoon. They'd been over to one of those tea dances they used to have at the K. of C. This must have been in the early fifties. There was a real downpour and any number of people from the dance were coming in."

I sipped Billy's drink. Another Queens rain, then: the raindrops themselves flashing black and silver in the air, darkening the sidewalk and the gray street and raising the smoky, dirty odor of wet asphalt and wet steel, the darkness of the afternoon making the neon lights in the various small storefronts, drugstore and Chinese restaurant and Quinlan's Bar and Grill, seem brighter than usual, even romantic, making the streets under and around the elevated seem a city unto themselves rather than the mere runoff—as they had always seemed to be to me—from Manhattan's surplus. Billy and Maeve, still younger-looking than anyone would remember them, hurrying along.

"I remember I saw Billy heading toward the bar with this girl in front of him, and my first thought was that she was someone he'd met out on the street or just inside the door. I thought maybe she was a stranger who needed to find a telephone and he was just helping her out. You weren't used to seeing Billy with a girl. It took me a few minutes to get it straight: that he'd actually taken her to the dance, picked her up at her house and brought her the orchid she was wearing. I must have seemed pretty thick, but it came as a surprise to me. You weren't used to it in those

227

days. Not with Billy. You were pretty sure he was a fellow who'd stay single."

Just as Billy must have been sure of it himself by then, five, six years since his summer on Long Island. And yet here was Maeve's very real elbow against his palm, yielding to his slightest pressure. Let me introduce you to my cousin. Here was another girl speaking into his ear—she'd just have a ginger ale, thank you—her breath mingled with the scent of the hothouse orchid on her shoulder, the one he'd brought her. Her face would seem dim in the new light of the crowded barroom, he would be aware of its downy paleness, her plain blue eyes. Thank you, Billy—maybe a little tremor as she lifted the glass and put it to her lips, a tremor of self-consciousness as she lifted her eyes to him over its rim.

Dan Lynch leaned forward a bit, cupping the stubby glass in both hands. "She was no beauty, was she? Maeve. A plain girl. I was going with Carol Wilson then, you know. Butch Wilson's sister, do you remember her?"

My father said he did. There was a beauty.

Dan sniffed a little. Her mouth was a bit too wide, he said. Not the brightest light either. He glanced at me as if to say there was a tale to tell, if it was just my father here alone. I suspected it would be a tale my father already knew.

"But Maeve seemed to be a good-enough sort," Dan Lynch said. "It didn't take much to see that she was wild about Billy. I don't know what Billy thought of her at that point, but she sure thought he was something."

Touching his own glass to hers in the bar where the crowd, just like the other couples at the tea dance that afternoon, was growing younger than them both. Time was passing. The christenings were beginning to outnumber the weddings among his family and his friends, the children born since the war, the nieces and nephews and cousins once removed becoming toddlers now, schoolchildren, startling him with their weight, their language, their blossoming lives. He touched her glass and sipped his whiskey and felt the watery veil cover his eyes. What could he have thought of Maeve, after the Irish girl, after that other future, the brightest of them, had shattered in his hand: Here was safety, here was compensation, here was yet another life, the one that had been waiting for him all along, even while he'd been busy imagining his life with Eva. "Pale brows, still hands and dim hair"—he would have found the lines in Yeats. "I had a beautiful friend / And dreamed that the old despair / Would end in love in the end—"

"When they finally decided to get married, I have to say it was another surprise to me. I never thought it had gotten to that point. Billy never even said that he was thinking of marriage. But I think maybe he was superstitious by then. I think he was afraid to say much to anyone about his plans. After what happened before."

"Could be," my father said.

Dan Lynch nodded and said, "I'm sure it's true."

Or did he think, leaning down to her pale face, the lipstick nearly gone from her dry lips, that here was the will to live, or the will to procreate, or simply the will to be joined to another, rising up in him again, all unbidden. Here was the familiar longing for peace, for sense, for happiness of some sort or another showing itself again in the form of this mild woman. Here it was, bidding him to go on, make plans, wed—weakening his resolve. His resolve to be true to his first intentions.

"All Billy says to me is 'Would you be my best man?' and I said, 'Sure. Who's the bride?'" Dan Lynch laughed, remembering. "I suppose he would have asked you if Claire hadn't been expecting."

He said it somewhat slyly and then seemed pleased when my father told him, "I don't think so. You were the man for the job."

Dan nodded to agree. "He showed me the ring. Just a plain pearl, not a diamond this time, which I suppose was more superstition still." He doubled his chin, looking into his drink. "I remember the way she shored up her old man, coming down the aisle."

My father smiled, nodding, showing that he remembered it, too.

"She did the same for Billy, when the time came. Maneuvered him when he couldn't maneuver himself."

"She was good at it," my father said.

Dan Lynch thought for a moment. A bit of wind picked up some raindrops and hit them against the glass, like pebbles thrown by a persistent suitor. "It was me who told Billy not to stay in the apartment with the two of them," Dan said softly, going on. "After he and Maeve were married. I knew he had some money saved. Working for Holtzman and all. I said, Buy yourself your own house and move Maeve and her old dad into it—or else you'll always be a visitor in their place. We were sitting in the back, at those little tables Quinlan had back there for a while, with the little lamps that had those scorched shades. Billy said Quinlan had gotten the whole set of them, along with the new waitress, at a fire sale somewhere. June was her name, the waitress. I took her out a few times. She did seem a little singed." He raised his eyebrows toward my father, shook his head again: another tale unfit for mixed company. "I said to Billy," he went on, "Tell yourself this is a way of the Irish girl giving something back to you. You took the job with Holtzman because of her, now use what money you've made at it to start out with Maeve. I don't know, maybe I was wrong to bring her up, the Irish girl, I mean. Billy never mentioned her himself." He shrugged. "But that's what I said. And Billy took my advice. He took my advice that time anyway."

Holtzman's money providing yet another down payment, then, this time for the house in Bayside. A narrow pale-brick house on a street lined with a dozen others, a small house with three high brick steps and a wrought-iron railing and a long white driveway that led to a narrow yard. They gave her old father his own room upstairs, moving into it the same bed and dresser and nightstand he had once purchased for his own young bride. The old black police scanner placed over the doily that covered the nightstand mumbling and squawking through most hours of the day that Maeve would spend cleaning and shopping and chatting with the neighbors while Billy was at Con Ed five days a week and Holtzman's Thursday nights and Saturdays, and even the two weeks of his summer vacation, since he would not go out there again.

("You and Maeve come out some weekend," Dennis would say when they met each other on the street or in the lobby or in the elevator at Edison, or when Billy and Maeve came by for supper or had Dennis and Claire over to their place. "Come mid-week," Dennis would offer. "Take a couple of vacation days. We'll be there with the children the first two weeks in July, you and Maeve come on out. Bring the old man, we'll make room."

But Billy would say no, shaking his head. "Thank you, Dennis, but no," he'd say softly. "I won't go out there." No need to ask him why.)

Dan Lynch said, "The real fly in the ointment as far as I could see was her old man. A drunk, pure and simple. And Billy so full of sympathy for him from the first, the way he'd lost his wife and a child and all. Billy thought it was reason enough for the man to drink. Reason enough for no one to deny him his whiskey, even though it was killing him." To me: "You only had to take one look at Maeve's old man to know that the drink was killing him." To my father: "Remember how he was, in his old slippers, the skin all mottled. That nose. Three sheets to the wind by four in the afternoon." He shook his head, shivered a little. "Maeve looking after him day after day. Not the best company for a newly married couple."

And yet Maeve's ordinary days alone with her father in the Bayside house could not have been much different from what they had been back in the apartment, before Billy, so much of the day, now as then, being predicated upon the dog. Her father coming into the kitchen to let the dog out in the morning and then pushing himself out of the living-room chair and into his clothes to take him for his first walk of the day; giving the animal his treat and putting the paper and the can of beer aside to give Trixie or Teddy or Joker a good scratch on the belly or to examine whatever it was that the dog was scratching at himself. Pouring the dog food at five o'clock and cutting up the chicken liver and gizzards that he would scatter on top while Maeve went upstairs to change her dress and comb her hair for Billy's return.

When she came down again, the old man would be in his easy chair in the living room, the dog licking his chops at his feet. He'd look up at her, noting the changes, the lipstick and the touch of rouge. Surely he loved his daughter. Surely he would have said if asked that he wanted to see her happy. But he also

233

had some stake himself in believing in the immutability of first affections, of promises made to the dead. No doubt he waged a kind of battle with himself before he said (no model of self-control), "Does Billy ever mention that other girl, the Irish one?" or "Did you know she was a redhead?"

Glancing in the mirror in the tiny powder room, Maeve might well have thought, Why bother?

By seven her old man might have already polished off a six-pack or fortified himself with more than one glass of Scotch, and Billy might have stopped off at Quinlan's after work, or had his lunch at some city bar-and-grill, but nevertheless, early on at least, there would be the ritual of a cocktail hour before Maeve served the chops or the cutlets or the casserole, the three of them raising their glasses, Good luck, Good luck, before they sat down—in the kitchen during the winter, at the lace-covered dining-room table come summer—the drink moving them along toward another closing of another day and Billy doing most of the talking, since he was the one who had been out working, collecting anecdotes and jokes and running into old friends in the dark and sparkling places where he took his leisure. Watching Maeve and her father watching him, you would be hard-pressed to tell what it was that gave them the most pleasure: Billy himself expending all this charm on just the two of them or their own satisfaction that one of them had managed to procure this entertainment for the other. You would be hard-pressed to tell, watching Billy at the head of the table, before his little family, talking and talking, making them laugh, the disappointment that lingered at his heart's core, disappointment and disbelief, disbelief that the faith he had sworn to an unrealized future should be so simply, so easily betrayed. "She looked into my heart one day / And saw your image was there / She has gone weeping away."

Then there would be the ten o'clock walk—the old man slipping a can or two into the kangaroo pockets of his coat, Billy going along for the fresh air and then—as the old man's legs gave out—going by himself, a cold beer can cupped behind his hand.

Walking through the neighborhood together, Billy and his father-in-law would have had little interest stirred by the lights in other living-room windows or the sound of other voices, shouts of an argument, the sobbing of a child, since all their talk ended up being about the past, about a time in the old man's life when he was a robust and redheaded young cop, the father of two little girls, when the city was what it used to be and the woman who made his life what it was still walked the earth. Billy adding his own recollections of what had once been but was no more. Billy sympathizing and telling him so.

Her father's physical decline, the slowing circulation, the water retention, the falls with their attendant concussions and sprains, the collapsed lung, the seeping capillaries, would have provided Maeve with enough to occupy her mind, consulting doctors now as she had once gone to the nuns, who went to the priest, getting the doctors, as the priest had done, to warn and reprimand him. Redheaded and fair-skinned, Maeve's father wore his dissipation boldly, blatantly, the same way, my father now said to Dan Lynch, he wore his heart on his sleeve.

But Billy called him Mr. Kehoe and took on the task of getting him up the stairs at night and into his bed. Maeve would be listening from their own bedroom with its Blessed Mother colors and the stiff-limbed baby doll that was either a stubborn hanging on to childishness or a balm for her inability to bear a child; a reassuring glance at the past or compensation for what had not been provided by the future. On the dresser before her, the wedding photo taken only minutes after they had made their vows. This will not change. Listening still as Billy made his way back downstairs again to pour himself another drink and lift the phone from the wall, or (Maeve still listening) lift his car keys and head out the door.

The drinking, down at Quinlan's, on his walks with her father, downstairs in the kitchen after she had gone to bed, would have been for her as much a part of Billy's personality as his slow smile, his multitude of cousins and friends, the letters and postcards that seemed to appear beneath his hand, to flow from his fingertips, in a nearly unbidden act of pres-

236

tidigitation. It was just Billy's way: this need to keep in touch, to keep talking, to be called by name when he entered the crowded barroom, slapped on the back, Glad to see you, have a seat. The drink a warmth across the cheeks, a watery veil that only brought into relief the gleam on the bar, the light in the mirror, the sparkle of a bottle, silver-topped, amber-filled, as it was plucked from its spot among the rows and rows of bright, silver-topped bottles and poured out again. The telltale aftertaste in the back of his throat that could only mean the one drink would have to be followed by another as the talk and the laughter turned, spiraled, not into the heart of his loneliness—he would not mention her now that he was a married man, he was that loyal—but toward the world where that loneliness existed, the world where change and cruelty, separation and loss, pity and sorrow refused to be forgotten, or forgiven, the world seen as it should be seen, through a veil of tears, where Uncle Daniel's life could be examined, or Bridie's troubles, his mother's loneliness and his father-in-law's grief, where the passing of time, the cruelty of war, the failure of hope, the death of the young could be discussed and examined (a young President, over the years, the young sons of cousins and of neighbors and friends, young children right over here in Kew Gardens, taken from their beds). A world where love (more difficult still) could be spoken of by a hand on the shoulder, a fresh drink placed on the bar, Good to see you, through welling tears, real ones now, Ah, Billy, it's always good to see you. Dark, sparkling, sprinkled with moments when the sound and smell and sight of the place, the taste at the back of his throat, transported him, however briefly, to a summer night long ago when he was young and life was all promise and she was there to turn to, to drink in, this was also the world where his faith met him, became actual, no longer as mere promise or possibility but as inevitable and true. No less than the cathedrals and churches and synagogues scattered throughout the city that had once sustained and amazed him, now the various bars he stopped into, for lunch, after work, between calls for Con Ed, and most evenings as the day came to a close, reminded him that what he sought, what he longed for, was universal and constant. Quinlan's was the best of them, sure, but each bar he went into offered the same familiar light and scent, the same company, the same talk. And in each of them, the force of his faith, of his Church, a force he could only glimpse briefly while sober—maybe for a second or two after Communion when he knelt and bowed his head, or for that brief instant when he pushed aside the heavy curtain and stepped into the dark confessional, or in the first rising scent of the incense at Benediction—became clear and steady and as fully true as the vivid past or the as-yet-unseen but inevitable future. A true redemption—it was a favorite word of his, after a few, Dan Lynch and my father agreed, a favorite topic—

238

a redemption that was not merely a pretty story grown up around a good man but a fact that changed the very fiber of the day, the moment. Drunk, when Billy turned his eyes to heaven, heaven was there. (Dan Lynch himself had seen it in Billy's eyes, he said again, years before, August 15, Feast of the Assumption, when they'd hightailed it over to Mass.) Heaven was there, utterly necessary, utterly sensible, the only possible reconciliation of the way he must live day by day and the certainty he'd felt that life meant something greater. The only redemption, the only compensation for the disappointment, the cruelty and pain that plagued the living, for love itself, because when he turned his eyes to heaven, heaven was there and Eva was in it.

Waiting up for him, Maeve would say a Rosary and think of the Bing Crosby song, counting her blessings instead of sheep: money was no problem and the house and yard more than she'd ever dreamed of; he never missed a day of work at either job and even in his cups never raised a hand toward her (not for years, anyway), hardly raised his voice, and never failed to give her his arm when they went out. He was kind to her father. He was a handsome man. And although the hour might be late and he might not make it up the stairs on his own, although she might have to call Dennis to help her get him in from the lawn or up off the floor, still he came home every night, eventually, managing always—it might have been planned—to stay conscious until he had at least stopped the car somewhere near the driveway or the curb.

She could manage his legs if Dennis could just get him under the arms. She could place herself between his knees, her elbows locked beneath his calves, her hips bearing whatever weight she could not bear on her forearms and maneuver him up the stairs, the landing the trickiest part, the little round table with the Hummel children being upset more than once (my father muttering, on his way back down again, "Couldn't you find another spot for that, Maeve?" telling my mother the next morning, reminding Dan Lynch now, of "her damn figurines"). She would be breathless by the time she got him to the bed, the backs of her legs black-and-blue from where his heels might have caught her, her arms weary, rubbed pink by the rough gabardine of his pant legs. Together they would undress him as well as they could, Maeve being the more adept, having cared so long for her old father. Dennis suspecting sometimes that Billy's determined unconsciousness was willful, even planned, a door he had sought and had stepped through and pulled closed behind him.

His body remained thin, the same long, thin legs and hairless chest, the same pale skin, chalk-white except for the raw patches of psoriasis and the nearly theatrically ruddy cheeks, so he looked for all the world in that moment before Maeve pulled the sheet up over him like some broken martyr, a tortured and heaven-bound saint. Billy Lynch in the flesh, in her own home.

Calmly, she would go downstairs and put the kettle on. A little sliver of cake with that, Dennis? Dennis sitting down with her in the tiny kitchen at all hours of the night to give her some company, to discuss a cure (AA, a drying-out hospital, a pill he'd read about that makes it impossible to hold down a drink), to let the hot liquid soothe the grief in his throat that told him that Billy, just like her old father, was determined to die on them. And that Maeve was determined to hang on to any kind of life at all as long as Billy was in it. The appearance of sobriety alone good enough. Good enough.

"From the very beginning," Dan Lynch went on, "Billy didn't buy the AA bit, even for the old man. He didn't buy this getting up and admitting that each and every one of them, every drunk, is exactly the same. He didn't buy this trying to freeze people out in order to make them quit, either. 'Billy's got to hit rock bottom before he'll quit,' Ted Lynch told me." He shook his head. "Jesus," he said softly, "nice sentiment. But look what Billy did: Billy sat with the old man and poured him his drinks and listened to his tale of woe because he knew that's what the old man needed. He sympathized." Dan paused, squinted into his drink. "I only wish we'd had sense enough to do the same for Billy," he said. "Maybe then he wouldn't have died out on the street the way he did."

My father said, "He didn't die on the street. He died in the hospital."

"Found on the street, then," Dan Lynch said, but it was clear that in his every telling of it in the future it would remain died in the street. "Found on the street like some bum instead of dying in his bed like Maeve's father did, because Billy had had the sense to feed him his whiskey at home and let him talk." Dan looked into his drink. "I tell you, Dennis, I've got some guilt about it all tonight. I think we should have done the same for Billy. Never mind this trying to trick him into staying sober, forcing him into it. You telling him he couldn't come over to the house to see the kids and me convincing Quinlan not to serve him. Jesus, there was a humiliation for the poor guy. And then Ted siccing his AA buddies on him like storm troopers. There's no drunk like a reformed drunk, Billy said. He made a joke out of it, sure, but they drove him crazy, puffing away on their cigarettes and glassy-eyed from all the coffee they guzzled at those meetings. They hounded him. And then Father Jim—who had a problem himself, you know—dragging him over to Ireland. His sisters wagging their fingers at him, the two husbands, too, although you can't tell me Peter Sullivan isn't in the same boat. And Maeve and her novenas. What were we thinking?" He looked up at my father. "We should have sat him here"—he pointed to the empty space of couch beside him—"and fed him his whiskey and let him talk. There was a pain in him that only alcohol eased. Who were we to tell him to give up the drink and live with the pain?"

My father held out his hand, palm up, a gesture that for me recalled and encompassed my life's entire experience of him, a plea for reasonableness. "That's not what we told him, Dan," he said.

"Essentially, it is," Dan Lynch answered. Stubborn.

"It's not," my father said. "He might have lived another twenty years if we'd gotten him to quit."

"He might not have wanted to," Dan Lynch said.

They were silent again, each one looking into opposite corners of the room, once more weighing words. I sensed that they both understood that this was not an argument either of them was up to pursuing or, for that matter, winning. Dan Lynch would not want to prove, finally, that they should have stood by, ready to pour, while Billy drank himself to death. My father would not want to hear Dan Lynch concede that Billy—their Billy, with his letters and his jokes, his loyalty and his broken heart—could have been cured of his affliction by rote, set back into his life by the simple application of some formula meant for everyone else. I moved the ice around in Billy's drink. Give the man that much credit.

Dan Lynch said, "You know, Billy never mentioned her again after he married Maeve." He lifted an eyebrow. "At least not to me," he added. "In all the nights we met and had a drink or two together, you know, before things got bad with him, you never heard him say a word about that girl, despite all he'd said about her before he met Maeve."

But my father sipped his drink, admitted nothing.

Dan Lynch sat back abruptly. "His sisters asked me today, Did Maeve know anything about her, the Irish girl? I told them I couldn't say." He seemed a little sheepish, as if he were reluctant to part with his authority—he, after all, had been the best man. "I said she must have known something."

My father shrugged. "Her old man had told her something. Billy had told him, early on."

"Much?" Dan asked, one smooth eyebrow still raised. With his bald head cocked and the stubby glass in his fist he looked like a cartoon prizefighter.

"As much as there was to know, I suppose," my father said.

"She can't have liked it."

My father smiled. "Claire was engaged once, too, remember. To one of those fellows who might not have come home if we hadn't dropped the bomb. I can't say it ever bothered either of us."

"But Billy didn't give up the girl. She was taken from him," Dan said. "That would make a big difference to a woman."

My father shrugged, lifted his drink. I wondered for a moment if he would say, Eva never died. Turn up the lights in Dan Lynch's little place and let the irony flood the room. It was only a lie. If you're looking for sense, Dan, you're not going to find it here. But what he said was "We're talking ancient history, Danny. Billy gave Maeve enough to think about day after day. She wouldn't have to go back that far to find something to fret over."

They were silent again, their glasses nearly empty. I drank from mine and listened to the rain, to a distant siren somewhere, to a few shouted words from down in the street, Spanish, Farsi. The two men looked into their drinks, ignoring it all, concentrating, it seemed to me, concentrating on conjuring something that they both understood would be fleeting, momentary, something that would be glimpsed only briefly if they managed to glimpse it at all. A way to make sense. Or else a way to tell the story that would make them believe it was sensible.

"Were they happy?" Dan said finally. "Billy and Maeve. Do you think? Were they ever close?" He would not look either of us in the eye, as if the question had embarrassed him.

"She put up with him," my father said, knowing it wasn't an answer.

"She chose to," Dan Lynch said. Now he raised his head. "She chose him, and as far as I can see he fit her to a T. Her old man all over again. Someone to maneuver, to shore up. An alcoholic with a shadow across his heart. An alcoholic because he had a shadow across his heart, the way I see it." He shook his head, squinting into the dim room. "I don't begrudge her her tears, of course, but I wonder, too. Would she have known what to do with a sober man, with the full force of the affection of a sober man who'd never loved another?"

Now it was my father's turn to lower his eyes. "Who can say?" he asked.

"I don't think so," Dan Lynch said, sitting back, a definitive nod. "I don't think she would have known, Dennis. I don't think Billy just as himself, without the girl there first, this Eva, I don't think Maeve would have found him so easy to maneuver. He'd had half the life taken out of him when that girl died and that could well have been just the thing that made him right for Maeve. Sure," he said—he raised his hand from his thigh and then placed it back down again—"sure, she put up with him all these years, but in other ways Billy asked very little of her. I'm certain he asked very little of her." He glanced quickly at me, trying to recall, it seemed, whether I was twenty-eight or twelve. "There were no children," he said. He nearly whispered it, as if the fact had been a secret. "And Billy loved children."

My father shook his head impatiently. He seemed annoyed. It might have been his natural disinclination to wholeheartedly agree with Dan Lynch about anything. It might have been his reluctance to consider the possibility that the lie he'd told Billy all those years ago was not merely the cause of thirty years of pointless grief but the very thing that

246

had made Billy's life with Maeve possible, and fruitless.

"Billy wanted too much," my father said finally. He leaned to put his glass on the coffee table, on top of the *St. Anthony Messenger*. It was both a way to dismiss the conversation and to show he was ready to take his leave. "He had some strange thoughts about the world, Danny, you know he did. About the way the world should be. You wouldn't have tolerated it in most other people. You would have said, 'Oh come on now.'"

He stood. I stood, too, Billy's drink still in my hand. My father's voice said he was at the end of his patience. His voice said, "Let's get to the bottom of things."

"Maeve made the same mistake we all did, Dan. She not only put up with him, she hoped he was right, in all his strange notions. She hoped the world would somehow turn out to be just the way he believed it to be. She hoped somehow that he'd turn out to be right in the end, with all his hanging on to the past. All his loyalty to the dead. Even if it meant she'd have no life of her own." He swatted the air.

"Billy didn't need someone to pour him his drinks, he needed someone to tell him that living isn't poetry. It isn't prayer. To tell him and convince him. And none of us could do it, Danny, because every one of us thought that as long as Billy believed it was, as long as he kept himself believing it, then maybe it could still be true. Jesus Christ, Danny," he said, and then stopped. In the silence that fol-

lowed, I fully expected him to say, *It was a lie.*
It was a lie and Billy knew it.

Dan Lynch sat in his seat, the empty glass
on his tattersall knee, his piles of books and
magazines, his mother's own pieces. He looked
at my father, his mouth closed, his eyes surprised and maybe a little hurt, but forgiving
him already for this outburst, because, you know
(he would tell them down at Quinlan's), it was
hard on Dennis, having to identify Billy and
all, it had been a hard week all around.

My father would not tell Dan Lynch the truth.
I knew simply by looking from one to the
other that he would never tell Dan Lynch
the truth. It was, after all, yet another sweet
romance to preserve.

"Jesus Christ," my father said again, but softly
now, that old, fading annoyance on his face.
"Sometimes the less said the better, do you
know what I mean?"

Dan nodded, clearly disappointed to have
the conversation pulled out from under him
like this (I had the sense that he'd have liked
to talk all night), but forgiving my father
already.

"Sure," he said. "Let's put it to rest for
tonight. Billy's ears must be burning."

My father smiled. "Gone but not forgotten,"
he said.

HE'D LEFT THE FLUSHING OFFICE at midmorning, driving in the rain to the VA hospital, where the girl at the information desk had said, "You're welcome, Officer," after she'd given him directions to the morgue. "Have a nice day, Detective," she'd called out when he left (the ordeal, at long last, over). She was smiling, he said, but with an edge to it. A young woman, Hispanic of some sort. No doubt with a boyfriend on Rikers Island.

That morning Maeve's neighborhood was sodden with the rain, the shingles and roofs a shade darker, surely, than they would have been in dry weather. Silver puddles in every pothole. A small river flowing along the crumbling curb. There were cardboard bunny rabbits and Easter eggs hung in storm windows here and there, marking the homes where children lived, or visited. Dorothy, the neighbor lady, was already over. Maeve was on the phone, and one of Billy's white shirts was already washed out and on a hanger, dripping dry into the kitchen sink. The undertaker's number was already written out, and the number for the rectory. She'd had nights enough, he supposed, to rehearse her every step should the worst occur, so that now that it had finally happened, it was all, for Maeve, part of an old routine. "She knew," Dorothy whispered, as if knowing, in Billy's case, required any prescience.

Sitting at her kitchen table, Dennis devised a list, writing on the back of an empty, windowed envelope, of the friends and relations he would call himself, and then copied it over again so Maeve would know they'd been taken care of. He called Kate and Rosemary from the phone in the kitchen. And half a dozen Lynch cousins. He brought Billy's best blue suit to the dry cleaners on the corner. And then there seemed for the moment nothing else for him to do but to go back to work.

It was shock that Billy had actually died of, not the cirrhosis, although the cirrhosis was certainly far advanced. Shock, as Dennis understood it, from his stomach being filled up with blood. He'd been found collapsed on the street, in Flushing, just off Main Street. Leaving some two-bit gin mill with his car keys in his hand—*still* in his hand when they found him, although his wallet was gone. It was a patrol car that found him (we're moving, Officer), not dead yet but dying. Dead three hours after they got him to the emergency room, one of the nurses there finally recognizing him and able to give him a name. Not Billy—Dennis's first thought when he saw him. A colored man, thank God.

When he left Maeve's, he took a minute to swing by Bridie's; it wasn't much out of the way. Standing at the top of her narrow stoop, he saw the curtain that covered the door glass move and had to shout through the wood. Bridie was out at the grocery store—it was the lady who sometimes took care of Jim and she had strict instructions not to let anybody in. He said that she should tell Bridie he'd call her later, he would not stand there in the rain, shouting the news. But of course by the time he called her, Bridie was able to say, "Oh, Dennis, I heard. I called Maeve. I had a feeling that was why you'd stopped by." When in truth he had stopped by mostly to see the shock on Bridie's face when he told her Billy was gone, the disbelief. Standing over Billy in that cold room (and soon enough the fat colored man they had shown him was transformed, by the familiar curve of his hairline, the shape of an ear, the smooth lips, into Billy himself), he had felt his hands form into fists and had turned to the young attendant to say, furiously, "Isn't this a damnable thing?" But how could the poor man respond? No doubt he saw such things every day—the husks of every kind of life carted out and carted away. Details like who he was, how he died, how the dusting of psoriasis on his bare leg recalled a bit of sea salt that had been there once, long ago, irrelevant now, barely interesting. What could the poor man say? Dennis had gone to Bridie's house in the hope of seeing in Bridie's eyes the acknowledgment, the shock—untempered by any premonition—that this was Billy they were talking about, Billy who had collapsed on the street (you could see the mark of the sidewalk on his dark cheek, one of those freckled bruises

251

Dennis had last seen on his children's knees), Billy whose life had ended this way. Billy Lynch. Googenheimer. Our Billy who had left us in this terrible and willful way.

Dennis had a call to make in St. Alban's, a Baptist church with a string of adjectives before its name: First Ethiopian Pentecostal Afro-Asian whatever whatever—so much exclusivity that you might expect the door of the chapel to be no bigger than a needle's eye. The pastor was the intellectual sort. A tall and handsome black man in his early thirties. Full of himself and his calling, his eyes always falling on a spot three or four inches above Dennis's head, his own head always drawn back a bit as he spoke, as if racism were a scent Dennis gave off. (As if it never occurred to the man that most of Dennis's customers these days, for years now, since he'd left Irving Place for the office in Queens, were colored.) And Dennis, to tell the truth, busy recalling all the while they spoke one of Billy's stories, about walking down a street in New York with his mother's sister, who was just off the boat, and a colored man passing them by, and then, minutes later, another, who was walking briskly. Billy's aunt had looked over her shoulder at the second man as he went by and then leaned to Billy, a boy then, and said, "He'll have to walk faster than that if he's going to catch up with his friend."

The pastor wanted to run a new separate line in for the nursery school and up the amperage in the sacristy (did they call it that?) and choir loft for a new sound system and music synthesizer. There was no urgency for the first, but the second "optimally" should be completed by the beginning of May, which was an anniversary of some sort. Dennis said his usual—The best we can—and dropped another "Reverend" into the conversation to show that he respected the man and his diplomas and his good work despite the fact that he himself was white and authentically Christian (i.e., Roman Catholic) and old enough to be this particular reverend's father.

He was surprised when the man walked him all the way to the door of the little church, thinking that perhaps he had, with his calculated deference, won him over. The rain was still coming down in sheets. The gray day still the one in which Billy Lynch had died. Dennis put on his hat and turned to shake the minister's hand and instantly felt the corner of a neatly folded bill prick his palm. "First week of May," the reverend said. "It's really a must." Now, finally, he brought his dark eyes down to Dennis's. He smiled, but not kindly, more as if (if you can picture it) he had looked into Dennis's shallow soul, had heard every "Damn nigger" he had ever breathed—over the newspaper, at the wheel of his car—as if he knew the narrow, ordinary, and ineffectual course of his life, of Billy's life, of the life of everyone like him. The superior smile of someone ennobled by true suffering, justifiable rage. Someone whose pain amounted to something. Whose love saved lives. Dennis nodded. He found himself searching for a joke to make, as if a joke might prove he was more than the sum of the things the man was sure he knew about him. "Dig we must," he said. But the S.O.B. had already turned away.

Standing on the sidewalk beside his car, Dennis unfolded the bill. A ten. There you go, Billy. And then dropped it on the sidewalk for some kid to find.

HERE'S THE THING, he said (we were on our way home, in the dark, in the now steady, heavy rain): Back in the sixties, when it was still Dig We Must, when it looked for certain that he'd be promoted to manager, a nearly twenty-year-old letter was produced from his personnel file. A letter from a Mr. Jacob R. Leibowitz, Jake—from whom, by then, he had bought four layette sets and maybe twenty pairs of footed pajamas, good wool Sunday coats, and at least a half dozen birthday blouses for your mother. The letter said that three weeks ago money was exchanged between him and a certain young man in your employ, a certain Mr. Lynch, with the understanding that as a result of said payment service would be provided in a timely manner, and yet service had only this morning been restored.

Dennis supposed he hadn't been called up on the carpet for it back then because he had plenty of friends in Personnel in those days—Mary Casey was there and his cousin Mal, Uncle Jim's son—but with the possibility of the promotion, the powers that be took a second look and found the letter that Jake had written in 1946 and so passed him over.

"We're passing you over this time," they said, apologizing, but there was little doubt in his mind then that it was for good.

That evening he took the subway home as usual, picked up the car as usual at Lefferts Boulevard, and drove the rest of the way to Rosedale. The kids were crowded into the kitchen, as usual, their mother at the stove frying fish, the dog underfoot. Homework and baths and prayers, not to mention the back of his hand to one or the other of them, and then the evening paper and a smoke before he's winding the clock again. Claire said, Oh, don't let it bother you, but there was the extra money as well as the boost it might have given his ego, and there were four college tuitions to think of. Not to mention the mark the letter left on his good name, his honesty, and the taint it might give to his friendship with Jake, whom you really couldn't blame in the long run because he had written the letter when Dennis was a stranger to him and the bitter taste of all he'd been through in the war was still on his tongue.

"How much was it?" Claire asked.

"Ten dollars," Dennis said.

"Cheapskate," Claire said, making a joke of it. "He could have given you twenty."

And then the phone ringing into his dreams at 2, 3 A.M., that godawful hour. Claire not even bothering to open her eyes for it. He stumbled out into the hallway where the phone was,

255

the only light coming from the dim lamps left burning all night in the children's two rooms. Billy's thick voice, in mid-sentence, it seemed, no doubt because Dennis himself had not yet come fully awake in order to catch the first few words, but giving him then, at 2 or 3 A.M., in the darkness, the impression that his cousin had been talking all along, all through the day and night, his steady stream of words an undercurrent to every moment of their existence.

He was thinking, Billy said, about the life she didn't have. Of all that had been denied her.

Dennis listened first for some sound in the background, some indication of where he was calling from. There was only silence.

Nights in a husband's arms, children, the movement of the seasons. The changes, melancholy or not, that came with age, with having a good span of years to look back on.

"Where are you, Billy?" Dennis said.

Billy said he was thinking about what a brief life it had been. The brevity of it couldn't have struck them then, they were young enough themselves, but now, as they themselves grew older, didn't it become clear that it was only a handful of years that she'd been given, only a blink to call her lifetime. Wasn't it something that as they themselves grew older, the cruelty of it, the unfairness, became more pronounced, more clear?

"Are you at home?" Dennis asked.

Billy said he was, but Dennis was only sure

it was true when he heard the dog moving around on the kitchen floor—this one would have been Trixie—scratching her neck and jiggling her collar.

"And where's the old man?" Dennis asked.

"In bed," Billy answered impatiently. Out cold, was how Dennis thought of it.

His own loss of her was one thing, Billy said. He'd long ago stopped thinking of himself in that regard. He'd had life enough himself, hadn't he? Here he was, a married man with a house of his own and two jobs and friends enough. His life had gone on, hadn't it? But he wasn't thinking of himself, you see. Tonight he was thinking only of her, of all she'd been cheated of.

"Go to bed, Billy," Dennis said.

Tonight the cruelty of it struck him. A girl so young, her childhood behind her, her life—marriage, motherhood—just about to begin. Was she born just to live these brief years and die? Was everything she'd felt and thought so utterly meaningless to her Maker? Where was the sense in it? There was no sense in it.

"Close up the bottle now, Billy," Dennis said. "Go upstairs to your wife."

There was a silence. Dennis was familiar enough with these phone calls to know that it could mean Billy had simply put the phone down to reach for another drink or had passed out or, if he was far enough along, had simply forgotten what it was he was saying. He might even have broken the connection. Dennis waited; he heard the muffled ticking of the clock, saw in the dimness the familiar shape of Claire's hip and shoulder under the dark blanket, felt his children's breath on the warm close air of the small house, in the middle of the night. There was the pull of indigestion in his gut, the same indigestion that had plagued him since early this morning, when he'd been called in and told that a letter had been found in his personnel file, written some time ago but troubling still...

"We have to rail against it," Billy said hoarsely.

"Go to bed, Billy."

"The injustice of it," Billy said. "The way she was cheated."

Dennis heard the sound of Billy's glass hitting the mouthpiece, the heavy swallow. He could almost smell the stuff on his breath.

"We can't be bribed into silence because we've lived long ourselves. We have to remember what she was deprived of."

"I'm not going to stay on the line with you, Bill," Dennis said patiently, although he well knew that as soon as he hung up Billy would be dialing someone else, Danny or Ted or one of his priests, keeping them up to all hours as well. "We both have to be at work tomorrow, Billy, that's all you need to remember. You're expected at work. You'll be sick as a dog if you don't close up the bottle now and go to bed."

"Death is a terrible thing," Billy said.

"Death comes to us all," Dennis told him. "But 7 A.M. will come sooner."

"Our Lord knew it," Billy went on. "Our Lord

knew it was terrible. Why would He have shed His own blood if death wasn't terrible?" There was another pause, another sip of whiskey. "You know what makes a mockery of the Crucifixion?" Billy said. "You know what makes it pointless? Anyone saying that death is just an ordinary thing, an ordinary part of life. It happens, you reconcile yourself, you go on. Anyone saying that is saying Our Lord's coming was to no avail."

Dennis heard the click of the glass again. "I'm not staying on," he said.

"What do we need the Redemption for?" Billy asked him. "If death isn't terrible. If we're reconciled? Why do we need heaven or hell? It makes no difference. If death doesn't trouble us, the injustice of it, then we don't need heaven or hell, do we? It might as well be a lie."

If ever Dennis had the chance and the inclination to say, "Billy, it was a lie," he had it now. But it was 3 A.M. and the indigestion was scratching at the back of his throat. And there was work tomorrow, when he would have to go back to his usual desk and his usual routine, loudmouthed McCauley with the Orange Crush—colored hair moving on to management, that single spark of small ambition that had ever flared in him extinguished now. Wife children house now the extent of his success.

"It's why I won't go back out to the Island," Billy said. His voice had lost some of its fierceness: even he, in his cups, knew this was covered territory.

"Jesus," Dennis whispered, to show Billy he knew it, too.

"I won't be placated by that beauty," Billy said. "I'll do that much for her."

"Go to bed, Billy," Dennis said.

There was another silence. "Is it still the same, Dennis?" he asked, his voice tinged with nostalgia. "Holtzman's place? East Hampton? Three Mile Harbor?"

"It's still the same."

"Are you going out there again this summer?"

"Who knows? She's talking about renting it out."

"I won't go there," Billy said.

"None of us will if she rents it."

"I won't see it again."

"She thinks it's a waste of money, keeping it empty all year. Now that Holtzman's gone."

"I'll do that much for her, Dennis. I'll stay away. She never went back and neither will I."

Dennis paused, trying to convey by his silence, as best he could, the end of his patience. "Close up the bottle now, Billy," he said softly. "You'll be dead yourself if you keep up this drinking."

He heard more silence in return. Another deep swallow. And then: "Are the children asleep, Dennis?"

"Of course," Dennis said.

"God bless them, they're a handful, aren't they?"

Resigned, wide-awake now, Dennis sank into the chair by the old phone table, pulling at the leg of his pajamas as he did, as if he had a crease to preserve. He glanced into his sons' room and saw the shadows strewn across the floor, sneakers and clothes, books and toys. "Some days," he said. He crossed his bare ankles before him, tucked his free hand under his elbow, settling in.

"No broken bones this week?" Billy was chuckling.

"Not this week," Dennis said.

"God bless them," Billy said again.

And another long pause. Another drink taken. Dennis considered telling him a funny little something one of them had said when Billy began to speak again, his voice growing heavier. "It's a pact with the devil," he said. "To be reconciled. Our Lord spilling His every drop of blood on the cross to show us death is terrible, a terrible injustice, and all the while we're telling ourselves that it's not so bad, after all. You get over it. You get used to it. Life is lovely despite the fact of a young woman dying, her children all unborn. Life's still good. What's beautiful stays beautiful. Life goes on pleasantly enough no matter who dies."

"It does," Dennis said wearily, although it struck him on this day, at this hour, that it was, for him, another lie.

"What's that?" Billy said. He was far into it now.

"I said it does," Dennis told him, raising his voice. Claire stirred, pulling the blanket up over her shoulder with a shadowy hand. "Life goes on, Billy," he said.

261

Billy whispered, "I won't let it."

"We don't have much say in the matter," Dennis said, but Billy was already off the line.

He sat for a few minutes in the dark hallway, a cold draft blowing across his bare feet. He wondered if Maeve would be calling in another hour or two. If he went back to bed would he go back to sleep. He thought of his father, the first and foremost (in those days) of the people he loved who had died. The very thought itself a prayer to the man in heaven, which he had surely earned, if only by dint of the flattery he had poured on God and every detail of His creation for the sixty-odd years he had lived. Or, if God required such things, by dint of the terrible pain he'd endured at the end. Even in compensation for the fact that for all the love he'd poured out for friends and family for all the years that he lived, he was never, let's face it, loved sufficiently in return. Not by the one being whose love he most sought, anyway.

He thought of his father, as he did so often in those days when his father was first and foremost of those he missed, the very thought of him a prayer of sorts (one that said, I'm weary, Dad, and discouraged; I've lost all sense of delight), although truth be told, it struck him that night, at that lonely hour, that his father in death was no more present to him, no more real, no more vivid than Eva was to Billy, in her just-over-the-Atlantic afterlife, pumping gas on the convent road in Clonmel.

Who can trace such things, he said, but it was perhaps the first tremor of the devastation that would strike him, knock him off his feet, in the weeks and months after my mother died. Billy's thirty years of misdirected prayer, Billy's tenacious, life-changing belief. His own lie.

FOR ONE OF MY MOTHER'S birthdays, my father wrapped a box of fifty matchbooks in bright tissue paper and then inscribed the card: *For a mate who is matchless.* It drew a great laugh at the dinner table that night, amid the remains of the sugary, elaborately iced cake, the already-opened birthday blouse from Jake's, and served as catalyst—at least as I recall it—for a discussion about which of them would remarry should anything "happen" to the other, which I suppose would have to place this particular birthday in a time when anything "happening" was such a remote possibility that speculation about it was benign and even pleasurable, a kind of flirtation. When a birthday gift of fifty matchbooks and a carton of cigarettes to go with them held no omen.

Coyly, my mother devised a list. There was a young widower down the street, and the son of the man who owned the delicatessen she shopped in—a good-looking Italian kid, she said, maybe twenty-five. There was the guy she'd taken driving lessons from when they'd first moved out to Rosedale, married, she thought, but she could still look him up. She could look up Bob O'Brien, her old flame, her old fiancé, the one my father stole her away from while he was still in the Navy, off cleaning up the Pacific. And his brother Ken, who'd had a crush on her all along and never did marry himself, as far as she knew. She could go on, she said, grinning, the cigarette held beside

264

her ear, the thick sweet icing still on her plate. The possibilities were endless. She still had some of the old charm.

"Should I go on?" she said, and my father bowed his head, laughing. "No," he said. "Don't go on."

"And what would you do?" she asked him. "Look up Irish Mary?"

My father shook his head, although we had heard him say, often enough, when my mother had run up a big bill at Gertz or A&S, or had forgotten to buy dessert or had dismissed him with a wave of her hand, I should have married Irish Mary.

"There'd be no one else for me," he said seriously. "I couldn't marry again. You could. You should. But there'd be no one else for me."

In the arc of an unremarkable life, a life whose triumphs are small and personal, whose trials are ordinary enough, as tempered in their pain as in their resolution of pain, the claim of exclusivity in love requires both a certain kind of courage and a good dose of delusion. Irish Mary, Eva's sister, would have been happy enough to accept my father's ring, I suppose, had Eva not chosen to stay in Ireland and marry Tom. My mother's first fiancé would have married her gladly if he hadn't been kept too long overseas by the Navy, if my father hadn't beaten him home, on points, a full year before. It might have been Cody or John in the car with your father, that day on Long Island. I might have been gone. Those of us who claim exclusivity in love do so with

a liar's courage: there are a hundred opportunities, thousands over the years, for a sense
of falsehood to seep in, for all that we imagine
as inevitable to become arbitrary, for our
history together to reveal itself as only a matter
of chance and happenstance, nothing
irrepeatable, or irreplaceable, the circumstantial
mingling of just one of the so many million
with just one more.

In the weeks and months after my mother
died my father grew silent about her, never mentioning her name and drawing his head back
just a little every time anyone else did. My
brothers and I noticed this about him and,
without ever discussing it ourselves, simply let
him be. We had all seen his reaction at the
graveside when my mother's sister, who read
entire books about such things and in church
prayed loudly, her eyes closed and her hands
raised to the altar, leaned into him and said,
"You can cry, Dennis. Big boys do cry." He
had smiled a little, looking over her head and
wearing the pained, polite expression the
early Christians might have worn as the
Romans lit the kindling at their feet. Without
ever discussing it, my brothers and I agreed
we would not torture our father with our
advice or our concern or with any well-
meaning injunctions for him to tell us what he
was feeling. We would let him be. He could
not talk about her, fine. He could not sit
through Mass without her, fine.

I was then in my senior year at the Mary Louis
Academy. During my mother's last hospital-

ization, my father had begun driving me there most mornings, stopping first at the hospital so we could say hello and then taking me to school before he went on to Con Ed, to put in an hour or two—face time—before he went back to the hospital again. He continued to drive me to school after she was gone, a convenience for me, an easy-enough detour for him. There was a morning radio show he liked, a father-and-son team, the father having been in broadcasting since before the war, the son clearly being groomed to take over alone when the time came. They cracked corny jokes and recited odd news items between traffic reports and weather updates and easy-listening ballads, and their soft and amicable banter gave us reason enough to say little to each other throughout the ride.

When I got out, I would slam the door and then lean down to wave goodbye through the car window. He would give a little salute and then drive on, his profile, in the last second I could catch it, tense and determined, leaning into the day, it seemed to me, heading toward what must be done and who must be attended to now that the passionate attention he had turned so exclusively to my mother in the past year of her dying was over and she was gone. Unable, he told me on the night of Billy's funeral, when we lingered for a few more minutes in the living room of the Rosedale house before he went up to his bed in the room that used to be their own and I went to the one that used to be mine, utterly unable, he said, to convince himself that the attention he had given her in that last year, the closeness they had felt, the assurance that they had achieved something exclusive, something redemptive in the endurance of their love, had been any more than another well-intentioned deception, another construction, as unbelievable, when you came right down to it, as the spontaneity of a love song in some Broadway musical, the supposedly heartfelt supplication of a well-rehearsed hymn, the bearing any one of Billy's poems about life and death and love and misery had on the actual way any of us lived from day to day.

He could not convince himself then, he said, in those days and months after her death, that heaven was any more than a well-intentioned deception meant to ease our own sense of foolishness, to ease pain. Despite his own years of vigilant Catholicism, despite his own mother's deathbed conversion, despite the promises he and my mother had exchanged, he could no longer see death as anything other than the void that met a used-up body, a spent mind. Not a mere moment over which you could sail, buoyed by love, by faith, but the abyss toward which you stumbled inevitably, part of the crowd. Put out a hand, if you like, to help someone along, surround yourself, if you like, with people who love you, who owe you, whose lives you've changed, but don't expect it to make a difference. It will make no difference; eventually, one after the other, every one of you will fall.

"And now?" I asked him, both of us standing,

not sitting, aware that there had been enough talking today. "Do you still feel that way now?" Aware, too, that we were edging close to it, to that embarrassing profundity he and Dan had feared, to that point at which too much had been said, but amazed, I suppose much as my father had once been amazed when his mother told him to get Billy to go out there, he's avoided it for too long—amazed at this kind of conversation, at this stage of the game. A conversation, it occurred to me, that Billy's life had spurred for us as much it had once spurred it for my father and his dying mother.

My father's eyes were a deep brown. He smiled a little, shaking his head. "Oh no," he said. "Not now."

How lonely they all seemed to me that night, my father's family and friends, lonely souls every one of them, despite husbands and children and cousins and friends, all their hopes, in the end, their pairings and procreation and their keeping in touch, keeping track, futile in the end, failing in the end to keep them from seeing that nothing they felt, in the end, has made any difference.

"It was only a brief loss of faith," he said. "It happens. They say it's not uncommon." And then he turned to climb the stairs on the night of the day Billy Lynch was placed in his grave. "I believe everything now," he said, his back to me. "Again."

Of course there was no way of telling if he lied.

S O BILLY RENTED a car and drove down to see her. The pledge taken, the last drink the one he'd had with Father Ryan on the flight over to Shannon. (Father Jim raising the tiny bottle and smacking his lips and telling Billy, "Dear Lord, if this isn't the blind leading the blind," setting the tone, so to speak, for their journey, whose seriousness of purpose— Father Jim was saying in his way—did not have to deprive it of its good humor.) The car was rented in the priest's name and the license Billy carried was the priest's as well, since his own had once again been suspended. So it was Father this and Father that at the rent-a-car office, despite the wedding band that he hadn't bothered to remove, couldn't remove if he tried, the way his hands were. A married priest, then.

Not, as Danny Lynch would say, to make too much of such things.

He'd planned, just as Kate suspected, to visit her grave. He foresaw a grassy plot and a granite stone engraved with her name, and the dates, the last not merely marking the end of her life but the end of his youth and that glorious and astounding possibility that he had once inhabited. He foresaw his own pale fingers, which trembled anyway, tracing the carved numbers and words. He thought of "Danny Boy" (he was in Ireland, after all, and the clouds were low over the fields he was passing, they were casting their shadows on the green and melancholy hills all around him), even hummed it as he drove—"Ye'll come and find the place where I am lying / And kneel and say an Ave there for me"—which in turn brought him thoughts of Uncle Daniel, and of Billy Sheehy's dad singing out all unrehearsed at the side of his grave. A moment that might have killed them all. The pain of it no less than the beauty. In his own prayer he would say he had not returned to the house on Long Island either, and never would: such was his sympathy and his outrage, both of them as keen as ever, regardless of the time gone by.

But first, he thought, he would go to her family. Mother or father if they still lived, Mary certainly, or one of the three younger sisters who would remember him no doubt as the boy, their sister's fiancé, who had sent them the American shoes. He knew her address by heart, of course, he'd written it out two or three times a year every year since Eva passed away, sending them a card at Christmas and always a line or two in late September, brief notes that said he was thinking of them, remembering Eva, giving Mary his best regards. Never more than a line or two, so he would never be forced to say that he had married, bought a house, carried on. Never really expecting a reply from the old folks and only briefly hurt that Mary hadn't been in touch with him. But Dennis was tied up with that part of it, he knew, her feelings for him, because even though she went straight home when Eva died, she could not have expected another girl—Claire Donavan—to take up Dennis's affections so soon. She could not have helped but feel jilted.

Driving the narrow wrong-sided roads between Dublin and Clonmel—parched, shaky, chilled to the bone by the dampness and the cold although the car's tiny heater was turned up full blast—he knew he would have to go to her family first and at some point tell them that he had a wife at home, a house, despite the number of times, over the years, he had written them to say Eva was in his heart and his mind and his memory still. He'd taken a wife and bought a house and for a good many years had kept fairly steady at the same two jobs he'd had then—one of them the very job he'd first taken simply to bring her back over.

No children, he'd say when they asked him. He'd say, A bit of a problem with the drink.

Clonmel was bigger than he'd imagined it and, as with so many of these Irish cities, not nearly as quaint. He might have been thrilled, or comforted, by the thought that this had been a place well familiar to her, that she'd once strolled these streets as a child, as a young woman, on the day before she left for her first appointment in Chicago—the beginning of her journey toward him—and the day she returned from New York, his diamond on her finger, but he had sense enough to know that the place was not the same city it would have seemed to her then, just before the war and just after it. He passed what looked like a Kentucky Fried Chicken shop, for instance. There was a shabby sense of change, of the modern, all about the place, that had little to do with the backward, quiet little city she had once described for him. He sensed that her ghost would have been as much a stranger here as he was.

And yet it was surely some sense of her ghost that made his heart beat heavily in his chest when, according to his map, not far from where he should be, he pulled into a gas station just outside town, off to the side so he would not block the pumps, and climbed awkwardly out of the tiny Fiesta to ask for directions. The attendant was a man about his own age, in the ubiquitous Irish cap and a filthy pair of mechanic's overalls. Billy and Father Jim had already shared a joke about how every set of directions given in Ireland begins "Go down to the church..." and no doubt that was the line he was fully expecting (delivered in its usual thick, nearly incomprehensible, mumbling brogue) when he asked the man how he could find the Kavanaugh place on Boylston Road. But instead the man squinted one eye and said, "An American cousin?" It seemed to Billy to be the beginning of a declarative sentence somehow cut short by a question mark.

"I beg your pardon?" he said politely.

The man pushed back his cap, a deeply lined face, the lines drawn deeper with grime.

Bad teeth. A once-good-looking face, perhaps. "Are you an American cousin?" he said.

Billy said no, he was only an old friend.

The man looked him up and down a bit, not unpleasantly, and then looked beyond him to a car that was just pulling in. The car beeped and the driver called, "Tommy!" and the man asked Billy if he'd mind stepping into the tea shop here, his wife would be inside, at the counter, and she'd be happy to draw a little map for him. It wasn't far.

But there was no one at the counter and only a single woman at a table in the corner, a blue-and-white cup before her, the newspaper in front of her face, a white plastic shopping bag at her feet. The place was small, it seemed to have been meant for another purpose—maybe as a place to sell windshield wipers and spare cans of oil, or as a waiting room for the garage next door. The windows were high and narrow and each covered with handmade curtains, blue-and-white cotton gingham. The walls were false stucco, perhaps aiming for a cottage effect, but the floor was pale linoleum, the tables and countertop a beige Formica. There were a plastic rose and a plastic fern in a white milk-glass vase on each table, and a Waterford vase filled with real flowers, tall and weedy things that nevertheless gave a nice effect, beside the register. Altogether, there was something hasty and false about the place—and this was not hindsight, he felt it immediately—as if it had been quickly rearranged to hide its true purpose. As if the woman, casually lifting her cup, intent on *The Irish Times*, had only seconds before been at the window, looking out for him.

He said, "I beg your pardon," and the woman quickly lowered her newspaper, as if she feared she'd been rude. Irish face number four: sharp chin, ruddy cheeks, good long nose, and too many teeth. Not unlike Helen O'Mara at home. He recalled one of Uncle Daniel's little ditties that ended "So I said, Mrs. Clemmon, you'd make a better lemon than you would a big red rose."

"The gentleman outside said I should ask in here for directions to Boylston Road," he told her. "The Kavanaugh place. He said I should ask his wife."

"Let me get her for you," the woman said, standing, smiling enough to show an impressive overbite. "Are you an American cousin?" she asked him over her shoulder as she headed behind the counter.

"No," he said. "Although I'm beginning to think I should be."

She laughed as if she got his meaning. "Well, the Kavanaughs have three of them, three of the girls who've gone over to the States. That's why I asked. Let me just get Eva for you."

She passed through the door behind the counter; he could see a small white enamel stove, a big stainless-steel kettle on top of it, a dishrag tied to its door handle. A shelf with some boxes of wholemeal biscuits, some tins of Earl Grey. A white enamel sink. He heard her say Eva again, and then a door opening, perhaps the back door to the place, and louder now, she cried "Eva!" out the door, into the wind.

For a moment, before the woman returned, he thought it mere coincidence. He thought it was, by some strange convergence of fact and fate, a sign of sorts, from her—no nothing so elaborate as her face in a glass, her actual voice in his ear as he slept, the kinds of signs he had imagined and hoped for so desperately in those first few months and years after her death, but a sign nonetheless, a mild comfort: to have pulled in here, to have been directed inside, to have asked the one woman who went off to fetch the wife whose name, it so happened, was also Eva. To hear on this day of all days, in this place, her name called out. It was a sign that said, You were right to come here, I am with you still.

And then the woman returned with Eva herself coming in behind her, the bouquet of ragged wildflowers only briefly blocking her face.

You could have counted on one hand the seconds it took for the two of them to know each other. Later, sitting with a cup of tea, Eva said for her it was the stoop of his shoulders, and of course those blue eyes. For him (and he, let's face it, had further to come, thirty years of distorted memory to cross), there was no single thing, certainly nothing physical, not at first, since she was so much heavier now, and the pale shade of her dyed hair no longer matched her mahogany eyes. He simply knew, after that initial tumble into disbelief, he simply knew this was Eva standing before him.

Well, what a lot of knots there were to untangle. He held out his hand at first, the homely lady still standing there, grinning between them. Held out his hand and said, "Billy Lynch," and Eva, drying her hands on her apron like some Brigadoon colleen, said, "Billy Lynch, I know it's you." Although the blush on her cheeks when she came in from the wind didn't fade inside the shop. She introduced her friend, Bessie Gordon, and called Billy the boy from New York—like a character listed in a *Playbill*.

"Oh sure," Bessie said, as if she was quite familiar with the entire cast. "The shoes," she said, nodding. The plot as well. "And all those little notes. I've always said I admired you for keeping up." She elbowed her friend. "And her scared to death to ever send a reply. I'm the one that was always telling her she was terrible not to reply."

Eva's blush grew darker and deeper; she was blushing to her roots. "Oh, Bessie's full of advice for everyone," she said in her old, laughing way. "I'm thinking of setting her up in a booth."

She offered him a cup of tea and scooted back around the counter to get it. She said she had some nice scones to go with it, or a ham roll, or some crackers and cheese, and when Billy refused all, she took a small chocolate bar from a pile by the register and slipped it onto his saucer. Bessie carried the cup for him to her own table while Eva poured tea for a group of workmen who had just pushed through the door, bringing the smell of dirt and tar and the damp outdoors in with them. Eva knew every one of them by name. And on their heels two mothers, one with a toddler on her hip—she knew them both as well. And then three elderly women, one with a canvas bag decorated with a cactus and the words *Flagstaff, Arizona*.

"The teatime rush," Bessie said—she made it sound like ruse. "No doubt it'll give Eva a chance to collect her thoughts before she has to speak to you. She's got a guilty conscience, you know. She's carried it for years." She looked at Billy, making sure he understood. Her eyes were a dishwater-gray, the skin around her nose full of scars from old blemishes and open pores. "About the money, we all know the story, the money you sent her to come back to the States. She swore any number of times she was sending it all back to you, but then there'd be another fuel crisis or Tom would get laid up or one of the children. And then she made up her mind to have this shop." She paused, studying him. It was apparent that her day had taken a delicious turn. "She's been guilty about it, though," she went on, leaning toward him. "Every one of us knew it. And your writing to her folks like that only made it worse. Her dad used to say you were calling in her loan." She drilled her bony fingers along the top of her cold cup.

"Honestly, you'd only have to say a single word to her and she'd pay you right back today, straight out of the till."

"I've never even thought about the money," Billy said. He was watching Eva, nearing sixty, matronly waist and breast, lean across the counter to chuck the chubby toddler under his chin. "She's welcome to the money."

Bessie Gordon drew her head back, eyeing him. He noticed that there was a wedding ring on her finger; who'd ever believe it, a woman so ugly—a lid for every pot, as his mother used to say. She closed her lips over her mess of teeth and then pulled them into a kind of smile, sympathetic, even pleasant. This was the face, chosen above a lifetime of other faces, some husband sought his solace in. "That's what I always thought, somehow," she told him. "That's just how I imagined you to be."

There was a small bell ringing somewhere, a far-off, fairy-wing, chinging sound that he gradually saw was the plastic rose knocking against the milk-glass vase, both of them set moving by the way his hand was trembling on the table. Bessie saw it, too, and bit her lip, all sympathy. No doubt she knew the true cause and would add that—a drinking problem—to the tale of Eva Kavanaugh's boy from New York.

He flexed the hand on the table. It was pale, bloated enough to strain against Maeve's ring. "A touch of Parkinson's," he told her, since he could not stop the tremor.

She nodded. "What a shame." And then added, "My mother had it, too." So that Billy had to wonder who was kidding whom.

When Eva finally came to the table, a cup for herself, a teapot to warm his, Bessie volunteered to take the counter for a while so they could chat undisturbed. She held out an icy hand. "It was a pleasure to meet you, Mr. Lynch," she said, and gave Eva a look that told her, at least to Billy's eyes, that here was a man better than she knew.

"Is this a holiday for you?" Eva asked brightly. It seemed to be the question she had decided on while she poured her customers their tea.

He said it was.

"With your family?"

He said he was with some priests. It was a kind of retreat.

"Lovely," she said. Her hair had been lightened to a honey blond and no longer matched her dark eyes, although the eyes themselves had stayed true. Her skin was rough and lined, a new downward turn to her lips, a second chin. She was back from the dead for him, there was that, but there was also half a lifetime of mistaken belief. He told her he was married, with a house, still with Con Ed, and he'd stayed at the shoe store until Mr. Holtzman sold it just before he died in '64.

She had four children, all of them grown now, two with babies of their own. One of them moved to the States, to Boston, with an American husband, one in London with the BBC. Two helping out here.

It wasn't only her being alive that took some getting used to, it was that she had lived, it was how she had lived.

She suddenly sat forward. It was a terrible thing she'd done, she said, leaving it to her sister to tell him she was marrying Tom, never sending him back his money. She couldn't imagine what he must think of her. She couldn't imagine what had possessed her back then. "What must you think of me?" she said again, lowering her eyes and catching him trying to steady the cup, spilling tea onto the saucer, darkening the red wrapper of the candy bar. He put it down, put his hands on his lap. He knew he'd stop at the first place he came to once he left here, get himself something to quench this thirst. "It was a long time ago," he said.

She said she would write him a check right now, would he let her? She would honestly like to, it had been on her conscience for so long.

But he said no, no. If it was a pub he first came to, well then, so be it. He could get himself a Coke at least.

She had her head bowed. She no longer wore a clean part. "I'm sorry, Billy," she said. "I've wanted to tell you so. It was cruel. It's just that I was afraid it would never happen, Tom getting this business going, us getting a place of our own. You know how it is when you're young, you're afraid your life will never get started. I got your money in my hands and I went a little mad."

"Dennis told me you died," Billy said easily. It was all part of a story now, and as story, it was nothing any of them had truly lived. He suspected there was a good joke in it, too, if he turned the tale around a bit, found the right way to look at it. He could see himself in Quinlan's, his glass to his heart, and Danny Lynch with his face gone red and his shoulders shaking the way they did when you really got him going.

Eva nodded. "We'd figured as much from your letters. Mary told me that's what he said he might do."

Billy nodded, too. "Did he?" He smiled a little. He couldn't risk another try at the cup although his throat was parched. "Like something out of *Romeo and Juliet*, hey?" He might even order a single shot, just one, to steady himself for the drive to Shannon. Because the oath he'd taken was part of a story, too, when you came right down to it. Nothing, when you came right down to it, was unbreakable, unchangeable, under threat of eternal damnation. Who was kidding whom?

"Well, we're both still here," Eva said.

"There's the pity of it," he told her, feigning a brogue to make her smile. One shot for the road and maybe a beer at the airport before he met up with Father Jim. A single glass of stout. Even Father Jim might excuse him, pledge or no, if he knew what he'd been

282

through this afternoon. If he could begin to appreciate this soaking sense of foolishness.

She said she'd known him immediately, as soon as she came through the door: the stoop of his shoulders, those blue eyes. She knew him as if no time had passed at all since the days they had spent on Long Island.

Sitting back from the table, his hands still in his lap, he said he'd be going out there again himself, to visit Dennis in Holtzman's little place, as soon as he returned to New York. He said he did so enjoy it out there, loveliest place on earth.

"How is Dennis?" she asked, and he told her. He said, "And Mary?"

Something came into her face then, something that had not been there before, during those days they had spent on Long Island, anger and determination and disgust, an old bitterness—something the span of years had taught her. Mary, she said, pulling herself up as if to keep her nose above it. Mary she doesn't hear from. Not since back then, if you want to know the truth. Not since Mary stopped hearing from Dennis. Since he broke off with her. Mary wrote to her at one point back then to say that Dennis might even tell Billy she had died rather than let him know she had merely been cruel. You're as good as dead to me, too, Mary wrote. You've ruined everything for me. "If you can imagine," Eva said, with that new bitterness in her face, in her voice, coming in strong and familiar and true, "a sister saying such a thing to her own flesh and blood. As if it was all my fault Dennis wanted no more to do with her. I wrote back to her and said Dennis was only doing what any decent man would do. It wasn't me who told her to be so loose and free with him." Her skin was dry now, lined, hinting at the dust it would, in another two or three decades, become. In truth this time. It was awkward, Billy thought, more awkwardness, to hear these angry words, these girlish concerns, on the lips of a plump old grandmother who long ago should have attained wisdom enough to dismiss this spleen. An old woman who should have wisdom enough to know that passion gone cold, gone way beyond its prime, was a pathetic thing. "She stopped writing me after that. My younger sister sees her in New York on occasion. She went to college, City College— the Mr. and Mrs. helped her out—and she ended up taking a job as a teacher, some- where near a city named Binghamton. Never married—" with some satisfaction.

"And you're not in touch?" Billy asked.

She shook her head. He might have said, until now, that time had not much changed her. "I'm as good as dead to her," she said haughtily. "And she to me, I might add."

AT HOLTZMAN'S PLACE, in the two webbed lawn chairs they had set up on the sparse grass of the front lawn because the low steps where they had sat for so many nights when

284

they were young were now too hard on their aging backs and sent pins and needles into their legs, Billy leaned forward, three sheets to the wind, and told Dennis that bitterness, then, was all that was left to it. Two old sisters locked in a silent transatlantic feud because of words exchanged about some boys they knew, thirty years ago—because one (you might say) had given too much and the other had given too little. That was it—all that remained of their lovely idyll in this lovely place. Faith inspired by anger outstripping any inspired by affection. There it was. There was the way it had ended. Nothing but bitterness, truth be told. Or pettiness at best.

What was it the poet said? More substance in our enmities than in our love.

My father shook his head. He leaned forward himself, his forearms on his knees. "You've been done more harm than good by your poetry," he said.

He knew he should send him packing. But Billy had refilled the flask in his pocket from the bottle he'd carried in his case and he was too far gone to be put back on the train. Not that Dennis had the strength now to do it. In the morning he'd send him off with a lecture he could already hear himself deliver, the one about killing yourself and maybe killing someone else as well. Think of Maeve. Think of Rosemary and Kate. Think of poor Father Jim and the trouble he took for you. Think of your friends, Billy. Think of me. He'd never said it before and would surely never say it again, but just this once he might tell him, Think of me, Billy. Without Claire, without even faith or fancy enough left to send her my thoughts, never mind my prayers. Put aside your nonsense, Billy, put aside the past and think of those who really love you, who've loved you all along. Every one of us living proof, Billy, that it's a powerless thing, this loving one another, nothing like what you had imagined. Except in the way it persists.

"I'm sorry, Billy" was what he said instead, shaking his head. "If it's an apology you're after, I'm sorry. I should have told you the truth long ago. But so much time passed. I suppose I began to think that it no longer mattered."

Billy sat erect, bleary-eyed, incurable. And yet still there lingered—was my father only imagining it?—that old longing to admire in Billy's blue eyes, Billy's own persistent love. "It was quite a thing to pull off, over all these years," he said softly.

Dennis agreed.

"Quite a story to tell."

My father nodded, leaning forward, the sparse grass at his feet still sun-warmed although the day was changing, approaching evening. The whiff of tar from the heated black road fading enough now to let the sweetness of the scented air once again come through. Air that was the very memory of that time itself, all those years ago. That was now the very scent of longing.

"Was it difficult?" Billy said with his thin smile.

"Only at first," my father told him. "After a while I suppose I believed it myself."

Billy nodded. "Mary never married," he said again, handing him something.

"And she was a pretty girl, too," my father said, refusing it. "Just goes to show you. You can never tell."

I approached from the road and only caught their attention when I had crossed the gravel driveway.

My father looked up, Billy turned a bit in his chair. I began talking right away, so I would not have to look into Billy's wet eyes, into my father's dark and troubled ones.

I met Matt West, I said, Mr. West's oldest son, the kid in the car this morning. Down at the beach, I said, not wanting to conjure the wide car, the lingering scent of marijuana. I was going to go out with him at seven, if the two of them didn't mind. Maybe a movie or something. I hoped they didn't mind.

My father sat back. "Billy's just here for the evening," he said severely. "It's not a good night to make other plans."

But Billy waved a hand, as my mother might have done. "Go," he said, and to my father: "Let her go. Why in the world would she want to spend an evening with a couple of old geezers?" He gestured toward the lawn and the road, the lengthening shadows and the still-blue sky. "On a night like this," he said, "a summer night in this lovely place." He looked at me, barely able to go on. "Go," he said, the tears welling, ready to spill. "Have a lovely night, dear, with your boy. Go."

THAT WAS THE NIGHT we discovered where our childhoods merged: on a summer evening, one of the last, I suppose, we had spent with my grandmother at the Long Island place. My brothers and I were playing a netless game of badminton in one corner of the yard, while my mother and father and grandmother sat in a semicircle of webbed lawn chairs in another. Fragrant late-summer evening, the sky streaked with brightness, pink and purple and gold, a touch of the bay in the cooling air that was itself touched with the very first hint of fall. There was a pitcher of martinis on an aluminum snack tray before them, a cracked plate of clams on the half shell beside it, each one dotted with a bit of red cocktail sauce, decorated with a slice of lemon. All they knew of heaven.

We could see the driveway from where we played, and so it must have been our slowing down and turning to look that first alerted my grandmother to her visitor, or maybe the sound of the wheels against the gravel. He got out of the car with the index card in his hand and seemed about to show it to us, as if to ask for directions, before he noticed that there were adults on the premises as well. My father getting out of his chair to meet him; my grandmother, knowing more, right behind. She overtook my father just as Mr. West was removing his cap and immediately directed him back around to the front of the house. We heard their voices inside through the screen in the kitchen windows and then again in the back bedroom. She seemed to be doing most of the talking. Her voice had grown huskier in her old age, still a redhead's voice although, spurning hair dye as she had spurned all self-deception, she had let her hair go white. My mother looked to my father and my father shrugged. They exchanged a few words. He stood to top off their drinks. When my grand-mother came back around the corner of the house, she had a number of ten-dollar bills in her hand and Mr. West had already once again started his engine.

He drove back to your house in Amagansett, where the long, loud argument that for you was your parents' marriage began again. He came in while you and your brothers were at the dinner table with your mother—something with catsup, you said, as you remembered it; as you remembered it, every meal of your childhood smelled of catsup (and then ducked your head to laugh, or because you had made me laugh). Your mother turned her back to him, this was the routine, and neither you nor your brothers were fooled by the icy silence—in a moment, you knew, it would crack. Your father went banging into the walkup attic, came banging down again with two suitcases, went banging into their bedroom. When he came through the kitchen again with the first suitcase, your mother asked, "What's this?" coolly, and he said, "I'm leaving." Oh sure, she mouthed to you and your brothers, who instantly wanted neither to take her side nor to believe him. She turned her back again when he returned, but when he came through the kitchen with the second suitcase, she sprang from her chair and followed him, through the kitchen door, down the steps, across the side lawn to the car.

There may be families, you said, who would lower their voices in the open air (mine, for instance, I told you, who at about this same time on that same night were listening quietly over our grilled round steaks to my grandmother's explanation regarding the sensibility of renting out the place all year, fond memories notwithstanding), but yours wasn't one of them. They were at each other a good ten minutes out on the side lawn, and then your father swung into the kitchen again, your mother right behind, trying to catch him by the back of his shirt. Both of them, with their eyes so bright and their jaws so set, with everything about them, you said, tunneled into their anger, unaware of, it seemed, blind to the three boys still at the table, over the remnants of another catsup dinner. Back into the bedroom. *You* was the operative word in these arguments, you said. *You* flung like a spitball. *You* peeled off and flung back again. Me? *You!* If they had only been able to decide which one of them was you they might have known for certain and at last which one of them

290

was to blame. They might have resolved something. (Ducking your head again to smile. I liked your mouth, your dark eyes, the leather bracelet on your slim wrist.)

Your father spent the night, perhaps the next dozen of them, on his boat, because it was September at least—at least school had started again—before he actually brought you and your brothers to the little house he had rented. You hated it, of course, the musty rooms and the blood-red shingles and the sense that whatever latent capacity your father had to become a stranger was now realized as he moved around the tiny kitchen, opening cabinets and drawers and mumbling, Now, where does she keep...frying eggs and bacon and serving them to you on faded china plates that were not his, not your mother's, that my mother had picked up, as a matter of fact, at the Opportunity Shop in East Hampton for a dollar or two (the remnant of another upheaval in yet another household) another summer years ago. You hated the little house because it was proof positive, or so it had seemed to you then, that your parents' marriage was over, that the days of the five of you living together were over. That the anger and the shouting would never, as you had always believed, somehow resolve itself into love again, peace. Don't even think about it, you told Cody and John. Don't even hope.

You slept in the room with the particleboard Buster Brown and Tighe on the wall. My room, I said, that's where I always stay—

"We've already slept in the same bed, then," you said, smiling, cutting all kinds of corners. Our amazement was at what we hadn't known until now, the parallels in our past no more delightful than what we were beginning to suspect our futures would contain, had contained for us all along, though we hadn't known.

This was the lesson it taught you, you said—we were already on our way, clothes falling off, as they did in those days, the sound of the ocean somewhere above us, the humid night, the same stars, our own summer idyll—this was your particular take on your particular broken home: that in the absence of love, the evaporation, the disintegration, the tossing out of the equation of love, came peace. This was your particular take: you had one or the other, paid for one with the other.

I agreed. It was, in those days, the way we all spoke about love: world-wise, open-eyed, without illusion. Lying, of course. Because what we truly believed at that moment—would believe on and off again for the rest of our lives—was that the whole history of Holtzman's little house—from its bankrupt builder to my grandmother's greed to your parents' bitter marriage—was, on this night, with our own meeting, redeemed.

IN THE MORNING, at the breakfast table, Billy was bloodshot but too skillful a drinker to seem hung over. He had showered and shaved with an electric razor and his hair was wet, combed back. The open collar of his pale blue shirt showed the aging throat, the blotched skin of his neck. Nothing in his face or in his manner indicated that he had heard a word of the talking-to my father had given him, in his room, before Billy, or I for that matter (listening to my father's voice coming from behind the wall where Buster Brown and Tighe were still hung), had even gotten out of bed. Killing himself and lying to everyone, and what about the trouble Father Jim went to, and what about AA again; it worked for Ted and for Mary Casey and for Uncle Jim, why not? Why not?

Billy's black satchel was already by the front door when he came into the kitchen. Seeing it there, he said, "Here's your hat, what's your hurry?"

My father was at the stove, frying eggs. He turned, smiling, and for a moment I thought he might relent. But he was as adept as his cousin was at keeping himself from what he most enjoyed. "There's an 11:17 train," he said.

At the table, Billy took a spoonful of coffee and lost half of it as it made its shaky way to his mouth, dabbling his plate and his lap and the front of his shirt. He swiped at himself with his napkin and then removed a small pack of postcards and a fountain pen from his breast pocket. He put both on the table beside his plate.

"Another thing about Ireland," he said. "We're all over there. All our faces." To me: "I saw your dad driving a Guinness truck in

293

Dublin. And his dad was moving a herd of sheep across the road up in the northwest."

He uncapped the pen and held it in one hand, but then put it down again when it was clear his trembling fingers could not manage it yet.

"I saw my mother," he went on. "Good Lord, I saw my mother in nearly every shop I went into, usually behind the counter. And my father's face was on one of the priests who said Mass at the retreat house."

He lifted the cards, shuffled through them. The duck pond. Home Sweet Home. The Maidstone Club. A sunset on the beach at Amagansett.

"Everybody," he was saying. "You and Danny and Claire. Both my sisters. Mac rented us a car at the airport. Ted Lynch was right behind us at a hurling match, and I'm sorry to say, Dennis, that he was pie-eyed for sure." He winked at me. "Easy does it, my foot," he said.

My father was smiling, an old habit. He couldn't help but get a kick out of Billy, even Billy hung over, lying to everyone, Billy incurable.

Billy placed the cards on the table again, white side up. He took another spoonful of coffee, steadier now than with the last.

"I didn't see anyone who resembled Kate's Peter, though," he said. "Which only proves what I've always said about that black-Irish bit being a lie. Sulinowsky turned to Sullivan, if you ask me."

He lifted the pen, turned the card over again to look at the photograph. Home Sweet Home. "Maeve, of course," he said. "And her father. Her father's face was a dime a dozen over there. Uncle Jim. Bridie Shea as a girl again." He began to write, slowly, carefully keeping control. "Wouldn't that be a gift for poor Bridie, to be a girl again? Sitting up there in her mother's window the way she used to. Not a care in the world. I told Father Jim that it was like a taste of the hereafter, going over there. I must have seen some version of every Irishman I know."

"What about yourself?" my father said. "Anyone look like you?"

Billy looked up from his postcard. He had written a single line across, two spindly words, as far as I could see.

"Oh sure," he said. "I was this young fellow in Clonmel. A regular legend around the gas station." My father laughed a little and Billy looked at me. "Get your father to tell you the tale," he said, although of course I never did, not then, my own future coming at me as it was. And I was too busy trying to make out what was written on the card under his hand. *Beautiful friend,* it looked like, just the two words.

And then I saw him address the card to Maeve.

THE LONG ISLAND HOUSE was squat, rectangular, red-shingled, and green-roofed, the shingles rough to the touch but sparkling in sunlight, flecked with mica. There were two windows in front, trimmed in deep green, a door between them, also green. Three wooden steps painted to match the door, the paint well peeled now, mostly showing bare board.

The lawn, in April, was pale green, the blades of grass wet and thin, newborn. Even the low weeds that edged the property seemed freshly sprouted, as did the tangle of honeysuckle vine that covered the wire fence along the side and that would, in summer, be tangled itself with the hum of bees. The gravel driveway was scattered with puddles. The road out front was still black from all the rain that had guaranteed Billy's swift ascent into heaven, but it was drying out now, a no-longer-solid brushstroke that by noon would have feathered back into dust along its edges. A road that on the hottest days gave off the same sharp odor it had had the moment it was spread. And swimming heat waves, of course, earth agitating air.

The suburban homes and sandy cottages were mostly silent, lights on in only one or two of them: another Saturday morning gained. The crescent of bay beach was deserted, the rocks and shells collected at its edges, the dark wash of lapping water running over them and back again.

The lot across the street was still empty

and still contained at its heart the remains of a crumbling foundation for a house that was never built, so well grown over by now that even in April the property was all fledgling weeds and dried stalks and last year's leaves.

This had always been the view from the front steps of the Long Island house: the pale green lot, the tree line, the blue sky that in certain kinds of sunlight seemed to be reflecting the mirror flashes of sunlight off the bay.

There was a screen door at the top of the steps, patched, as all screen doors in summer homes seem to be patched, against wire-cutting mosquitoes with a two-inch square of mesh—upper-right-hand corner of the top screen (always). A heavy green door behind it.

The door opened onto a narrow room, a breath of mildew, of ocean dampness. A small rag rug at the door, another larger one under the heavy coffee table. Three damp *Reader's Digest*s on top, and a blue-and-white schedule for the Long Island Railroad, East Hampton station. A wood-framed couch with tweed cushions worn white along the edges. A dark rocker, a plaid wingback. A table and lamp beside it, the base of the lamp a shellacked coil of rope. An old Cinzano ashtray, an ancient, useless pack of matches from Jungle Pete's. A wrought-iron floor lamp. There was a trace of last summer's sand on the wood floor, under the couch. A trace of dust in every corner. Charcoal along the baseboards meant to discourage mildew.

At the other end of the room, and open to it, the kitchen with its heavy Formica table and red countertops and domed refrigerator. The sink was against the back wall, under a long row of narrow windows hung high enough to block the view for all dishwashers 5'pr2";dp and under. A back-yard door beside the sink that contained the only curtained window in the house, all others being covered by yellowed shades. Another door beside the refrigerator that led to a narrow corridor that led to the three bedrooms. The only bath at the end of these, chipped white porcelain fixtures, the sink wobbly on steel mosquito legs, the cracked gray linoleum.

Across the hall, the largest bedroom by an inch or two and the brightest due to a second window was painted yellow and decorated with eight wooden shoe-store daisies tacked by my grandmother in an unfathomable constellation across the far wall. A tall dresser with a long bureau scarf. A night table with a milk-glass lamp, a magazine opened and folded back to show a white page filled with black print, unrelieved by photographs, a pair of reading glasses placed over the page, placed there the night before because it was too late to finish and there were too many words and it was all about how much the citizenry loved the President, who was just an actor when you got right down to it, an actor reading them his lines.

On the double bed, dark mahogany headboard, no footboard, white chenille spread folded back, thin floral sheets washed pale, my father opened his eyes to the same room he had gone to sleep in. The same room he had gone to sleep in: then the shadowy circle of the milk-glass lamp, now sun-shot early morning, ebb and flow of it as the breeze sucked in the bottom of the yellow shade and then let it go again (a child in a swing) to snap back against the sash. The very sound that had awakened him. Distant ringing of the buoys in the bay (Oh, but she's a girl). Scent of new grass and of ocean, of mildew, of the Long Island house, of eastern Long Island. I am still here.

He swung his feet out of the bed and sat for a moment. Nothing changed but the light, the magazine on the table, eyeglasses there, clothes in the chair, daisies, dresser, Dopp kit on the bureau because his daughter was here with him and liked to keep her makeup bag on the back of the toilet.

It was there when he made his way across the hall, pale pink and blue, plump. He nudged it gently when he lifted the lid.

Back in the room he raised the shade up above the open window so the snap of it wouldn't wake her—and then heard the same sound, faint but persistent, coming from the shade and window in her room next door. They had both kept the windows open all night, then, despite the cold air. There was still mist on the gray grass, mist all along the vine-covered fence. There was no place in the world he'd rather wake to.

He stood for a moment between the dresser and the bed and offered himself as some elemental part of understanding: the same room he had gone to sleep in, consciousness dropped and then picked up again, only the light changed. The return of day.

In the kitchen, he put the kettle on. Cut oranges and squeezed them under his palm on an old-fashioned glass juicer. The very one, in fact, his mother had used when he was young, in the apartment in Woodside. The very one, washed up on this shore somehow after what he imagined had been a long, newspaper-wrapped odyssey, box-bound, from that tiny kitchen in Queens to the basement of Holtzman's house in Jamaica (years passing there, light in the narrow basement window and then darkness, light again, a thousand times over while he himself returned from overseas, met Mary, met Claire, married, had children) until someone—himself? Holtzman? his mother?—hoisted the box marked *Kitchen Things* and brought it out here to the Long Island house, where it dropped out of his sight for years and then returned again as something he shared with Mr. West while he was still "my mother's tenant" and not yet "my daughter's father-in-law" and then found himself on this morning in April, the second morning with Billy in his grave, surprised and even delighted by the thing, by the things that ride out time.

He poured the juice into two short, thick glasses, washed and dried his hands. He pulled open the back door—frame sticking, curtain swinging—on a stage the whole wall would have moved with it. He stepped out onto the narrow back porch, where the brush-strokes in the dark green paint were his own, and Billy's. Marvelous sweet spring air of eastern Long Island. New grass and sweet blossom and tang of sea salt. In the bright green of the pale trees, high up, narrow shafts of yellow sunlight, theatrical as well. The sound-track birdsong: gulls and sparrows and distant crows.

He did a few calisthenics. His arms winter pale, the fine hairs on them mostly gray, certainly grayer than Claire had ever seen them. By sundown his arms will have turned a ruddy brown, what with the work he had planned, clippers and scythe and scraping some paint. He touched his waist, his shoulder, raised his hands above his head, looking for all the world like a man giving praise. The return of day.

Inside, the plumbing was moaning and clunking, the sound of water rushing through the walls as if the place had been framed in pipes, not lumber. His daughter in the shower.

He took the breakfast tray from under the counter, placed cups and saucers on it, bowls, cereal, sugar, spoons, a carton of milk, a jar of jam. He toasted four slices of bread and poured water into the teapot just as she came into the kitchen, barefoot, sweatpants and an old T-shirt, her hair wet and smelling of shampoo.

"Good morning, Glory," he said, and she said, "Good morning," the towel draped around her shoulders. She had already been out for a run, she said, down to the beach and back, and he realized that the shade he'd heard had been snapping in an empty room. Tomorrow they'd drive back to Rosedale. Tomorrow evening she'd fly home.

He lifted the tray and she walked ahead of him through the living room. She once more unlocked the green door, pulled it open, sunlight and birdsong transforming a long shaft of the damp, dark room. She stepped outside, holding the screen open for him.

He said, "Thank you, ma'am," and then caught the door with his elbow to let her go first. She went to the bottom step and then turned to take the tray from him, but he said, "I've got it," and let the screen door close behind him as he stepped down and turned to place the tray carefully, crockery rattling, on the top step. He sat beside it. She sat below him, at his feet, shaking out her hair, running her fingers through it, and wafting a shampoo that was some false yet strenuous version of the scent of the spring air. He lifted the teacup and poured for her. She reached back.

"Thank you," she said.

"You're most welcome."

She sipped from the cup. The breeze that had woken him had grown weaker in the sun, but something of the cold dawn still lingered. One did not dare say to a grown daughter, a married woman with children of her own, Are you warm enough? Do you need a sweater? Wouldn't you rather wear shoes?

He said, "You'll have to give the in-laws a call while you're here."

I said yes, I had already told them I'd stop by.

"There's a happy pair," my father said, meaning Mr. West and his wife, united again now that their three boys had grown, and flown. Nesting again, as you yourself had said, in the Amagansett house, nesting among the ruins. What was more tenacious, you'd said, than the desire to be connected, especially in old age, more tenacious than fact, than memory. Your parents would turn away, wide-eyed, whenever you or your brothers said, But you hated…They'd only needed space, they would tell you, turning our own words against us. They'd only gone through a rough patch in their marriage that had, unlucky for you boys, more or less corresponded to your childhoods…

Sitting on the steps of the Long Island house, Billy two days in his grave, my father and I discussed what the little house needed to have done to get it in shape for summer, for his retirement next year, when he would put the Rosedale house on the market and live out here permanently. Another overhaul, long overdue. Insulation, plumbing, heating, paint. Redoing and then supplementing all that work he and Billy had done years ago. New furniture. A real garden, once he was out here permanently, plenty of visitors, too, what with a good six months to schedule them, April through September at least, maybe October, too. My three brothers and their families would each take a turn, and he hoped I'd come in from the coast with the children. Take at least a week or two.

My father sat on the step above me, the step he would begin to scrape and sand that very afternoon, and looking toward the blue sky above the bay and the crescent beach behind the treeline, he described for me all the ways he would spend his time in this lovely place, still old Holtzman's place when you came right down to it, his surprise inheritance from a mother who hadn't put much stock in elaborate emotion but nevertheless had married twice and loved him and had said at the end, having scattered Holtzman's money to the charitable winds, Bring Billy out there, with his wife, because when you got right down to it, there were all kinds of things in her heart and in her mind that we never knew. There was, for instance, her capacity to believe. There was as well her capacity to be deceived, since you can't have one without the other, each one side of the other.

He'd have the Quinns out, my father said, Mickey will be retiring soon, too, and all the various Lynches, sure, Danny, too, and Bridie when she needed a break in a beautiful place from taking care of poor Jim. He'd have the Caseys out and both sets of our Rosedale neighbors, my mother's sister Louise with her family, although she drove him crazy. And, he said, he'd ask Maeve.

I looked at him over my shoulder. I'd been

thinking, as he counted off the names, how clear it was that Billy's was missing from the list, although Billy over the years would not come, and I thought then that my father mentioned her name just for that, for Billy's sake. He said, Maeve's never been out this way, as far as I know. She should see it. She would enjoy it.

I nodded. Sure, I said. I could imagine her, I supposed, getting off the train at the East Hampton station, tentative and slow, her hand on the rail beside the steps (the plain pearl ring) for much longer than was necessary, lingering there until the conductor offered her his own hand to help her down. (Dorothy or maybe Bridie behind her, since it would not do for her to come out here all alone.) A simple dress, or a pant suit for traveling, her round face and her short hair. My father would take her bag, take her for lunch across the street, take her on the usual tour past the beautiful houses (cottages, he'd say) that neither one of them would have ever thought to own, or even to enter, but would be content, as we'd all been content, to merely pass by and admire. Billy's idea of heaven, he'd tell her—the idea itself sufficient alone.

Early evening in the lawn chairs on the sparse lawn, a cocktail, then dinner in town, or maybe something on the grill. The far bedroom, for privacy's sake, with the bed turned down. Fresh, worn towels from the Rosedale house on the dresser for her. A laugh over the smiling pressed-wood seahorse on the wall—another decoration from Holtzman's store.

Holtzman with his literal wealth the one in the long run who had changed the lives of them all ("Even my daughter," he would say. "She met Matt out here, you know.") Figurative wealth changing nothing, in the long run, except maybe the stories that were told.

"If it comes to a choice between love and money," my father would tell Maeve, repeating an old joke, "take money."

And then bringing her back to the station on Sunday afternoon, after Mass and a bit of breakfast. The gorgeous people on the platform with her, most of them young, all of them transformed by a weekend in the sun, fruit and wildflowers in their arms.

Maeve would be working by then, two years, three years, after Billy's death. A little job Ted Lynch found for her with the archdiocese once she'd convinced him that whatever inclination she'd had to enter a convent had disappeared long ago. The sweet Indian couple meeting her at the Bayside station and driving her home to the narrow house where she now lived alone with the dog; peacefully, she would have to say. Where she would begin to wonder, no doubt, when Dennis would invite her out again, because it was so lovely out there and because Billy had so loved the place, regardless of how vigorously and for how long he had deprived himself of it. He had, after all, deprived himself of much that he loved best, poor man.

Hoping he would invite her out again, because when she and Dennis sat at the table last night with a piece of toast and a cup of tea, the dead were there with them, just outside the circle of light. Billy and Claire, not forgotten, no less mourned, but silent, for now, in dreams their faces always turned away, so that the course of other lives, the lives of those they'd loved, could be completed, could go on.

Surely just as the Irish girl, whom Billy had loved when he was young, just back from the war, had eventually turned her face away.

No less remembered, no less mourned. My father would say it himself in another six or seven years' time, as we sat together on these steps again and I watched our children playing croquet on the lawn (wondering, counting, how many more years would such summers continue, my father alive, our children still children, how many more were enough). No less loved now as then, my father would say, breaking the news, but still life goes on. Some relief is required. Some compensation.

I would look at him over my shoulder. Was it penance, I'd want to ask him, was it compensation for an old and well-intentioned lie, for the life it had deprived her of? Or was it merely taking care, more taking care? A hand held out once again to whoever happened to be nearby.

I couldn't ask, of course. And it was impossible to say. His capacity for sympathy was no less than Billy's for self-denial. Their faith, both of them—all of them, I suppose—was no less keen than their suspicion that in the end they might be proven wrong. And their certainty that they would continue to believe anyway.

They were married in March of 1991, my father and Maeve. At the little church in East Hampton, Most Holy Trinity now, no longer St. Philomena's—the poor woman having been tossed out of the canon of saints in the mid-sixties because some doubt had arisen about whether or not she had actually lived. As if, in that wide-ranging anthology of stories that was the lives of the saints—that was, as well, my father's faith and Billy's and some part of my own—what was actual, as opposed to what was imagined, as opposed to what was believed, made, when you got right down to it, any difference at all.